CUPID'S BOW

A MINA KANE NOVEL:
BOOK THREE

AMANDA CARLSON

CUPID'S BOW
A Mina Kane Novel: Book Three

Copyright © 2020 Amanda Carlson, Inc.

This book is a work of fiction. The characters, events, and places portrayed in this book are products of the author's imagination and are either fictitious or are used fictitiously. Any similarity to real persons, living or dead, is purely coincidental and not intended by the author.

ISBN-13: 978-1-944431-16-7

Email: amanda@amandacarlson.com

Published in the United States of America.

Cherubs aren't the only ones who go missing in 2105

Finding Vincent Kramer, the colonel-in-arms of the French Protectorate, has become a must-do on Mina's task log, but that's before she discovers Veritus is planning a deadly vendetta against the city. The killing ring is still operational and finding them takes precedent over locating the colonel. According to the intel, Mina and her team have less than twenty-four hours to complete the task.

Instead of actively searching for the perpetrators, Agent Kane and Agent Adams are forced to retreat underground, where they meet up with a crafty superhacker who holds the answers to the Cupid's Bow. After the case breaks apart like a space rock exploding into ten trillion quarks, Mina teams up with an unlikely companion who's already in pursuit. Mina has no choice but to join forces and trust he knows what he's doing.

Too bad only one of them is telling the truth.

Other Books by Amanda Carlson

Jessica McClain Series
Urban Fantasy
BLOODED
FULL BLOODED
HOT BLOODED
COLD BLOODED
RED BLOODED
PURE BLOODED
BLUE BLOODED

Sin City Collectors
Paranormal Romance
ACES WILD
ANTE UP
ALL IN

Phoebe Meadows
Contemporary Fantasy
STRUCK
FREED
EXILED

Holly Danger
Futuristic Dystopian
DANGER'S HALO
DANGER'S VICE
DANGER'S RACE
DANGER'S CURE
DANGER'S HUNT
DANGER'S FATE

Mina Kane
Futuristic Thriller
TOTAL ENHANCEMENT
PERFECT PLANT
CUPID'S BOW

 Chapter 1

MINA WOKE TO the smell of bacon. *Odd.* She opened her eyes and realized she could actually hear it sizzling. She slipped out of her platform by rolling to the edge and climbing out, because she hadn't gotten the settings just right, and it was still too soft.

Once on solid ground, she grabbed a modest wrap to put on around her gown, belting it as she walked, and padded into her living area to see what was up with the bacon.

The scene took her a moment to comprehend, as her synapses weren't fully firing. She rubbed her eyes.

Lee, the unseasoned rookie who'd been irritating the hell out of her only a short time ago and who'd helped her take down a serial killer the night before, stood at her island, frying bacon on what looked to be a molecular induction skillet she'd had no idea she owned.

His head was still wrapped with thick gauze because said killer had tried to saw off his ear. Shockingly violet hair stuck out all over like some kind of ridiculous enhancement gone all kinds of wrong. A fake goatee, dyed the same deranged purple, was peeling off his chin. He looked like he'd gotten into a fight with an old-fashioned potato peeler and lost.

He smiled. The goatee flapped. "Good morning." He poked at the bacon with a long contraption she also hadn't known she owned. Or maybe he'd printed some specialized bacon-flipping tool? Once fully awake, she'd find out. Or not.

The rookie looked nothing like the baby chick who'd fallen out of a tree last night. This morning, he was more like a lunatic escaped from a bad-hair asylum hell-bent on eating perfectly crisp bacon.

"What are you doing?" It was the only thing she could think of to ask. A cup of coffee sat on the counter, slightly creamed. "Is this for me?"

He nodded.

She picked it up and took a sip. "*Ahhh.*"

"One of my only memories of my father is eating bacon together," he said. "I woke up thinking about him, so I asked your Magnito to print me some. But everyone knows printers don't ever get the crispy part right, even a top-of-the-line unit like yours." He shrugged. "So I looked around and found this skillet. I'm making breakfast partly as a thanks to you for taking me in last night and partly because I'm feeling nostalgic. I appreciate you letting me stay here. You didn't have to."

Well, jeez.

Hard to argue with dad bacon.

Mina pulled out a stool and sat, clutching the warm mug between both hands. Lee asked Eggie, her now-cooperative meal printer that had created this excellent cup of coffee, to make two orders of scrambled eggs and two orange juices. Eggie complied.

Once the printer had provided the eggs and juice, Lee deemed the bacon ready and added it to their plates. Then he took the seat next to her.

Mina raised an eyebrow as she picked up a slice of the bacon. She brought it to her nose. Smelled like bacon. Was greasy like bacon. She took a bite.

"*Mmm.* That's really good." She took a moment to savor, chewing slowly. "I haven't tasted decent bacon in, I think, forever." Who took the time to cook something twice? Mina barely had time to eat the meals Eggie gave her. "Thanks, Lee. Greasy goodness is a really great way to start the day."

Neither of them mentioned it was almost noon.

Lee picked up a piece of his bacon. He closed his eyes.

Mina gave him a moment. Lots of big things had happened last night. Veritus, a serial-killing crime ring, had been brought down after being on the Planet's Most Wanted list for over twenty-five years. The kingpin, Franco Tedesco the Third, who was also a full-blown psychopath, had been responsible for the death of Langley Adams, Lee's father. None of this information had been helpfully imparted to Mina ahead of time, so Lee had been forced to face his father's killer on his own, with almost no warning whatsoever.

Intense for a seasoned agent, unthinkable for a rookie.

He'd made mistakes—like creating a pixel mirror to expose sensitive data to the world without prior approval—but in the end he'd gotten the job done and had helped bring a nefarious and previously out-of-reach criminal to justice.

As far as Mina knew, Tedesco was still alive, even though he'd taken a hit to the abdomen from a mini hydro-bomb. Neither she nor Lee had been debriefed by their director yet. They were technically on leave for the next sixty-something hours. Mostly to recuperate from an emotional op, but also to conduct some necessary off-duty research.

Lee opened his eyes. "Are you sure I'm not getting fired?"

"Not that I know of," Mina answered, shoveling in a forkful of eggs. Eggie had nailed them as well. The consistency was A-grade fluff.

"That's good." Lee was fairly low-key. It seemed he needed some cheering.

Mina reached across the counter and grabbed the black armored Midas box he'd looked over last night and slid it toward him. "This encrypted locator is going to need your attention as soon as breakfast is over, but *after* you take a turn in my soaker with some dissolvers. That horrid violet needs to go, and I can't even discuss that goatee for fear of ruining this delicious breakfast."

Last night, Lee had posed as superhacker Jordan Maybach, who went around looking like that on purpose. Some people couldn't be trained. Mina appraised Lee and added, "That is, if your ear and neck are all healed.

The medi-specialist said you could take off the bandages this morning. I don't see any blood. That's good. Does anything hurt?"

"Not really, just kind of a lingering ache." Lee popped the last of the crisped perfection into his mouth, then wiped his hands on a cloth. The kid had thought of everything. He picked up the Midas box, opening the lid. "Why did Vincent Kramer send you a Cupid's Bow?"

"Why in the *hell* is it called that?" The words tumbled out with more fervor than anyone anywhere would have deemed necessary for the situation. They just kept coming. "It's an encrypted locator. It has nothing to do with love." Why had she immediately jumped to the L word? Maybe she didn't want to think about her childhood pal, who'd turned out to be quite the international heartthrob, sending her cutesy little love symbols? It was a reasonable assumption.

Judging by the look on Lee's face, Mina had overreacted to a stratospheric degree. She shoveled in another forkful of eggs.

"Um, because it's small and cute?" Lee plucked out two data chips that were nestled inside some serious gel-cush. A tiny bow and a tiny arrow. No hearts anywhere, thank goodness. "I don't think...um...love was on the mind of whoever created this. I think Cupid is considered sneaky. This device is actually pretty rare, very costly, and really well-made. I've only known of a few hackers who can crack them." He demonstrated placing the arrow in the little niche of the bow without actually doing it. "The arrow fits into this groove. If you place them together, a signal is generated, and the encryption is downloaded from the remote database where it's cloaked and waiting. To receive the location without a hack, you have to have a Cupid reader that inserts right here." He tapped the end of the bow where Mina noticed a pinhole connector. "The trick to hacking this cleanly is to figure out where the database is located without actually connecting them. Once you have the coordinates, it's fairly easy. You just siphon the information, while trying not to alert the sender of what you're doing."

He was sounding more Lee-like by the second. Nothing like a good geek-out to get a techie back on track.

"I never thought I'd get to play around with one of these. It's pretty spec."

Mina finished her eggs and took a swig of juice. "Well, today's your lucky borrow credit day." Her voice was jolly, verging on singsongy, which she normally abhorred, but everyone forgetting about the angry-love stuff was a high priority. "The reason the colonel-in-arms of the French Protectorate sent me that is so he can be located if he goes missing. He was supposed to contact me last night between eighteen hundred and midnight, but didn't. So technically, by the parameters I made him agree to, he's missing. He asked me to deliver that"—she bobbed her head toward the tech—"to Chaz Burquist, the head of the International Judicial Committee so they can start an inquisition into his whereabouts." She glanced at Lee to find him studying her with a quizzical expression.

"If he's missing, shouldn't you deliver it now?"

"Technically, yes. But there are questions with his vid

chat that don't add up and are making me think twice. I've been going over it in my mind a kiloton. Originally, he didn't want any set check-in times, which was odd. Why not give me a specific timeframe if a real threat was breathing down his curved eurocollar? If I waited too long, it might be too late to help." Mina listed the other issues, which helped organize them in her mind. "He had a possible black eye, he was uneasy and fidgety, he was quiet and appeared vaguely unsure. He presented a stark contrast to the confident guy who took me to dinner." Lee nodded along. "I mean, why ask me, of all people, to go to Chaz, when picking a colleague in France would've made more sense? Chaz is located in Italy, which is much closer to France. Vince and I only reconnected like a week ago. We hardly know each other. I'm ill-suited, as the trilinguist he believes me to be, to provide any real help or even to carry out the request, even with my name on a list." She took her empty dishes to the grinder. "Even though there's a lot of issues, I do plan to take his request seriously. If you can't break the encryption, and we can't locate him fairly quickly, I'll go to Chaz." That was definite. She didn't want anything to happen to Vince. "But all these discrepancies are making me cautious. We'll have to get an okay from our esteemed director to hack, of course."

"Of course." Lee looked thoughtful. "I trust your take on this. You're good at spotting all the details. It seems like we should try to hack it." He shrugged. "There's a possibility Vince wants you to. I mean, there could be a message hidden in the device because he feared he was being monitored and felt he couldn't tell you something secret over a regular channel."

Mina's eyebrows rose as she considered. "That didn't occur to me, and it should've. Lee, you're brilliant." The rookie blushed and looked away. "A hidden message is a possibility. Once we check in with McAllister, I'm sure he'll make the hack a priority."

Veronica, Mina's home sim, announced in her light, plucky British accent, "A vid chat request from Kaylee Poston is coming through. Do you wish to accept?"

"Yes, screen at fifty."

An image of Mina's best pal and fellow federal agent popped on the wall a second later. Kaylee was dressed for work in functional charcoal tuck pants and an orange flow shirt, her black blunt-cut bob perfectly styled, not a strand out of place.

Unlike Mina, who was still in her sleep clothes, hair uncombed and tumbling around her shoulders, and Lee, who still wore the ruffled green two-sizes-too-big medi-patient scrubs from last night.

"It's nice to see you two are finally up and at 'em," Kaylee announced. "While you were snoozing the day away, I was off doing my patriotic duty chasing an ID-smuggling thug through a city park. Good times. After I brought that creep in, I went to headquarters to do a deep dive on a currency bandit. Apparently, some punk thinks it's funny to gather up other people's solid currency and toss it out of megas. Not only is it utterly stupid to waste coin like that, but falling hunks of silver from four hundred stories up can actually *kill* someone.

Thank the great cosmos above nobody's died yet. I think I've narrowed down his position. He's either a kilometer away or somewhere in Nebraska."

Chucking, Mina said, "Seems like you've had a busy morning, but you didn't bring down one of the Planet's Most Wanted last night by almost blowing him in half. We did such a stellar job that McAllister ordered us on leave. We're off for another sixty."

Mina left out all of Lee's emotional dad stuff, as Kaylee already knew lots of it from last night. Also his emotional mom stuff, since she had basically left him when the rookie had been just sixteen and was refusing to return now, which was why Mina had taken him in, all of which Kaylee also knew.

And they weren't technically *off* off. They were going to hack stuff—like the Cupid's Bow—and hopefully start investigating the Plush issue that had come up when Mina's brother's new friend had had a bad reaction.

"Last night was child's play." Kaylee swished her hand. Then she leaned forward, squinting. "What's wrong with your face, Lee? You look like you're molting."

Mina was waiting for the rookie to add his dishes to the mix before she initiated the grinder. Having another person in her home was weird. "Lee has a date with some dissolvers very soon. Then we're going to deal with the Cupid's Bow."

"Cupid's Bow?"

"Apparently, that thing Vince sent me when you were here yesterday is called a Cupid's Bow. And it's not what you think. It has *nothing* to do with love. Lee thinks there might be a message coded inside. He's going to hack it once we get the okay from McAllister."

Kaylee tossed her head back and chortled so loudly that, Dag, her big, lovable dog, barked along in tandem. Once Kaylee recovered, she squealed again, slapping her thigh. "He sent you something called a *Cupid's Bow*. That's completely adorbs. See? I was right! This is even better than gemstones. He's declaring his love after one date. I'm sure there's a supersecret message inside. Afterall, I watched that vid chat with you. Something was off." She held a single finger in the air that looked as big as a toddler because Kaylee's image took up half her wall. "One date. That's all it took."

"It wasn't a date. It was an impromptu dinner. There's a difference." A dinner where Mina had stupidly allowed the media to capture her image. Since then, she'd been forced to wear annoying disguises so civilians wouldn't recognize her. "And he's *not* declaring anything. There's nothing adorbs about it. He could be in trouble, we're just not sure yet. Lee said the bow"— she refused to say the Cupid part—"is *super* rare and *super* complex. It's going to take him time to hack." Since Lee was a Level XIII hacker, that was saying something. She waggled her finger at her friend. "I know that look. Don't you dare go there."

"Go where? To Love Town?" Kaylee hooted. "Can't stop me, the mag-lev has already left the station. I'm shooting fric-free straight to *Looove* Town." She started humming a beat from a popular song and snapping her fingers. "He shot an arrow through my *so-oul*. He doesn't know where this is going to *go-oh*. It might take an awful *to-oll*, but in the end he'll score a *go-oal*."

"Those aren't even the right words," Mina groused.

"They are now," Kaylee countered, still giggling. Dag wagged his tail, ears perked, ready to play.

Lee glanced between the two of them like they'd lost their minds. They probably had.

"The man is not in love with me. We've seen each other *one* time in seven years. We hardly know each other."

"He could've sent you a regular encrypted locator that's not associated with the cherub of love," Kaylee offered.

"Too easy to hack," Mina replied. "Obviously, it has to be secure, because if it was intercepted, then everyone would know his business."

"He could've sent you a coded quantum drive."

"Yes, but he didn't."

"He could've sent you an obelisk," Lee offered helpfully. "Those are sealed up *tight*. It would take me a week to hack one of those."

Mina shot him a look. "That's not helpful." Kaylee hooted some more while Lee resumed his confused face, which in his lunatic state made him look manic. "Never mind," she told him. To Kaylee, she said, "We have pressing matters to attend to, like getting Lee into the soaker before his goatee sheds all over my floor. Is there anything else you need before you go?"

Kaylee hiccup-laughed as Dag bounded to her, dropping his ball in her lap. "No. I'm good. I'm going to take this big lug out. I just wanted to check on you and make sure you're both up and functioning after your huge Planet's Most Wanted night. I can see you are. After that, I'm heading back to the grind, because, you know, someone has to deal with the bad guys while you two are off relaxing."

Mina snorted. "The last time I relaxed was 2086. I was seven."

"Good luck with the *Cupid's* Bow. I bet once it cracks, the message points straight to Love Town." Kaylee held up her hand, cackling. "Fine. *Fine.* I'm going. Lee, take care of that issue with your face and hair." She swirled a palm in Lee's general direction. "Tag me back later. Kevin, end vid." She popped off the wall.

Not even two seconds later, Veronica announced, "Quinn Kane and guest are requesting entrance from the transpo hub on level twenty. What would you like to do?"

 Chapter 2

"Authorize entry with DNA swab," Mina ordered Veronica, who would convey the request to the transpo hub's sim, who would convey it to a bot or an air breather, whoever was in charge of letting nonresidents into the building. Mina glanced at Lee, who stood at her counter still looking slightly baffled, the Midas box clutched in his hand, the bow and arrow tucked back inside. She shook her head and muttered, "It can't be helped."

"What?" He looked helpless. More birdlike now, less escaped madman.

She made the same motion Kaylee had, swirling a palm in his direction. "Your violet lunacy. My brother's on his way up. He knows I'm an agent, but he thinks I work in Street Crime. We are not saying anything about Tedesco or what went down last night. We were never there."

"Okay." Lee deposited his dishes in the grinder and pressed the button.

Once the dish dust had been sucked down into the bowels of the mega, Mina said, "I mean it, Lee. We were never there. Last night, we were chasing down a petty thief who broke into a kiosk to steal some treats. You're as easy to read as a tot waiting for a celestial gift. You have to learn to conceal your emotions." She headed down the hallway toward her sleep room. "At the very least, unwrap your bandages. I'm going to throw on some regular clothes before they get here. At least I can fix *something*."

Not three minutes later, Veronica intoned, "Tube arrival in forty seconds."

Mina walked to her door, clad in jet leggings, which were one step up—or to the side, depending on your viewpoint—from comfort pants, and a navy tunic, her hair bundled in a knot on top of her head. She settled her thumbprint on the handle and positioned her eye in front of the retinal scanner. The locks disengaged. She opened the door just as the tube doors engaged, and her baby brother stepped out, along with his new female friend, Daphne, a tall, dark-haired beauty dressed sedately in cropped green tuck pants and a white blouse. Daphne was carrying flowers.

"Hi, sis." Quinn waved. His hair was the same color as Mina's, basic brown with a few sun-streaked highlights, but he wore his shorter and wavier than his big sister did. His clothing was neutral tones and casual, his style of choice. "We wanted to come by and give you our thanks in person. If you hadn't helped us the other night, Daphne would've lost her job. That would've been a crater-sized disaster."

Daphne smiled, dipping her head, a slow blush creeping along her cheeks.

Mina had stepped in to help when Daphne had had a bad reaction to Plush, a relatively new pharma designed to enhance sexual pleasure. Highly embarrassing for anyone but your lover to know, much less your new lover's sister.

Daphne glanced at her. "I'm so thankful for your help. I just want you to know…I don't take drugs on a daily basis… I mean…I was just trying something new…"

"No need to explain any further," Mina interrupted smoothly. "I was happy to help. Come inside."

Quinn whistled low. "Wow, this is amaz—" He abruptly stopped when his eyes landed on the spectacle standing at her meal counter. Then Quinn moved forward, his hand out, a genial smile on his face. "Hi, I'm Quinn Kane, Mina's little brother. I didn't know she had company." He shot an inquisitive look at his sister. "I guess I should've called first."

They shook hands, and Lee said, "Hello."

Mina responded, in the overly joyous singsong she just couldn't quit today, "Don't be silly! This is Lee Adams, my new partner at work." So weird to acknowledge out loud that they were now officially partners. But McAllister had deemed it so. So it was so. "We were in a bit of a scuffle last night. Lee ended up at the Medi Center and needed to be watched overnight, so he came here."

She sounded slightly manic. "He's on his way into the soaker to use some dissolvers. You know street crime." She shrugged, lofting both arms like street crime was such an enigma. "Sometimes we have to track down the bad guys in disguise."

Lee's expression went from confused to bewildered.

How was it that Mina was entertaining guests before she'd fully awoken? This never happened. And by the looks of it, it never should again.

"Quinn told me all about your job," Daphne said to Mina. "It's so cool you're a federal agent." She glanced at Lee. "Both of you. I think your disguise looks terrific. I'm certain I couldn't do a job like that. I'm such a scaredy-cat." She handed the flowers to Mina. "These are for you. We picked them ourselves over at Meadow Scape Sanctuary, just outside city limits. They let you do it for a small fee. I'm not sure what I would've done if you hadn't come to my rescue. I really appreciate it. And I want you to know I've learned my lesson. No more Plush for me. Or anything, for that matter. I'm totally clean from now on."

Mina took the flowers, unsure if she should have Eggie print a tall glass with water, or if she had some kind of a vase around here somewhere. For now, she set them in a shallow basin next to the grinder. "Thank you, they're beautiful. I'll put them in water soon."

"Speaking of federal agents, have you seen the screencasts this morning?" Quinn moved into her living area, facing her wall. "They took down Veritus last night. It was crazy. All of a sudden, all these files beamed into various media outlets. It was some kind of pixel mirror thing. I dunno. Way above my currency credit grade. Anyway, the media had breakfast, lunch, and dinner with it. They're still reporting. Turn on your screen," he encouraged, gesturing at the clean white expanse. "I've never seen a fully integrated floor-to-ceiling. Let's go."

Mina had no choice but to comply with her baby brother's wishes. She shot Lee a look as she ordered Veronica to turn on a media screencast.

A second later, Melissa Socorro's face took up the entire wall. The screencaster wore a different outfit than the red sparkles of last night, this one a more sedate yellow with capped sleeves. She looked weary, but Mina had to hand it to her, she had pulled an all-nighter and into-the-next-dayer with style and grace.

Several data points hovered next to her. She was telling her audience, "And we still haven't found out who set up the pixel mirror. The feds are being very tightlipped. But we have tech experts on the trail and journalists out in the field trying to dig up that very info for you, our loyal watchers..."

Lee made a small mewing noise. Mina elbowed him.

Little did her brother and his new friend know that the hacker who'd made the complicated pixel mirror was standing right in front of them with a peeling goatee and awful hair.

Luckily, Quinn was mesmerized by the screen. He moved forward. "Holy cosmos, this is insane. I've only known a few people who live in a mega, and no one up this high. Everything is so streamlined. You can't see any seams or anything. It just looks like a wall." He hovered, inspecting, then made his way toward her solar-catch windows, which displayed an amazing view of the city and beyond. Daphne joined him.

"Wow, this is incredible," she breathed. "You can see so far, but everything looks like it's a miniature version of the real thing. Look…" She pointed. "I think that's where I live, but it's just a teensy speck."

"Or is it spec?" Quinn laughed, settling his arm comfortably around Daphne's waist. They looked cute together. Mina hoped this was the start of something special. Her brother deserved to be happy.

"Franco Tedesco the Third, the purported head of Veritus," Melissa Socorro announced, catching everyone's attention, "remains in critical condition. My sources tell me he was hit with a mini hydro-bomb, though none of them could say how it happened…"

Mina knew how.

With crafty hand movements, that's how.

She'd taken the bomb, which had been disguised to look like a camera, from her pocket, flicked it to Lee while he'd been searching for another cam on the floor. Lee had handed it to Tedesco, who in turn had activated it when he thought he was powering it down.

It'd taken both luck and skill to get the hydro-bomb to Lee without Tedesco catching sight of it. If that bit of choreography hadn't worked, Mina wasn't certain how everything would've gone down. A short time later, Mina had uttered the keyword, *ballpark*, and her director had authorized the detonation. The rest was being reported by Melissa Socorro now.

The scene on the wall suddenly switched to the press conference Director McAllister had given last night, moments after the drone she and Lee had boarded took off from the roof and was en route to the Medi Center.

Her director looked completely in charge and all business in his suit, his SWAT vest unclipped and open for effect. "At twenty-one oh seven this evening, the federal Street Crime Unit apprehended the head of Veritus, Franco Tedesco the Third. He has been taken into custody. His son, Franco Tedesco the Fourth, identity-chipped as Frankie Four, died tonight during an altercation that did not involve Street Crime agents. On my order, all of the incriminating files from Veritus have been mirrored…"

Quinn pointed at the screen. "That dude looks fierce as hell. I wouldn't want to step inside his trajectory."

You don't say.

"I heard Frankie Four was stabbed in the neck by his own father." Quinn brought his hand up to massage his throat. "Can you imagine witnessing a father take out his only son like that?"

Lee made an indecipherable sound, and Mina found her own hand snaking up to her neck.

Time to redirect. "Screen off," she commanded. "Sorry, Quinn, there's only so much crime news Lee and I can take in a day, since we live it. I watched last night, and I'm getting interdepartmental updates." She cleared her throat. "While Lee dissolves his alt"—Mina propelled a thankfully quiet Lee toward her shower room—"is it okay if I ask Daphne a few questions about her experience with Plush?"

Quinn shot Daphne an *I told you she was going to ask* look. Daphne nervously fidgeted with her shirt hem.

Mina reassured her, "I promise everything you say will remain private and within the confidences of me, my partner here, and my director." *The same guy you just saw on screen,* she didn't add. No reason to upset anyone. "I was going to get a hold of you anyway, so it's a happy coincidence you came by. I've been tasked with researching what's going on with Plush and Bliss Corp following your incident." *Incident* was the most delicate way to put *blacking out after taking a sex drug.* "Your assistance will be very welcome and helpful to the investigation."

"Yes," Daphne said. "Of course. I understand. I just wasn't prepared for any of this, you know. I just got it from a friend..." She trailed off.

"You won't be penalized for anything you tell me. It doesn't matter if you didn't have a prescription. In fact, I'll mark you down as an asset, which in my line of work shields you from prosecution. Just let me get Lee set up with the dissolvers, and I'll be right back." Mina didn't wait for an answer, instead hurrying Lee into her shower room.

"Wow, this is great," Lee said, glancing around, running his hand along her soaker.

It *was* pretty spectacular. Mina had a huge tub, a double sprayer and dryer, a medi-pod, two sinks, a beauty printer that could handle small, personal stuff, and a grinder.

"Veronica, fill soaker," Mina directed while she walked

to her vanity, where she stored the dissolvers she'd used to get rid of her own semiperm alt. McAllister had ordered her into disguise for her last op because the media had caught her out with Vincent Kramer. The very same man she now needed to find.

She handed the package to Lee. "Dump this in. It'll bubble up. Then get in and scrub that crap off." Another palm circle. "Throw it in the grinder when you're finished. If you want the temp hotter or cooler, there are manual dials you can adjust. Any questions?" The soaker was almost half full already.

"Um, no, I'm good."

"I wish I had something for you to change into. Your regular clothes were covered in blood, so they ground them up at the Medi Center, but I don't have a clothing printer."

Clothing printers were expensive and required custom mixing valves. Mina preferred to stick with the professionals when it came to anything fitted and made of fabric. Jeni Crisfold at Dutiful Duds was an artistic maven when it came to design styles. When Mina needed the basics, she could order them from Jeni and have them delivered within an hour. That was good enough for her. Plus, when she'd had a printer at home in the past, she'd tended to go crazy, always wanting the newest and trendiest styles. That had proved costly.

"That's okay." Lee glanced down his front, seeming to realize he was still in the scrubs from last night. "This is fine. You've done enough for me, really."

Mina gently took hold of his shoulders. He still seemed

a little dazed. "Listen, Lee, it's going to take time for you to process everything that happened last night. Really big things went down. Your brain is trying to catch up. But in the end, you have to remember you got justice for your father. You took down his killer. Tedesco is going to pay for what he did. Not everyone who loses a parent the way you did can say that. Hold on to it. It will help you get through this." She cleared her throat, dropping her arms. "And I'm sorry about your mom. She really wanted to come and see you, but..."

Lee's mother had said nothing of the kind when Mina had called her last night. In fact, she'd seemed unable to even process what Mina had told her. In the end, she'd refused to come to Lee's side, even though a mag-lev could've gotten her there in less than an hour.

Lee blushed. "You don't have to make excuses for my mother. She's not all...there anymore. She had a hard time with... I mean, she's never been the same since my dad, you know, died. She did her best. Once I explain to her what happened, I'm sure she'll understand and be grateful."

"I'm sure she will, too." Mina glanced around, busying herself grabbing a large cloth out of a bin under the sink. "If you need anything, let me know." She set the cloth on the edge of the soaker. "Veronica, allow Lee Adams, voice signature on file, to operate home apparatuses until further notice."

"Allowing access," her sim announced.

"Thanks," Lee said. "I appreciate that."

They stood awkwardly together for a couple more seconds before Mina patted him on the shoulder, feeling it was more appropriate than giving him a friendly slug. "Don't come out until you look like you again."

Lee chuckled. "I won't."

"YOUR ORDERS ARE to follow up at the Pleasure Emporium and find out what you can from Harri Hampburg," McAllister ordered from his projected placement on Mina's wall.

Harri was a former dalliance of Mina's. Now he was a person tied to her Plush investigation, which could become a very big deal in the future. Life was strange, more than occasionally.

"You're to go in as yourself, as a civilian inquiring after a family member, not in full official capacity," he continued. Daphne wasn't family, but close enough. "But with a discreet alt so passersby don't recognize you."

Mina wasn't surprised to hear she still had to be at least somewhat cloaked whenever she went out. Because she'd dallied and was photographed in the company of Vincent Kramer. Dallying was her thing, apparently.

"While you're interviewing Harri," McAllister went on, "Lee will focus on decoding the Cupid's Bow. I agree with your assumption that there's more to it than we understand at the moment." Her director had viewed a recording of the vid chat between her and Vince himself. "Agent Adams thinking there might be a message of some kind embedded there makes some sense. If we find nothing, I will authorize an immediate trip to Italy to meet with Burquist."

Lee exited Mina's shower room, looking clean and refreshed and wearing his scrubs. At least they were blood-free. "Here he is now," she told McAllister. To Lee, she said, "Quinn and Daphne just left. McAllister called right after. I filled him in on what Daphne told me, which wasn't much, unfortunately. We were waiting until you were finished to do the full debriefing on the Tedesco op."

"Sorry." Sheepishness crept in. "That soaker was amazing. I dozed off for a few minutes."

"Well, you look like you, and that's all that matters." Mina turned back to the screen. "We heard from Melinda Socorro that Tedesco is still alive. Is that true?"

What the media knew and what the government knew were oftentimes two distinctly different things.

"Tedesco is indeed alive," McAllister answered. "The hit he took with that hydro did major damage, but they got him into an intensive care pod immediately. They worked on him all night, medi-printing various organs. It's a good thing, too. The storage unit that required the elusive key Frankie Four was willing to kill for turned out to be empty. Tedesco was toying with us. We don't need any of the physical evidence to put him away for the rest of his life, but intel suggests that he has a cache of his signature killing gas hidden somewhere, which could be accessed by an accomplice, or several, for a possible vendetta scenario against the government to avenge their fallen leader. Either that, or to continue their criminal network without Tedesco in charge."

Mina whistled. All of those options would be bad. "Do we know how far-reaching Veritus is yet?"

"The Serial Crimes Unit is working on verifying that, but they believe it's grown into a global organization. The files that Agent Adams mirrored last night have provided specific locations, but no names. Tedesco referenced the players by a combination of numbers and letters. SCU has teams around the world rounding people up based on location. But we need to find that cache soon. The longer we take to track it down, the more likely the contents could be used against us or someone else."

"Is SCU going to need our assistance?" Mina asked.

"We're on standby," McAllister confirmed. He turned his attention to Lee. "Good work last night, Agent Adams. Your quick thinking assured us a victory. Bringing down a Planet's Most Wanted is no small feat. Agents go their entire careers without achieving such a thing."

Lee fidgeted. "I want to apologize for working without authorization—"

"No apologies necessary, Lee," Mina cut in. He had to learn their ways, and he was going to do it via her stellar mentoring skills. When their director told them they did good work, they accepted it. It wasn't up for discussion. "You did what you had to do to ensure the mission was a success. I confirmed with you via your ear node that you had the authorization before you completed the mirror. Therefore, you did your job with the backing of the agency."

Telling anyone he'd gone rogue would not be in the CIU's best interest. Luckily, their unit was secretive by nature, so that wasn't really an issue. And was it technically *rogue* when he ended up getting approval? Blurred lines abounded.

"As I specified last night," McAllister said, "you will be receiving a commendation as soon as I get word from the top. Due to the fact our department is under the radar"—way, way under—"you'll be receiving that accolade in front of a small group of your fellow agents sometime in the next week or two. As I said, good work, Agent Adams. You've proven to be an asset to this department." He picked up his handheld to inspect something.

Quinn was right—Duncan McAllister was intimidating. Even while he was reading, he looked ready to give a stunning rebuke. His sharp features, neatly shorn hair—dark on top, gray at the edges—and no-nonsense pursed lips made him seem like he wouldn't put up with much. Even so, Mina had never met a more morally sound and fair leader. He was intelligent, ridiculously competent, and had shown a humorous side lately. Odd, but not unwelcome.

"Now, back to the colonel-in-arms of the French Protectorate," McAllister said, setting down his board. "Agent Adams, Agent Kane has briefed me on your conversation about the Cupid's Bow this afternoon."

That's right, it wasn't technically even midmorning anymore. "You have my permission to hack it. It's your first priority. I've just received some interesting intel from a few of my connections in Europe, and the results seem to add to our assumption that the colonel could be trying to convey a message to us through this locator."

Before becoming the director of the CIU, aka the Corruption Investigation Unit, McAllister had spent twenty-five years as an undercover agent with the FBI-CA, aka the Federal Bureau of Investigative Crime Abroad. He was damn good at his job and had made many loyal contacts.

"From the reports, no one knows about any secret mission the Protectorate is involved in, and several agents swear that Ambrose Bernard has not left the country." Vince had clearly stated that he was with Ambrose. "There have been sightings of the leader of the Protectorate as recently as yesterday. Of note, something is afoot with Colossal Bank, located in the heart of Paris. They have suspended their borrows, which is unprecedented for a bank of that size, but are thus far keeping things well cloaked as to the reasons why. It seems France is currently involved in more than one issue at the moment. I'm unfamiliar with a Cupid's Bow, other than the name. Do you think it'll be an issue to hack, Agent Adams?"

"No, sir," Lee said. "I have all the tools I need. If I run into a problem, I can discreetly contact some of my resources. I'm looking forward to it."

"Approximately how long do you think it will take you to complete?"

"Should take the better part of the day, possibly into the night."

"I'll expect a report as soon as you're finished." McAllister nodded, turning to Mina. "As for the Plush investigation, I trust you can make an immediate appointment at the Pleasure Emporium?" Now it was her director's turn to look flustered. "Well, not an appointment, per se." He coughed into his fist. "I mean a one-on-one interview with your personal connection there?"

Now everyone was flustered. Clearly, it wasn't just love that was hard to talk about. It was every branch of that particular, um, tree.

Too bad Kaylee wasn't here to sing about it. Although, that would take a *to-oll* on Mina's patience.

"I should be able to secure an appointment with Harri, no problem," Mina replied easily, trying not to singsong anything. "My brother gave me his updated contact info before he left. I'm sure Harri can squeeze me in, especially if I lay on the charm." Mina could ooze charm if she needed to. "He won't be happy to discuss one of his clients who might be providing people with illegal prescriptions of Plush. I'll have to assure him that everything between us will stay confidential. If I have to, even though I'm going in as a civilian inquiring after family, I'll pull out the Federal Crimes Accomplice Act of 2045, which supersedes the rights of the clients of the Pleasure Emporium."

"If that doesn't work," McAllister offered, "threaten to charge him with obstructing a federal investigation."

Mina's eyebrows rose, pushing to hairline level. "That's not something a civilian would do." Though, whipping out the FCA Act of '45 wasn't really either. They were treading a line here. Mina didn't mind, as it was a line she was eager to formally cross.

Seemed McAllister was in agreement. "You are free to use your job as a federal agent as a threat. Mr. Hampburg does not need to know this visit is as unofficial as it is. Put everything he says on record. Take your veribox and read him his FCAA rights." A veribox was a verified recorder that was government-allocated and tamper-proof. "The more I'm looking into these allegations, the larger and more complex this potential case is becoming. If Bliss Corp is releasing unvetted pharma into the general population to test it on people without their consent, it's a High Crime Against Humanity. Since I have no direct orders to pursue this, gathering as much proven and verified testimony as we can is all we've got to anchor this case. With that verified information, I should be able to secure official permission to take up a federal inquiry. However, the pushback I will receive will be on a large scale. Bliss Corp is a multitrillion-dollar Big Pharma company. They are linked arm in arm with the banks and many elite government officials. By my best assumption, it will be a complicated, ongoing fight to get this case operational. But I refuse to relent when so many innocents are potentially at risk." His face was set. Mina was proud to work for him. "This investigation begins with Harri Hampburg. Since you have a past together"—cough, odd throat-clearing noises—"it would be foolish of us not to utilize that connection to its fullest. I have no doubt that you'll be able to extract the necessary details from him to give us the solid lead we're looking for."

"I will do my best." Although, they were talking about the same guy who'd left out a very important piece of information the night Mina had spoken with him on screen when Daphne was in trouble. Daphne had told her before this call with McAllister that at a recent gathering, Harri had introduced her to the man who'd given her the illicit pharma. In fact, this man was one of Harri's clients.

"If Mr. Hampburg fails to cooperate," McAllister said, "he will eventually pay the price for obstructing and more. Feel free to stress that."

"Got it," Mina said. "Just so we're clear, I'm going in unofficially, interviewing him in a semiofficial capacity, and using official means to get the information necessary to secure this case officially."

McAllister grinned, breaking his stern countenance for only a brief moment. No jokes today. "That's exactly correct. Same goes for you, Agent Adams. You are unofficially hacking the Cupid's Bow as a favor to your fellow agent. Then, if need be, we will make whatever data you find official if the missing colonel requires further aid or investigating. You are both technically on leave, so if anyone asks, you are pursuing these avenues by choice."

"Once Agent Adams hacks the device"—*no Cupid, no Bow*—"he can contact us both simultaneously," Mina offered. "That way, if I'm in the field, I can head back here. Or to your place." She turned to Lee.

Lee blushed. "I prefer to meet here. My place is... ancient and really small."

"That will be remedied soon," McAllister announced. "CIU agents must live in government-approved residences that are equipped with upgraded security, among other things. Now that you've passed your trial initiation period, I will task the housing department with finding an appropriate residence, as soon as this afternoon. You won't qualify for the kind of upgrade Agent Kane has, as she has been an agent with this department for a number of years, but I'm certain whatever they deem appropriate will be an improvement over where you are now. I'll be waiting. Signing off."

Mina's wall went clear.

"Hey, you're getting a new place," Mina said to a stunned Lee. "That's pretty spec." When the rookie continued to maintain his frozen countenance, she asked, "Lee, what's wrong?"

"I just...I just thought I'd have to stay there."

"Like, forever? That's silly." Mina clapped him on the back, guiding him toward her door. The Lee Sleepover was officially over. "Lee, you're a Level XIII hacker. If the government hadn't netted you over illegal dealings, you'd likely be above borrows in the millions now."

"I don't think so."

Mina unsecured her door and tugged it open. "What do you mean?"

His eyes were on the floor. "I promised my mom before she left that I would never make currency off of hacking. She wanted me to be an accountant like my father and earn an honest living. The thought of me stuck in a box was too much for her after everything that happened. So I made a promise to her, and I've kept it."

"You hacked for *free*?" Mina couldn't hide her astonishment. Sometimes it was okay for emotions to show, she decided. Now was one of those times.

Lee shrugged as he stepped into the hallway. "I mean, people gave me stuff, and I had enough borrow credits for rent from my dad's death benefits. I just never saw myself having the means to move into something better."

Mina had seen only the outside of his building, a squat old brick brownstone. He likely had only one room in addition to his waste room.

"Well, you need to start envisioning life with a brand-new view. Usually, once rookies pass the monitoring stage, they get their choice of a single room on a government campus or shared status one-tiered, where you bunk with another rookie from the department in a modest residence. But since you just brought down a Planet's Most Wanted, I wouldn't be surprised if McAllister elevates you to second- or even third-tiered status. That means a minimum of three rooms, all to yourself, in a high-rise."

Lee's owl eyes blinked open twice. "A high-rise? Are you sure?"

Their city had only a handful of megascrapers, but there were hundreds of high-rise buildings topping two hundred stories. Many were new and decked out. Mina had had a pretty nice setup before she'd moved.

But her last place hadn't had integrated wall screens or lux finishes. Eligibility for that came at the six-year mark for a CIU agent.

Mina chuckled. "Yes, I'm sure. Start researching mover-bot companies. I used Smart Move, and it was smooth and efficient. Now go home and earn your currency. I'll summon a private ride home for you on hub twenty. Just give the attendant your name." She shook her head as she closed the door on a bewildered Lee.

The kid really had to learn to control his expressions.

Chapter 4

IT'D TAKEN SOME prodding on Mina's part to wrangle an appointment with Harri. More than she'd anticipated. After she'd thrown around fun phrases, like *government inquiry* and *obstruction of justice*, Harri had finally relented and scheduled a meeting within the hour.

Because Mina was going in private, she'd taken her own craft. Very few citizens had enough borrowing power to afford their own transpo unit, as they were costly to maintain. But as a government agent, she received a subsidy for a craft, as well as her residence. It was mandatory for her to have access to transpo whenever the need arose.

For customers who had an appointment at the emporium, there was public landing on the roof. This emporium's name was Pleasure Emporium South. There were four emporiums in the city, each named after a direction, all owned by a corporation called Panorama.

A brief background check had revealed that it was a subsidiary of Bliss Corp.

Having it all intertwined sounded about right.

From the roof of the emporium, Mina took an automated glass tube to the lobby. There had been no floor numbers, and everything was sim activated. But judging by the short ride, the lobby was near the top of the building.

The doors slicked open, and Mina stepped into an elaborate waiting room. The floor was covered in a thick pile of gleaming white. Ultras, on low and covered with frosted ovals, were dotted around the room for effect. The name Pleasure Emporium South was laser-etched into a gigantic piece of metal that hung, embossed in gold and accented by backlighting, on the far wall. Numerous private single-person loungers were discreetly set up away from one another, covered in glimmering pearl tones. Nothing said *sex it up*, apparently, like pearl.

As she moved into the area, a woman with hair perfectly styled in a complicated updo colored a normal shade of blonde, flawless skin, and exacting enhancements rose from behind an enormous white marble desk. Her nails didn't blink, but she definitely gave Suzanne the mega rep a run for her currency in terms of flawless application. "You must be Mina. Welcome."

Mina refrained from showing surprise. Score one for the agent who could keep her emotions in check. "Yes, that's me."

"Come right this way. Harri is waiting for you." She

stepped out from behind the desk, which had nothing on it. It might have a board embedded in the top somewhere, which had alerted her to who was coming, but Mina couldn't tell. The woman walked on impossibly high scissor heels dyed the same matte black as her suction dress. She led Mina toward a glass wall. Once the woman was in range, a piece broke away and swung open on its own.

Impressive.

Mina followed the woman with no name down a well-lit hallway with a white marble floor and small, intricate geometric paintings on the crisp-ivory walls. Since this place was owned by a multitrillion-dollar company, the marble was probably real. Just so they could say it was.

Mina had no idea if the closed doors they passed led to offices or pleasure rooms. To think about what might be going on behind them was weird. Or kinky. One or the other. Mostly weird.

The woman paused at the end of the hallway and pressed her hand onto a palm plate. A hidden door opened, revealing a stairway. She said nothing as she entered. Mina followed her scissors heels as they clacked up the staircase. More marble, because why not?

The woman turned at the top landing, slightly out of breath. Apparently, she wasn't used to taking the secret staircase. She leaned in, whispering, "I'm doing this as a favor for Harri. He's just so nice. Follow me. When you're done, use this stairway to leave. It will lead you to the roof and back to your craft. The plate is not coded, so you can just place your hand on it."

"Okay." More weirdness. What did this nice, perfectly coiffed woman think Mina was about to do with Harri? Did she think Mina was here to engage in an illicit quickie? How could Mina's brain not go there? She was literally creeping up a secret passage in a sex palace to meet a man who worked here.

They reached a room at the end of another well-appointed hallway. The woman eased the door open and ushered Mina inside.

Low lights blinked on as the woman said, "Enjoy your stay."

Then she closed the door behind her.

Mina inspected the place as a polite female sim intoned, "Please make yourself comfortable. If you would like, I can be shown in hologram. If that is preferable to you, please say *yes*."

"That's a strong *no*." No hologram was necessary in what looked to be an upscale bedroom complete with a large, cushy platform that had four posts of winding, plated gold rising up toward the ceiling at each corner. It was covered in deep-chocolate-colored sheets that carried a high sheen. Mirrors and screens took up every centimeter of wall space, and a curio cabinet that Mina had no desire to open stood opposite her. Her imagination had already stocked it full of...supplies. It made her a little uncomfortable.

Harri had indeed decided to meet her in a sex room. Mina had no time to be angry or even confused, as the door whooshed open, and a harried Harri hustled inside, shutting it behind him like he was a fugitive, flattening his back against it, arms splayed.

"Have you been waiting long?" he huffed as his eyes darted around the room.

He was rattled.

"Honestly, a few seconds in here feels like an eternity," Mina retorted. "Why are we meeting in a...pleasure room?"

"They're called passion porticos, and they're the only spaces in the entire building that don't have active cams. It's illegal to have them inside the rooms. Thank goodness." He unstuck himself from the door and began to pace.

Mina didn't remember pacing being one of his things, but they'd been together for only a short time. He was still as cute as she remembered, even though he was freaked out. He ran his hands through his short, curly, black hair a couple of times. His outfit was decidedly elegant—black panel pants and a nice button-up in midnight blue with a rounded European collar.

He finally stopped moving. "You were quite insistent on the phone. You mentioned Geoff Ramsey, but like I told you, I can't discuss client information with you. It's confidential. No exceptions."

He resumed pacing. Mina had no choice but to join him, as there was no place to sit except the bed, and there wasn't currency high enough to coax her onto that platform. "Harri, you're going to have to make an exception."

He shook his head, curls bouncing. "I can't. I'll get fired. I need this job. Mina, please." He stopped, piercing her with eyes almost as wide as Lee's when they went owly. But they were diffracted an eerie blue, instead of Lee's normal light brown. Mina saw a small tic flutter at the corner of his left eyelid. "I can't go against my NDA with this company. As you probably already discovered, all the Pleasure Emporiums are owned by Bliss Corp. If they find out I've been talking to you, they could not only fire me, but they can strip me of all my borrows and throw me in the outskirts!" He was bordering on frantic. "I can't let that happen!"

"Nobody's throwing you anywhere, Harri. I need you to calm down." This wasn't going to work with a panicked Harri. Mina needed him steady so she could gather the information she desperately needed. "As I already stated when I contacted you"—which had been on a secure line—"the federal government supersedes your NDA with Bliss Corp. People are getting sick from Plush, and this will turn into a full-fledged federal investigation very soon. No one—not even a multi-trillion-dollar company—is allowed to experiment on humans without their consent. If you don't choose to cooperate now, you'll just have to do it in an official capacity later. I *can* protect you from that and make sure your testimony stays anonymous, but I'll only do that if you cooperate with me right now in this room. I'm not giving you a second chance."

Mina pulled a veribox out of her pants pocket. She'd changed into a more professional outfit for the occasion, a brown tapered pantsuit with flared shoulders and an ivory blouse. She didn't want to admit that she had unwittingly matched the décor of the room.

Harri shook his hand back and forth in front of him like he was trying to ward off a demon. "Oh no. I'm not talking into that."

"You don't need to talk *into* it. It's going to simply record whatever we say." Within a twenty-meter radius. "I'll set it here." Mina placed it on the edge of the platform, the only available space other than the floor, and the way Harri was pacing, he would crush it to dust in thirty seconds flat. "I'm going to read you your rights according to the Federal Crimes Accomplice Act, and once you agree, you will be protected as a government asset, and Bliss Corp cannot take any action against you." This visit was turning out to be less civilian than intended, and not private or low-key, but things needed to get done. Mina couldn't afford to be picky.

Harri rushed to the other end of the room as if to physically distance himself from the veribox.

It's not going to work, Harri. It can still hear you.

"I don't think you understand who or what Bliss Corp is," he said. "I've only dealt with a few of the higher-ups, but they're scarier than an impending meteor strike. They come in with a roving eye, and if they think for a millisecond anything is out of place, people get fired, or worse."

What was worse than being fired? Currency was king, and if you didn't have a job, you had nothing.

"That's why I had Zelda bring you up the back way.

Workers here have been known to sneak in a tryst or two. They won't fire you for that. Talking to a federal agent is another story." He visibly shivered.

Mina glanced around. "Okay. Let's take a few more precautions, then. Is there anything in here that we can turn on for background noise? Voices would be better than music. Maybe a screencast?" The veribox was advanced enough to separate each voice sig.

Harri looked confused for a moment, then thankful. "These screens are not connected to the outside, for fear of hacking. So no screencasts. Um, we can use the aural system. But the programs are of...the passion variety."

Not great, but okay? There was a possibility that Bliss Corp could be spying on their customers in these rooms—er, porticos—even though that was highly illegal and trampled every personal privacy law citizens had. Harri would be protected by the federal government after Mina read him his rights. But it wouldn't hurt to try to make it harder for Bliss Corp to spy. "Turn it on. But pick something...tame." For the love of the great cosmos above, he'd better pick something tame. Mina didn't want to think overmuch about the technician who would have to do the formal decoding on the veribox. Now everyone had a reason to shiver.

The lighting was too low for Mina to see if Harri was blushing as he addressed the sim, "Audrey, select a level-one portico feature, audio only."

She and Harri had been intimate when they were dating, so Mina had to block her brain from digging up any juicy Harri memories.

Mina cleared her throat. Then she cleared it again as sensual voices began to issue out of the aural speakers. A man and a woman who seemed to be engaged in some kind of role-play.

Blocking out the words *hunky* and *built*, Mina said, "I promise I'm going to keep you safe... Harri, look at me."

Harri glanced up, his face creased with worry.

"I will protect you during this investigation. You and I were only together for a short time, but you got to know me. You know I have integrity. I know you do, too. That was part of the reason I was attracted to you." He looked surprised, then embarrassed, then resigned. "That integrity has to stand up now. Innocents are at risk. People who didn't agree to be experimented on were given a new formula of Plush and are having severe reactions. You saw it happen to Daphne. Quinn is your best friend, and he was beside himself with worry. You also know it's illegal and harmful for Bliss Corp to do what they're doing. You care about your clients, and that's fantastic. I swear to you that Geoff Ramsey, and whoever else you decide to tell me about, will never know of your involvement. Do you trust me?"

His expression was pained. "I do. But you won't be around all the time. These Bliss Corp people are vindictive. Not only do they fire people, but they make sure they lose everything. It's how they silence them, removing them from the equation permanently. And they do it for infractions not as big as this would be, like stealing VR goggles or accidentally double-booking clients. I've *seen* it happen. Those people leave this job destitute with nowhere to turn."

"I understand, and I'm assuring you that if something like that happens, after I read you your rights, the federal government will consider their action against you a crime. We can and will fight them. In this country, we protect people's rights. Bliss Corp cannot get away with what they're doing with Plush or intimidating their employees. With your cooperation, the innocents who have fallen victim to this drug, as well as future victims, will be spared. I'm going to read you your rights from the Federal Crimes Accomplice Act now so everything is verified. Okay?"

Mina recited the rights, including the Witness Protection Act that Harri would also be entitled to. As she recited them from memory, she did her best to ignore the background voices, which were getting decidedly more...active. *Eek.*

Harri seemed to relax by a few degrees once she finished. He seemed to be having zero issues with the symphony of moans echoing around them. She guessed that in his business, it was just business. A small relief.

"Do you understand your rights?"

"Yes."

"Okay, now tell me what you know about Geoff Ramsey. How many years has he been a client of yours?"

"Just about two."

"You and he socialize outside the emporium, correct? You invited him to meet up with Quinn and Daphne on a recent night out. Is that something new? Was he a friend of yours before he became a client?"

Harri refrained from pacing, which was nice. "I didn't know him before. I met him for the first time here. He was Kressa's client first, then he changed over to me. Sometimes you get to know clients, and they become your friends. Other times, they keep to themselves. Geoff is social. He's a great guy. He didn't do anything to Daphne on purpose, I swear."

I'll be the judge of that.

"Daphne said when you guys were out together that Geoff brought up Plush on his own with no prodding from her. He discussed it in detail, in fact. He suggested that Daphne and Quinn should try out the Pleasure Emporium for themselves. When she declined, as she's not flush with enough borrows to book one of these"— Mina gestured around, ignoring the panting and short gasps—"porticos, he offered her a free sample of Plush. He assured her that she wouldn't get caught and that he simply had more than he could use this month. He arranged to meet her at a café two days later. She said he was fairly insistent that she try it soon, the quicker the better. He told her that after she ingested it, she should contact him. He wanted to hear about her results, see if she liked it. He told her if she did, he could set her up with a doctor who could offer a severely discounted prescription. He's since tried to contact her three times. She hasn't answered. She's terrified he will come to Primal, where she works on the waitstaff, and demand a meeting. This whole thing has been a lot for her."

Poor Daphne. She was so sweet, and now she was caught up in all this drama. But if it weren't for her,

Mina and her agency would be in the dark about what was going on with Plush.

Harri couldn't hide his surprise. "That doesn't sound like Geoff at all. He's totally laid-back. He'd never pry into someone's life like that. He also knows that giving prescription pharma to someone who doesn't have a prescription is illegal. Whether it's extra or not."

"Was Geoff aggressive in pursuing a friendship with you? Did he initiate your first get-togethers? Did he often make the plans? Or offer up meeting places?"

He scratched his head, thinking. "Yeah. At least at first. Then it was mutual." Harri was getting defensive. "Now we both contact each other."

Mina couldn't blame him. Harri was going to have to sit with whatever knowledge they uncovered about his relationship with this Geoff guy.

"Does he regularly ask to meet your friends? Has he been in personal contact with any of your other long-term friends after they were introduced to each other by you?"

Harri huffed, taking a few stomps around the room. "What are you implying? That I unwittingly set my friends up with some kind of Bliss Corp predator?"

"I'm not implying anything." *Yet.* "This is how an investigation works. I ask probing questions. I do background checks and full lifechecks, then I get to the bottom of exactly what's going on. And it seems to me that your new friend Geoff has an agenda. He may have switched from Kressa to you on purpose, based on your private contacts. This morning, when Daphne relayed to me what happened, she was shaken. She doesn't want to speak to Geoff again. I'm trying to figure out how he approached you in the beginning so I can find out what he was after. I need you to answer the questions honestly. Do you hang out together, just the two of you?"

Harri came to a stop in the middle of the room. "Not really." His eyes squinted shut as if he was trying to remember. "I mean, not anymore. He likes to party. He prefers groups of people instead of being one-on-one."

"Did he say that specifically?"

"Yes. Come to think of it, I asked him the other day if he wanted to do a holo game at Sandbox. He said no, but asked when the next party is. He refers to every social event as a party. His term, not mine."

"Have any of your other friends received any Plush from him?"

"Not that they've told me."

"Would they keep it a secret?"

"Sure. I mean, people in general are private when it comes to pleasure."

No kidding.

Come here, big boy. How about this time you put that...

Mina coughed, bordering on a full-on hack attack. It was time to wrap this up. Conducting this interview against a backdrop of sex and seduction was not optimal. She'd meet with Harri again in a more secure location. She just needed one more thing from him before she gratefully departed the premises.

"I'm going to need Geoff's contact information."

"I can't do that," Harri said. "I don't even care about the federal crimes stuff. Sharing his information crosses a big line for me."

Okay. Understood. "Let's try another path. Has he been to the emporium recently? Is there anything here that contains his DNA? If I *happen on* his DNA, I can do a lifecheck. Harri, I need this. Remember, you're protecting innocents. I know you care about them as much or more than you do this Geoff guy."

Harri looked defeated. "He keeps a private locker here."

"Great. Lead the way. You can pretend you're showing around a potential client. I'll act accordingly." Honestly, anything to get out of this room. No way in hell she'd ever be a client. This place gave her strange vibes.

Mina wasn't antisex, but she was anti whatever this was.

Chapter 5

MINA WAS ON her way home with a few of Geoff's hairs secured in a tube in her pocket when her cuff beeped with a call from her director. "Dolly, integrate incoming cuff call to craft system." It was easier to communicate that way. And yes, her craft was named Dolly. After her grandmother on her father's side. Dolly the Adored.

Dolly announced, "Integrating call. Line is open."

"Agent Kane here."

"Have you finished up at the emporium?"

"I have, and I've acquired some DNA from one of Harri's clients. My priority is to do a lifecheck on him. From what I gathered, this guy has an agenda. He's the one who gave Daphne the Plush."

"That's good, but I need you to reroute. Tedesco is awake, and he's refusing to cooperate. I want you to interrogate him. We need to know where that gas is located. Since you're the one who took him down, he might break for you. He's in a secure medi-cell at Government Four.

I've cleared a rooftop landing and expedited entrance. Agent Darian is waiting to escort you down."

"Got it. On my way."

"You have permission to interrogate as you see fit."

"Understood. Dolly, line off," she instructed. "Change course for federal government building number four. Rooftop."

"In order to make a directional change midflight, please insert your finger into the helix." It was already there. Mina had several levels of authentication on her craft. She was cautious like that. Once the micro-skin scrape sample was given, it took the sim only a second to digest. "Rerouting to Government Four. Rooftop landing."

They touched down four minutes later.

Mina exited her craft. Agent Darian stood near the entrance, which was a large plexan skybox. This agent was in her second year, a short blonde with an athletic build, hair knotted efficiently at the back of her neck. She wore a formal black pantsuit and reflective sun-shielding chromes. She looked every bit a federal agent, which was fine for agents in the CIU as long as they worked primarily inside government spaces, which Agent Darian did. She wasn't often in the field, but Mina enjoyed her company. She was smart and competent.

"Welcome, Agent Kane."

Mina nodded. "Nice to see you again, Agent Darian."

Agent Darian held open the door, and they both entered a waiting tube, each placing a finger in yet another helix and leaning in for a retinal. A beep sounded, and Agent Darian said, "Level double G, preauthorization granted. Expedite."

A sim directed, "For expedite, please use handrails. Ride may be unsteady."

The women took hold. The tube whooshed down quickly. Usually, you couldn't feel anything because the acceleration was carefully controlled, but when you were going at expedited speed, it messed with your balance.

Agent Darian leaned in. "I just have to tell you that was excellent work last night. Really amazing."

"Thank you."

"I know gushing is not the norm for this department, but it was an incredible thing to witness. You brought down a Planet's Most Wanted, and you did it with a mastery I can only dream about."

Mina had no idea what to say, so she simply said, "I appreciate that."

"I hope Agent Adams is okay."

"He is."

"He was incredible, too."

"I'll be sure to tell him." The doors opened, and they both stepped out. The low ceilings and lack of natural light were immediate giveaways that they were below ground.

Two guards in full military, including beefy lasers sticking out of their belts, moved ahead of them, leading the way. The government wasn't taking any chances with a mass murderer who had eluded capture for over twenty-five years and had enough wealth to pay heaping currency for an escape. Mina was glad to see the added security.

They passed through two more blockaded entries, giving their DNA each time, until they came to a stop in front of a door bracketed by two guards in the same military garb.

One guard broke away from his position. "Agent Kane and Agent Darian with Street Crime?" They both nodded. If this guy only knew. "I'm Agent Williams, with the AIA." Army Intel Agency. "Agent Montel, with SCU, is inside. I'll alert him you're here. The room is being monitored, full eyes and ears. The prisoner is secured to his platform by his wrists and ankles. He's a cantankerous SOB. Once we get the location of the gas, five teams will be deployed, including a bomb unit and a specialized poison unit. Good luck in there." No pressure. His eyes raked Mina's body. "Are you carrying concealed?"

"I have no weapon on me."

"You might consider taking one of mine."

"Why?" Weapons of any kind weren't an everyday necessity in their line of work. Civilians had limited access to weapons. If they printed them illegally, time in a box was hefty. Too risky for petty thieves, and hardened criminals like Tedesco wouldn't carry them every day. Too crass. "You said he's secured to his platform."

"Yeah, but Veritus is notorious." He glanced over his shoulder like he thought a member could materialize out of the wall, brandishing a fumigator full of noxious gas aimed at their faces. "We're on high alert until otherwise notified."

Mina didn't want to remind this highly trained agent that she'd just passed through three separate double-verified stations to get here. No one without authorized DNA could get where she stood right now. But she didn't remind him, because he was obviously worried. Maybe she should be, too. "Fine. Do you have a knife?"

His eyebrows rose. "Yes, but my backup laser would be much more effective."

"Just give me your blade. I happen to know that the man in there has an affinity for them." He'd tried to saw off her partner's ear and plunged a knife through his own son's neck right in front of her after all.

There was no way Mina was going to use the knife on Tedesco. Especially since the man was restrained. That would never be her style, even though she was authorized to do the interrogation *as she saw fit.* That designation meant she had leeway to use physical force to intimidate, if need be. But having a prop wouldn't hurt. What Tedesco didn't know could help her. She'd take all the help she could.

Agent Williams pulled a knife out of a sheath inside his vest. It was half the length of the one Tedesco had used on Lee last night.

Mina took it, realizing she didn't have a good place to stash it, so she kept it in her hand. Visible was good. "Open the door, please."

Agent Williams nodded, giving a head directive to his partner, who jumped to attention, placing his hand on the palm plate and completing a retinal. Once he was finished, Agent Williams did the same. Then Agent Williams stepped back and motioned for Mina to do it.

Three levels. That was good.

A low beep sounded, and Agent Williams pulled open the door, walking in ahead of Mina, briefly chatting with Agent Montel inside the room. Montel approached Mina. "I couldn't get much out of him. He somehow thinks he's going to evade this situation. He keeps talking about a private island." He shook his head. "He's too cocky for his own good, but he's definitely running scared, so that should help. A psychopath feeds off structure and routine. Once their stability is upended, they make mistakes."

Mina was counting on it.

"Thanks for the info," Mina told him. "I'm not sure if I'll be able to get any more out of him than you did, but it can't hurt to try."

"A lot is resting on this." As if she didn't know that. "You don't look familiar. Are you with Serial or High Crimes?"

"I'm with Street."

He couldn't hide his surprise. "Street? Okay. Well, then, good luck."

"I'm sure luck will play a part. I mean, it did last night when I took him down. It was lucky he put the mini hydro in his pocket after I tossed it. It was also lucky he stopped trying to saw my partner's ear off because he wanted a piece of me. But I'm banking on pure skill today. Skill gets the job done." She spun the knife in her hand and grinned. She couldn't help herself. Getting the same dubious reaction from agents outside her department was beyond old—it was ancient. Street Crime was the lowest tier in the agency. But Mina knew plenty of very talented and capable agents who worked Street. In fact, her bestie had chased a thug through a park just today. No one should be above doing the job, whatever it entailed.

Montel raised an eyebrow and had the decency to look abashed. Just slightly, but it was satisfying. "Well, in that case, I'm sure you'll get something." He walked away.

Agent Darian leaned in, grinning. "That was awesome. I'm going to watch from the communications room down the hall." She gestured to the left. "Go get him."

Mina took a breath and entered the room.

The first thing that struck her was how old and frail Tedesco looked after only one day. His enhancements had faded—his hair showed gray, his eyes had less diffraction, and there were deep creases where the Wrinkle Cement had worn off. He looked pale, and his eyebrows, oddly, had gone from big, bushy, and black to white and sparse. He'd aged at least twenty years and now resembled his true age. On file, that was sixty-three, but Mina thought he was more likely around eighty. A guy like Tedesco had the means to alter official data about himself, so eighty sounded about right.

What hadn't changed was the confidence and scheming in his gaze. When he spotted Mina, those keen eyes narrowed like a hawk sighting prey. She hoped Tedesco saw something similar in her own eyes.

"Seems you're a little tied up at the moment," she said.

Nothing. He simply stared.

Mina moved a chair closer to the bed and sat. She

rested her knife hand in full view on her thigh, fiddling with the grip, which was freshly oiled, shiny carbon. "This setup is a far cry from your penthouse in the sky and your beloved gardens. You probably miss your plants, though that's likely a pretense, as psychopaths such as yourself generally have little feeling for anything except themselves. You've enjoyed accumulating currency, but as we both know, it's all about the game, not the gain. You love winning above all else. So how does it feel to lose so badly? You're all tied up with no place to go. You killed your kid for nothing. That's got to sting."

Mina would normally approach a psychopathic narcissist like Tedesco with flattery, but this particular psychopath was already unstable, so she hoped that poking him would work better. If not, she could alter her course. Already, she could tell she'd hit a nerve. He was blinking rapidly, and his eyebrows kept twitching like he was going to sneeze. For him, that was facial Olympics.

"Frankie *deserved* to die," he replied through a clenched jaw. "He's the one responsible for this, not me. He was the mastermind behind everything."

"You're not trying to pin this on your dead child, are you?"

"Frankie was in charge." Tedesco pulled on his restraints.

Agitation was good. At least for now.

Tedesco seemed to be forgetting he'd attested to his crimes on audio and vid last night. She wasn't going to remind him just yet.

"So by your reasoning, since Frankie was responsible, you should go free?" She leaned forward, examining his bandaged middle. That red was seeping through meant it was bad. Medi-staff and medi-pods could fix almost anything these days. They'd released Lee with a mended ear only a few hours after he'd arrived at the Medi Center. "Man, that wound has to hurt. I bet you weren't expecting my partner to hand you a bomb. You fell for our trick so easily, too. It was like printing a treat for an itty-bitty baby."

Tedesco snarled, "Enough of this. I want to make a deal."

"That's nice, but the government doesn't need to make a deal with you. We have everything we need to lock you up nice and tight. You're never going to see the light of day again, Tedesco. This is it." Mina gestured around the room. "Low ceilings, no natural light, bland walls, no greenery. Just what a killer like you deserves." She'd infused a fair amount of glee into her words, which honestly hadn't been hard. "Box life will be an adjustment, one you won't like, but as you know, you don't get a say."

Tedesco seethed, fighting his restraints, not getting more than a centimeter of movement. Physically acting out was way out of character, so really, things were going according to plan. The break wouldn't take much longer, by Mina's estimation.

"How did that bogus key work out for you?" Tedesco asked. "You thought I was stupid. Frankie thought I was stupid. Now you're all scurrying around, trying to find the storage units. But you won't. Not without my help!"

Mina leaned forward. "Units, plural. Thank you." The break had come quickly. She called toward the door, "Hear that, guys? There's more than one storage unit." She played on his slip, knowing it would make Tedesco even more crazy.

This man had viewed himself as infallible his entire life, likely from a very young age, and being in this predicament—under arrest, restrained, interrogated by a *girl*—was unacceptable. Realizing he was fallible would break his carefully crafted hyper-sterile containment bubble.

The bubble Mina was busy sticking carbon needles into right now.

"See, they sent you here to find the gas. You care about the units," he sneered, calming by a few degrees, apparently thinking he still had an advantage. "It's made especially for me, you know." He settled back against his pillow. "It requires a stable environment to maintain. Scientists will have a wonderful time trying to figure out the formula. That is, if they don't die trying." He smirked. "It's a very specific combination of hyper-rare plant-based neurotoxins that deliver the greatest amount of pain and embody the greatest efficacy in killing."

It sounded simply wonderful.

"One can't have the pain go on indefinitely," he went on, "but the aim is for maximum discomfort. Then, after it kills, it evaporates into nothing, like the magical compound it is." He ended with a dreamy look on his face.

Gross. This man was beyond mad. Only a few perpetrators Mina had ever come across were this clinically deranged. As he'd spoken about his beloved killing gas, his eyes had danced. *Danced.*

Mina fought hard not to gag on the bad taste flooding her mouth. "You think your beloved gas stuck in storage units is keeping us up until twilight? Not even close. Did Agent Montel share with you that we've picked up at least a dozen of your cronies in the last hour? You were pretty tricky with your identifiers, but there was one thing you overlooked. Their locations were integrated into the code. That was negligent on your part." Another carbon needle inserted into the bubble. "We've been snatching them up like berries off a juniper. So easy. One of them is bound to talk."

Tedesco appeared fearful for less than a second before he regained control. "No one knows what I know."

"Are you sure about that? Not even Frankie, the supposed leader of Veritus?"

"Frankie was good for some security aspects."

"So Frankie *wasn't* the leader? I'm confused."

Mina wasn't confused at all. A narcissist wasn't capable of letting someone else take credit, particularly with something as big as Veritus, which Tedesco considered his life's work.

Sure, a narcissist could throw someone in front of a mag-lev with no compunction and watch them go splat, but at the end of the day, they were not capable of giving credit to anyone but themselves.

When Tedesco remained quiet, Mina quirked her brows together. "So you're innocent? Or you know everything? Which is it, Tedesco? I'm running short on time here." She glanced down at her cuff. "I have another pressing engagement to get to."

He gave her a maniacal grin as blood began to seep through his teeth. "I'm going to enjoy watching you die."

Chapter 6

Mina resisted the urge to jump up or summon medi-staff, something she was sure Tedesco wanted her to do. He was hoping for a fear reaction, waiting for it. He wasn't going to get one. There was no way he'd managed to ingest anything or get a hold of anything deadly. He'd been under constant government surveillance since last night, as well as had undergone multiple rounds in a medi-pod, which had included transplanting new organs. He was clean.

So, Tedesco was either gnawing the inside of his cheeks or clamping down on his tongue in frustration. Either way, the sight of the blood on his teeth was like something out of a horror vid.

It was time to change up the dynamic. Do something completely unexpected.

Mina stood quickly, bringing the knife up to his cheek as she bent over him, causing him to cringe back against the bed.

Her position of power would induce rage. She needed rage. He'd already broken once because of it.

"What? Do you think I'm going to cut you?" Mina scoffed. "Using this knife on you would be much too easy." She tossed the knife onto a side table, well out of his reach. "I'm not stooping to your level, Tedesco. I have something more interesting planned." She bent over him again, mere centimeters away. He arched back, spittle on his lip. "When bad guys get locked up for life, their currency reverts to the government."

His eyes narrowed.

"*Ah*, by your reaction I see you already know that. What you don't know is I get a say in how we spend yours." She didn't. She just had to make him believe she did. "The first thing I'm going to do is turn your penthouse into an outskirts charity."

His eyes widened. No more order in his home. Things would be out of place.

"Poor folks are going to sleep in your platform, they're going to eat their messy meals on your pristine furniture, and I'm going to let them take whatever souvenir they'd like from your vid shrine." Tedesco had invested millions in vids. He had a whole room devoted to vid crap and novelty items, all lovingly arranged. They obviously meant something to him. Maybe his mother never let him watch vids as a child. Regardless, the thought of anyone tampering with his things would continue to drive him crazy.

"You can't do that! Those things are *mine.*"

Come on, rage.

"Not yours anymore." Mina grinned, still up close and personal. "Then I'm going to have all your precious plants uprooted."

"You wouldn't dare."

She needed more. He didn't believe her. "I would. I'm not even going to replant them. They're just going to be left to rot. All your prized fruit trees. Gone. All your Japanese yews. Gone. Your beloved roses. Gone. Do you want to know what's going to go in their place?"

More blood leaked between his teeth. *Good.*

"Syncrete. We're going to scrape the entire space and make it big and open for all the charity events we're going to hold there. Every time we get together there, we will all laugh about your bungled operation. People will write about it. They will sing dumb songs about it." Kaylee should be here. "You will be known around the planet as the worst, most inept, dumbest criminal on the face of this planet. It will be glorious."

The opposite, in fact, was true. This man had eluded capture for over twenty-five years. Veritus would go down as one of the most successfully run killing rings in history.

"Enough!" he seethed. *Perfect.* "You will leave my things alone. I am not inept. I am *brilliant.* You've never met someone as smart as—"

"Not smart. Nope." She interrupted him on purpose. Another insult. She set another needle in. "You're incredibly predictable," she proclaimed in a bored tone. "You're obsessive. You're particular. You like things just so. You'd want your precious gas close, where you could monitor it. Envision using it. Remember how you felt when you unleashed it." She pretended to be talking to herself. "I don't see you sneaking off to some high-rise storage unit to ride a tube up to a plain, boring room. No, you would want more pizzazz than that. More fanfare." She studied his face. "This killing stuff is your pride and joy. It gets you off. I bet the entire space is decked out with fancy coolers and tubes and extra-shiny titanium storage containers. I bet you use a buffer on them."

"You have no idea what you're talking about." Blood flowed over one lip. "The gas is very far away from here. I would never keep it close. You couldn't get to it even if you tried." His pupils expanded. Just a bit.

"I hate liars." She readjusted, flashing him her clean teeth, adding a little growl to throw him further off-balance. "Other than killing, there are only three things you love—or pretend to love." She scrutinized him. "Your precious gardens." No reaction. Too close to home. "Your ridiculous vid productions. The ones you've spent so much currency on and audiences hate anyway." Nothing. "And your shipping empire." His eyes darted to the side before he tried to resume his don't-care attitude.

She rose off the bed, making sure Tedesco saw her disgust.

To the room, she announced, "I believe Mr. Killer here is keeping his poison on a ship or in one of his warehouses close by. Start in an area close to his offices and move outward. Look for tricky spaces, hidden doors, and lots of carved wood."

Tedesco's eyes flicked around the room.

"He *loves* carved wood. It will be a space that only he has access to. His employees will know what we're looking for. They'll have noticed him slipping away or receiving strange shipments of things and then taking them in a certain direction."

Tedesco sputtered, outraged. "You're wrong! It's nowhere near my ships! I said it's far, far away. You'll never find it!"

The bubble had burst.

It'd taken only three needles.

Mina settled her hands on her hips. "It's my turn to ask if you think I'm stupid. Screen flash, I'm not. You have clear tells, Tedesco, and it just so happens I'm good at reading them. If your precious gas isn't near your shipyard, I'll eat a plate of your currency for dinner. It's only a matter of time now. So much for your deal."

Mina picked the knife up off the table and walked purposely toward the door. Her business here was done for now.

She could be wrong, but she didn't think so. He was easy to read, but only because he was at a severe disadvantage. In his normal life, he would've been devoid of any emotion. No tells to find. Shrewd. Confident. Very, very hard to read.

Tedesco couldn't seem to comprehend what had just happened. "We will make a deal," he shouted to her retreating back. "That's how this is supposed to work! I have currency. I will go to my island and stay there indefinitely. Frankie will be blamed for Veritus. You have to make a deal!"

Mina placed her hand on the palm plate as she glanced over her shoulder at the wizened man now sputtering in his bed, yanking at his restraints. "I realize that when we're together, I confuse you. I don't act predictably, and you're a man who lives and breathes structure. But I can assure you there's been no mistake. There will be no deal. We will find your gas, and you will be placed in a box for the rest of your life, as it should be. My hope is I never have to lay eyes on you again. You give filth a bad name."

He seemed to get his wits about him at the last moment. His eyes narrowed to no more than slits. "You will pay for this with your life. I swear it."

The door popped open. Mina grabbed the handle. "I doubt it. Enjoy your box."

⸻

Mina bit into the zesty chicken sandwich Eggie had just printed for her. She'd toyed with adding bacon, but after this morning, she'd just be asking for disappointment.

"Computer, list matches with various spellings of Geoffrey Alan Ramsey, including with a G and a J, and pair them with work in the service and pleasure industries."

The hair strands she'd collected from the emporium had already been identified as belonging to one Geoffrey Alan Ramsey. So far so good. He'd been born in Memphis, Tennessee. He was twenty-seven years old and had two siblings. Both his parents were still alive. He'd moved to the city six years ago, worked a few odd jobs, the last two as server at a printed restaurant with specialized trace elements and as overseer of cleaning bots in an office building. His current job was listed as consultant, but not for what.

After that, the trail had run dry or was blocked by layers of security she couldn't access.

"There has to be more," Mina grumbled, taking another bite of her sandwich. She was using her supercomputer, the data displayed on her wall screen for easy viewing.

As the computer populated info about other Geoffrey Ramseys so she could see if she could find a connection, she set down her food and picked up her tea. Eggie had done a pretty decent ginseng, even without the trace elements.

She'd come straight home after dealing with Tedesco and having a short in-person debriefing with her director, who had visited on-site. Units were being deployed to Tedesco's shipyards, which happened to be vast. It would take some time for the professionals to comb for hidden chambers and hidey-holes.

She glanced at her cuff. She hadn't heard from Lee in a few hours. She was getting impatient. "Veronica, contact Lee Adams, vid request. Mark it priority. Living area, forty percent. Display immediately."

If the call was marked as priority, Lee would take it unless he was otherwise disposed.

Less than twenty seconds later, Lee popped on her wall next to her Geoffrey Ramsey data. The rookie had changed out of his scrubs, but he still looked tired.

"Any news?" Mina asked hopefully. Only Lee's face was visible. Mina knew he was self-conscious about his accommodations and likely had only a small screen for viewing on his end. But that would be changing soon.

"I was actually just going to call you," Lee said. "I'm getting close."

"To a location or finding a message?" Mina stood, moving toward her wall.

"I'm not seeing a data or voice message, at least at the layer I'm at right now, but a location is solidifying. I've narrowed it down to a wide span south of here."

"Here in *this* city?" That was unexpected. When Vince had mentioned a secret mission, Mina had figured it was in some far-flung place.

Lee glanced down at something in his hands. "I'm not one hundred percent, but it's looking that way."

"That's something to ponder." Why would Vince be here?

"In order to home in on the exact location, I might need to contact a friend of mine. He has this super-cool locator map set up for the city. It scans and renews its data every millisecond and goes per centimeter—"

"Whatever you need to do to pin this down. We need this information. Be as discreet as you can. Don't let on that we are tracking a colonel in the French Protectorate." Discreet wasn't Lee's specialty.

"I understand. Why do you think he's here?"

"I have no idea. But I can promise you we're going to figure it out."

"Do you think he knows you're an agent?"

"It's a possibility." Everything at this point was a possibility. Having Vince close meant that they could investigate quickly, which was a bonus.

"Maybe someone's taken Vincent Kramer hostage," Lee offered.

"Could be. Or he knew they were planning something and sent the location. It's too soon to speculate. We need more." Mina replayed an image of Vince from the other night asking for help. Wouldn't she have noticed if he'd been in a hostage situation? She'd like to think she would've. He would've been stiff and mechanical, relaying a predetermined dialogue. *Hostage* didn't ring for her, but nothing else really did either. "Let me know what you come up with as soon as you can. I want incremental updates. Tag my cuff if I'm not home."

"Okay."

"And, Lee, make sure this stays well under the radar."

"I will. What happened at the emporium?"

"I was able to get Harri to talk. There's a high probability Bliss Corp has eyes and ears everywhere in that emporium. Harri was worried about being monitored, so it got a little...strange." She didn't elaborate on the interesting background noises or that a tech at headquarters was now sorting through it all. "But I got DNA from the guy who gave Daphne the altered Plush. I'm running a lifecheck now, and the trail just ran dry, so I'm—"

Veronica interrupted, "Incoming vid request from Director McAllister. Do you wish to accept?"

MINA SWITCHED OVER. Her director looked grave. It was a theme with this op. "You were right. They found the gas storage unit at Tedesco's shipyard. It was concealed behind a moored ship and was marked as a defunct cooling unit. It was also empty."

"Empty, as in it hadn't been used in a long time? Or empty, as in it was just cleared out?"

"The latter. There's no vid surveillance in that area, for obvious reasons. But other cams caught two drones setting down in an unauthorized area just before dawn this morning. Six people went in, all of them dressed in dark clothing, faces obscured. They cleared the area in less than thirty. We have technicians working on craft recognition, but so far the trail is cold."

Mina whistled. "Do you think they're operating on Tedesco's orders? He's been cut off from communicating with anyone since he was taken in last night."

McAllister shook his head. "They're likely following a

long-standing order that if the boss goes down, there will be retaliation. We tried to get to it before they did, but that didn't happen. Good work on figuring out where it was, by the way. You were able to get what others could not."

Little good that did now. "What does that mean for us?"

"CIU is taking this threat very seriously. As of right now, the media does not have you or Agent Adams' names as key actors in this case. As long as Tedesco is out of contact with his followers, your identities should remain protected."

She knew what it meant if that didn't happen. "You gave the media briefing last night. They now assume the agents who took Tedesco down are with Street."

"Yes, and Street has been informed. They will be taking every precaution as well. In the meantime, we need to function on high alert until that gas is tracked down. It kills on contact, within moments, painfully. Once the drones that took it are identified, things should move along quicker."

"Should I try Tedesco again? I might be able to get something more from him. Maybe names of the players?"

"No, but I want you back on the inside."

"Inside where?"

"Tedesco's residence. Tactical units have examined every square centimeter of tech and possible hiding places in the home, but I want you to take a look, both inside and outside, covering the roof and his gardens. There could be clues to networking and Veritus members' identities they missed. We need any and all the insight before this gas is used on our people in retaliation."

"Got it."

"A government craft is on the way now. You will swing by and pick up Agent Adams. I'm making this a priority over the Cupid's Bow for now, as this is a direct threat against our agency and people. The drone will transport you to the roof of The Mega. Again, Agent Darian will be there to meet you. You and Agent Adams are officially back on duty."

"I'll be ready." Mina hadn't expected their downtime to last the full sixty anyway. When agents had a hot case, it was to be expected.

Her director popped off screen, and Mina went in search of a few tech toys.

"It's weird being back here again." Lee wandered into Tedesco's office where, just a very short while ago, he'd almost lost his ear. He fiddled with a few items on the desk and opened and shut a few cabinets.

The situation had to be hard for the rookie, but there was no way to help that. "Every centimeter of this place has been analyzed by a tactical forensic team," Mina told him. "Let's just give it a cursory glance. Then I want to head outside to the gardens."

"The gardens?" Agent Darian asked. She pulled a book off Tedesco's shelf and leafed through the pages. "Why would he store anything of value outside?"

Mina turned, hands on her hips as she analyzed the space. "Because the gardens were his pride and joy.

He loved them as much as any psychopath could love anything. Likely because they represent something he could never have for himself—real beauty. I have a hunch if we're going to find anything on the premises, it'll be out there."

"Like some kind of secret bunker?" Lee asked.

"Maybe. Or just a box buried in the dirt with one single chip in it that could contain details we could use to track down the other players involved in Veritus."

Mina was reaching, but it could be true. They were here to turn over every stone—literally.

"That could take days," Lee said. "His gardens cover the entire roof. There's more than an acre of greenery out there."

"Yeah," Mina countered, "but he favored the roses and the annuals. He lingered over those more than others." She'd been told that the first day she'd worked in the gardens.

Agent Darian shrugged. "It's worth a try. With that noxious gas out there in the world, we're all on edge. Nobody's going to settle until it's found."

She was right. No one was going to settle. When one agent was targeted, they all were.

"We can exit this way." Mina strode through Tedesco's kitschy library room that held all his prized vid memorabilia and through the big living area that she'd just snuck through a few days before, with its grotesquely oversized couches and chairs. All the bots had been confiscated, so there was nothing around to stop them.

She pushed through the door set into the wall of glass. Once outside, she passed the large entertainment area Tedesco had set up with tables, meal printers, grills, and lounging furniture. Lee and Agent Darian followed.

Mina wandered around, rolling up one of the grill shields to take a look. It looked pristine, never used. She shut the cover. Mina didn't think Tedesco would hide anything where he did his entertaining, but a cursory look couldn't hurt. The other agents did the same.

"Let's head up to the tiers." She rounded a corner and went up to the third gardening tier and the rosebushes she'd been tasked to look over when she'd begun posing as a gardener. Agent Darian and Agent Adams were right behind her. It was sunny, but not windy, because Tedesco had installed a gigantic windscreen around the entire roof of the residence. It really was something. The city and beyond were spectacular in the most awe-inspiring sense. The view stretched for hundreds of kilometers in every direction.

"What are we looking for, exactly?" Lee asked.

"Anything out of the ordinary. Maybe a bush or a plant that's not spaced correctly, or a tree that looks fake. Not really sure." Mina bent down to inspect one of the rosebushes she'd used her secret solution on. The black spot on the leaves that she had treated actually looked a little better. She chuckled.

"Did you find something?" Agent Darian asked, peering over her shoulder, her voice hopeful.

Mina stood. "No. I was just thinking that gardening was surprisingly enjoyable." Maybe Mina would consider it as a hobby down the road. "I think we should split up.

We can cover more ground that way. If you come across something, don't hesitate to dig it up or move things around. Tedesco won't be coming back." She wondered for a moment what would happen to this place, then shook her head. It was none of her concern. Likely, the property would be sliced up and made into more reasonably sized units. "Lee, you take up top where the hydro-garden is located."

That's where they'd taken a stunned Andy after they'd discovered he was actually a plant for Frankie, Tedesco's son. "That would be a convenient place for Tedesco to go," Mina continued. "Since the interior stairs lead there and to where his craft was usually parked. Agent Darian, you head down to the main tier and make your way all the way around, inspecting the annuals. They're planted up front and center, lots of colorful flowers. I remember Doreen"—the cheerful head gardener with hair the color of sunshine—"telling me Tedesco loved his impatiens and zinnias. Look them up and pay close attention. I'll head to the delivery area where Cots had all the plants droned in. There may be something I missed while I was in that space. There were plenty of tables and shelving units to squirrel away something."

Mina had worked for Cotswold Higgins for exactly one day and three hours. She was certain Cots was still reeling that he'd lost his main client and most of his income in a matter of moments. His hawkish nose was probably still sniffing the air, trying to sort it all out. She felt kind of bad for the guy. He was really passionate about his craft.

"Will do. And, um, you can call me Anna," Agent Darian said, flashing Mina a grin. "No need to be formal when we're all working together." She looked pleased to be on the hunt with them.

Mina nodded. "Okay, Anna. Let's meet back here in"—she glanced at her cuff—"one hour. Tag me if you find anything."

Mina followed the third tier around, inspecting the roses and the other bushes and shrubs as she went. Nothing seemed particularly out of the ordinary. There weren't any overly heaped mounds of dirt, and everything was evenly spaced. If she hadn't already known the bushes and trees were real, she'd know it now because of the smattering of petals and leaves on the ground.

When she reached the wall of the delivery area, she headed down to the main level. It was quiet, no gardeners bustling around. No drones about to land. All the hoses were coiled up. Most of the gardening implements were stacked on shelves. A few overturned pots and dribbles of dirt were here and there, which came with the territory, as Mina had learned quickly. Gardening was a dirty job.

She opened a large metal storage unit that she hadn't investigated before. Rakes, shovels, and other tools hung inside. She moved them aside, checking the back panel to see if it opened. This didn't seem like a likely place for Tedesco to store anything. Too much work and hassle. He would want something easy and sleek.

She wandered over to the shelving unit, where she'd

added the soap and a few other ingredients to make the black spot cure. She moved canisters around. Seeing nothing, she moved over to where the printers and a grinder sat. The area was clean. Nowhere to hide anything of consequence.

Unless, of course, Tedesco had packed something into the back of one of these machines, which didn't seem likely. Again, too much work.

There were only two doors. One led into a cramped waste room, the other she wasn't sure. She was relieved to find it unlocked, not wanting to go through the hassle of finding a key or breaking the door down. The space was dark.

"Ultras on," she ordered, assuming there wouldn't be a voice-sig requirement in a space like this. An instant later, the ultras popped on. It was another storage unit, by the looks of it. Possibly for hydro-garden items, as there were large barrels and nets, including some hook gadgets with seaweed dangling from the tines.

The delivery area was looking like a bust. It was too bad, because this was the only other place outside that could have potentially led into the residence or given Tedesco easy access to hide things he didn't want anyone else to find.

Mina exited the storage room, shutting the door behind her. As it snapped closed, she turned, picking up on a strange sound.

The noise was coming from the waste room.

She edged closer.

Was that humming?

Mina hadn't brought a weapon with her. Why would she need one when the residence was supposed to be empty? Instead, she shoved her hand in her pocket and drew out a lock disengager. It was metal. It would have to do.

A moment later, the waste room door opened, and Doreen the gardener emerged, not noticing Mina at first.

Doreen's face must have mimicked the surprise on Mina's once she caught sight of the agent standing there with a disengager at the ready. The gardener, with her halo of puffy yellow hair, gasped, clasping a hand to her chest as she registered her shock. Then one of her hands dipped into her smock pocket.

When she withdrew it, she wasn't holding a garden tool.

She was clutching a laser.

CHAPTER 8

"EASY THERE, DOREEN," Mina said, slowly raising her hands. "No need to point a weapon at me. I'm not here to hurt anyone."

Doreen seemed momentarily confused, then her face rapidly morphed into an expression that looked shrewd and conniving. Not a look Mina had seen on her before. Doreen had played the role of jolly gardener to a T.

"I knew you'd come back." She waved her weapon around erratically. "It took me a moment to recognize you, because you look different. But I'd know that voice anywhere. It's annoying as hell. Why'd you ditch the blonde hair? It looked so much better." She leaned in, inspecting Mina's features. "And your nose is different. Cheekbones, too. Such a shame. Now you just look ordinary. I bet Andy wouldn't think you're such a hot lava drip now." She shook her head sadly, indicating that she thought how Mina looked without her semiperm alt was such a pity. "Why my love put any trust in that man is beyond me. He was just a dirty, dirty UPS—that's an *ultimate pleasure seeker*, for those not in the know."

You don't say, Doreen.

"That Andy would do anything to get his pecker pecked. And he was an incompetent gardener as well!" She ended on a huff, like inefficient gardening had been the worst of Andy's offenses. Hardly.

Mina kept her mouth shut. Her brain had become a superdroneway of thoughts all colliding in midair. She had a pretty good idea who this *my love* was.

"You were involved with Frankie." Frankie Four, born Franco Tedesco the Fourth, was the heir apparent before his parent ended up parting him from his heirship with a sharp stick to the neck.

Doreen's face hardened. "I was more than involved with Frankie. We were in love." She added a foot stamp. "Now he's gone because of you!" She gestured with her laser, which looked like a Sunray.

Seemed apt for a gardener to carry a weapon named after the strength of the sun. Especially a gardener who had bright sunny hair and weird, diffracted, mustard-colored eyes. A few days ago, Mina had thought Doreen's eye color was a cute choice for a gardener. Now they just looked wicked and cruel, especially with the Sunray positioned between them.

"I had nothing to do with Frankie's death," Mina assured her. "That's all on his father."

"I know his father killed him!" Doreen was rattled, a state that, if prolonged, would lead to instability. Not what Mina needed when she had a hot laser pointed at her face. "But it's because of you. Because you were there! You pushed him to the limit."

Him meaning Tedesco?

Mina was trying to keep up with all this shiny, new information pouring out of the gardener like water shooting out of a spigot, soaking everything in sight. There was no way Doreen could have known she was in the room with Tedesco last night, so this laser-pointing madwoman was only guessing.

Mina glanced around, wondering where Doreen's transpo unit was parked. And if Doreen didn't have a craft here, how did she get in? This location had been secured since early yesterday afternoon, not to mention the kiloton of motion cams and alarms set up around the premises by tech agents. Doreen would've triggered something if she had come back to try to find her love. Or whatever.

"I mean it," Mina stated calmly, trying her best to talk down an agitated Doreen. "I had nothing to do with Frankie's death. Tedesco had plans in place all along for Frankie to take the blame." Mina peered at her, trying to figure out where she had gone wrong in her previous assumptions. This happy-go-lucky gardener had fooled her completely. Mina had taken her as a nice, albeit loud and slightly irritating, gardener when they'd first met at Cots' shop. This turnaround was epic. Like a comet streak with a neon-yellow tail. She cursed her inner dar for not sensing any threat from this former slice of sunshine. *Damn.*

Mina tried a new tactic. "You know Frankie was involved in Veritus, right? The serial-killing group."

Maybe she could appeal directly to the woman Doreen had been *before* she'd gotten together with Frankie, the woman who might possibly still live somewhere inside her. When nothing registered, Mina added, "Killing, as in ruthlessly ending lives by way of noxious fumes that make people scream in agony and bleed out of their ears." Still nothing. "Lots and lots of killing and death. Veritus left a swath of wreckage littered with broken lives and grieving families in its wake." Lee's among them.

Doreen's eyelids shifted to slits, her stony stare boring right through Mina. She lowered the laser to chest level. Maybe that would hurt less than a blast to the face? "I saw you. I *heard* you. My Frankie died because of *you*."

Wait a second. She *heard* Mina? *Saw* her?

Mina finally realized why she hadn't spotted Doreen's craft parked nearby.

"You never left. When Cots and the other gardeners went home for the day...you stayed behind? How? Where?" Mina searched the delivery area. She'd missed something key. Had Cots been so confused after Mina had left with an out-cold Andy that he hadn't realized Doreen wasn't among the other gardeners when they left?

"Of course I stayed! It wasn't hard to do. I told Cots I was being picked up by private transpo, and he bought it. My love contacted me. Used our secret signal. He needed my help. Things were going down. When Andy disappeared over the shoulder of that hulking, faux gardener Grigg, I knew something wasn't right. I should've stopped you right then and there, but I didn't.

I follow the rules. I was told to keep a low profile. So I let you go." She grinned, her back stiffening to show she was confident she could've stopped two federal agents—maybe three, as Mina didn't know who Grigg was affiliated with. As *if.*

Mina glanced over Doreen's shoulder, knowing this woman had come out of the waste room, wondering if there was something to that. "I'm assuming you have a secret way inside the residence from here?" she asked, ignoring Doreen's severely misplaced bravado.

"What, are you stupid? Haven't you been listening to what I've been telling you? I don't need to be *inside* the residence to know what you've done," she sneered. "I have my own hidey-hole out here. My love made sure I had a place to go if everything came tumbling down, which it did."

"Through the waste room?" Maybe Tedesco kept his secrets through there. Mina had to check it out.

"Why don't you find out for yourself?"

That worked.

Doreen stepped back and to the side, gesturing for Mina to move toward the waste room. "Open that door," she commanded. "And don't try anything funny. I'm itching for revenge. Just give me a reason. A single reason. Blowing a hole through you would make my day so much brighter."

Mina moved forward cautiously, her hands still in the air. At some point, she would need to hit her cuff to send out an alert. She settled one hand on the lever and pulled open the door. It was a tiny space. A single toilet sat at the back, and a small sink was mounted on the wall.

Nothing advertised *escape pod* whatsoever. It was hard not to feel bad that Mina had overlooked it the one time she'd been inside. That time, she'd been trying to hear Tedesco and Frankie talking... She remembered now that Doreen had repeatedly pounded on the door, interrupting her.

Things were adding up.

"What would you like me to do now?" Mina asked once inside.

"Take off your cuff. No, let me do it. I trust you about as far as a jetty can fly with a broken prop, which is about a meter if you're lucky. I'd pay to see that. I bet you'd land right on your skinny ass and break a few bones." She chuckled. When Mina didn't comply quickly enough, she growled. An actual growl. It sounded feral, like the sound a woman would make if she lost someone she loved. Which, if everything Doreen had said was true, she had. "Hold out your arm. If you don't, I'll sever it. This laser is so hot it cauterizes as it cuts. Don't believe me? Give me a reason. Hard to do your dumb job without an arm."

Mina had to hand it to her—or not, depending on how you looked at it—this woman was a walking, talking hard-ass. It was becoming less and less surprising that Doreen had chosen a life of crime. Mina held out her wrist. This was a government cuff, and if it was tampered with by hands other than Mina's, it would send out its own alert. So it was basically the same as Mina doing it.

Doreen reached for it, then stopped. "You take it off," she commanded. "You government types are sneaky and sly, but not sneakier than my love, and he taught me everything. And if you say anything or touch anything that sets that off while you're doing it, you're a dead woman without a head. I'll just stuff you back in there, and nobody will ever find you." She was gleeful. The thought of cutting Mina's head off made her giggle like she was in middle school programming.

Mina was beginning to think that killing her would fulfill the revenge clause for Doreen very nicely. For a man involved with Veritus, Frankie would have lived by revenge. Depending on how long they'd been together, Doreen now likely shared that same mentality.

Mina had no choice but to do what she was told. She didn't want to give Doreen the happiness she so desired with her untimely death.

Once the cuff was off, Doreen motioned for Mina to place it in the sink. Then Doreen leaned over and shot it with her laser.

Mina arched back as it exploded and then watched in morbid curiosity as it melted into a gummy pile and began to drip through the hole Doreen had put in the sink. Lasers were hot like that.

Dang. Mina had liked that cuff. It'd been good to her.

But unlucky for Doreen, destroying it had just triggered a homing signal. She guessed Frankie hadn't known *everything.*

"Move," Doreen ordered.

"Where to?" Mina asked. "There's barely enough room for the both of us in here."

Doreen grabbed the door and closed it behind them. "It only works if the latch is secured."

She grunted as the laser jammed into Mina's ribs from behind. It wasn't a very comfortable feeling. One slip of Doreen's wrist, and Mina would be lasered in half, or at the very least have a big, gaping, scalding-hot hole seared through her insides.

"See that backup flusher lever? Right behind it is a button. Push it and then take a step back."

Mina did as she was told. Stepping back meant placing herself against Doreen and the laser again. Luckily, Mina didn't have to wait long. The entire wall behind the toilet began to shift backward, exposing a small opening.

"This was my Frankie's idea," Doreen espoused in a dreamy voice that did not fit the current situation. "No one would be looking for anything in here, he said. He was right! You didn't even know it existed. I thought maybe you were trying to get inside it when you spent so much time in here the other day. That's why I pounded on the door. But it looked like you'd just gone to the bathroom. See, my suspicions were right about you earlier. Frankie thought you were just a gardener, but he put me and Andy on extra alert just in case. We knew the feds would be on to us sooner than later. I thought to myself that you were just too pretty to be a gardener. You should've just showed up how you look now with no alt. No one would've paid you any attention." *Ouch.* "Go on, then," Doreen urged, jabbing the gun harder into her ribs.

Mina moved forward, stepping into the new space. The first thing to hit her was the smell. Musty, like it hadn't been opened in a while, overlaid with a syrupy-sweet scent, like candy. Then Mina saw the wrappers.

So many wrappers. This space must not have a meal printer, but someone had stocked it full of what appeared to be maple treats and something with a strong strawberry scent. Pink smears coated half the wrappers.

"Don't mind the mess." Doreen shooed Mina farther into the room, which was a surprisingly large space. Doreen ordered, "Show screens."

Immediately, a false wall lowered and exposed a wall full of monitors. Mina's heart sank. Several of them showed Tedesco's inner sanctum. Doreen had indeed seen exactly what had transpired last night.

Mina addressed the former happy gardener, surprise ringing in her voice, as something dawned on her. "You're the one who contacted Tedesco's allies and told them he'd been taken into custody." Mina considered herself a good judge of character, if not above average in the body-language department, but Doreen had just exploded all that. Mina had noted zero—absolutely *zero*—of her tells.

It was more than a little humbling.

"Taken into custody?" Doreen said. "I thought he was dead. You nearly blew him in half!"

"The media covered it soon after. Everybody knew he wasn't dead," Mina countered. "They all reported that he'd been taken to the Medi Center and was still breathing."

"That came a good thirty minutes after you hydro-bombed him—not that I was sad, because he took out my love right in front of my eyes—but I *saw* it happen. By the time the screencasts were reporting, I'd already raised the alarm." She flashed a set of perfectly micro-enameled teeth.

"You have to move quickly in this organization. Veritus doesn't abide by losers and lollygaggers."

Good to know. Or not at all good?

"We have rules, and I followed them with honor."

Honor was clearly not the right word. More like *complete disregard for human life.*

Mina's mind raced as she tried to remember whether this woman knew her real identity. Had Mina mentioned anything of note to Tedesco about herself or Lee? Doreen had known her only as Marilyn Leonard, the better-than-average-looking gardener. But if Doreen had captured still shots of her and Lee from the screens in this hidey-hole, Veritus would have images of Mina in a black wig and Lee with violet hair and a goatee. That could be enough for them to work from to try and track down who they were.

"What is Veritus planning to do with the gas they just took from the shipyard?" Mina asked, hoping she sounded matter-of-fact and not at all cagey or needy.

"Why the great cosmos above would I tell you something like that?" Doreen made a face. Something between annoyance and exasperation, her eyes shooting upward. "But you needn't worry your boring little head about it. I'm taking care of things here. Now we just have to get that hacker, and all will be right with the world."

They still thought Lee was superhacker Jordan Maybach. That was good, as Jordan would have his identity and traceable elements locked down tight. They would have trouble getting any intel on him.

"'Right with the world' as in Veritus is done killing forever once you take care of us? Or 'right with the world' as in you got your revenge, now you're going to regroup and start where you left off gassing people to death?"

"You ask too many questions, you know that? I bet you're a drag in real life."

Mina was *not* a drag. She was a kiloton o' fun.

"Taking everything so serious all the time will give you an ulcer," Doreen said. "I'm living proof of that. You have to learn to go with the flow. No one needs to know everything all the time. It's just not right. We have to save some secrets for later." She cackled. Doreen had mastered the role of evil villain, complete with super-dyed hair and weird yellow eyes.

"I'd prefer you reveal your secrets before you kill me with a super-hot laser," Mina said simply.

Doreen pushed up into her personal space, sneering, "Well, I'm not going to tell you. How do you like that?"

Mina blew out an exasperated breath and rolled her eyes. "I guess we're going to have to do this the hard way." She raised her arm and brought the edge of her hand down on Doreen's wrist, snapping it hard. Predictably, the woman let go of the laser. Mina caught it with her other hand as she pivoted and sent her booted foot right into Doreen's gut.

The woman crashed backward, hitting the edge of a sleeping pod with considerable force, then tumbling to the floor, gasping for air, clutching her belly.

A shout sounded from outside. A moment later, Lee appeared in the secret doorway, which was still open,

Agent Darian right behind him with her blaster out. At least somebody had brought a weapon.

Lee glanced down at Doreen, mouth agape, then back up at Mina. "Your cuff sent out an alarm and a location. McAllister just called. He's sending reinforcements."

"I know," Mina replied as she moved toward Doreen, who was now crying and cursing at the same time. "Anna, I need a pair of e-restraints."

Agent Darian came forward, pulling a pair out of her pocket. "Who is she?"

"Information we were hoping to find." Just not of the tech variety.

Chapter 9

MINA KNELT BY the whimpering Doreen. It was her turn to cackle. "Stop sniveling like a tot," Mina ordered. "You're going to help us, and this is how it's going to go. I'm going to sit you right over there in that chair, and you're going to answer every one of my questions like it's your job."

"But...but...I can't," she wailed.

"You can. And you will."

"They'll kill me if I do." She hiccupped. "I'm just a gardener. I wasn't meant for any of this!"

Mina refrained from rolling her eyes all the way to the back of her head. "You were just talking like a long drone hauler two minutes ago. What the hell happened?"

"I was...role-playing." She sniffle-hiccupped. "Frankie said I was very good at it. He said they should film a whole vid production with me as the star. He said if I ever got in trouble, that's what I needed to do. I had to act tough or die!" The dramatics were in full effect.

Mina sat back on her haunches. She felt a little better

knowing it had all been an act. Not spotting Doreen's tells stung a tiny bit less. Okay, a *teensy* bit.

"It was all an act?" Mina stood. "Well, you're good at it, though it was clear you'd never handled a weapon in your life. You were waving it all over like your arm was made of elastomer. But that doesn't matter. We need to know what you know. End of story. After we debrief you, we'll take you into protective custody. That way, the Veritus goons can't off you."

"No." She shook her head so hard her sunny halo of hair bounced around. "You can't take me in! They have people on the inside. They'll get to me!"

Lee made a surprised sound, and Agent Darian muttered something unintelligible.

Mina squatted in front of Doreen once again, her voice hard. "*Who's* on the inside?"

"They...Veritus..." For the first time, the not-so-jolly gardener looked unsure. "They have people inside the government. In high-powered positions. They did Tedesco's bidding. They made things happen for him. They're in on it. Even if they weren't involved with the killing stuff, they got paid kilotons of currency. They can get to me if you take me in."

Mina grabbed hold of Doreen's shirt and pulled her off the ground, startling her like she'd meant to. "I need names. Right now. I need to know who's involved in this network. This isn't a game anymore, Doreen. This is not role-play. Frankie's not here to protect you. People are going to die, and I'm not going to let that happen."

"I don't know," she wailed. "I was too new. They didn't

trust me with anything. Frankie said I had to prove myself. I did. I sent out the alert after you took Tedesco into custody! I did what Frankie told me to, even though he's not here anymore to see it." She ended with a series of sobbing barks that morphed into quieter weeping, tears rushing down her cheeks.

Mina let go, allowing her to fall back. Frustrated, hands fisted, she asked Lee and Agent Darian, "Where's the backup? I need to talk to McAllister. Someone get him up on holo now."

Agent Darian obliged.

"Report, Agent Kane." McAllister's image floated above Agent Darian's wrist.

"I was checking out the delivery area and came across the gardener Doreen, surname unknown. She pulled a laser on me, recognizing my voice from both gardening and seeing me on screen with Tedesco last night. She destroyed my cuff and took me into a secret room behind the waste area. It's filled with monitors and tech, a sleeping pod"—Mina turned—"and empty candy wrappers. She's Frankie's love interest and was the one who sent the alert to Veritus last night, after Tedesco went down. I had her talking until she wasn't anymore. So I disarmed her, and Agent Adams and Agent Darian arrived. We e-cuffed her, and now I'm interrogating her. Sir, she says that Veritus has people on the inside. Government people. She's scared to talk and doesn't want us to bring her in."

Veritus having links to the US government was appalling. None of this was good news. "Since she was the one who raised the alarm," McAllister said, "she must have access to other information."

"That could be, but I'm not entirely certain." Mina inspected the room. She homed in on a red button on the wall. She walked toward it. "She might've just pressed this."

In Mina's absence, Lee had crouched next to Doreen, trying to calm her down. "Is that true, Doreen?" Lee asked, coaxing. "Did you press that button?"

"Yes…yes…that's all I did. I swear!"

"What does the button do, Doreen?" Mina asked.

"Frankie said that everybody would get a signal, and they'd know how to respond."

Mina was disgusted. She walked swiftly toward Doreen. "What do you think their orders were? What did you think would happen?"

"I don't know!"

"Yes, you do. You know exactly what would happen. You were standing there lecturing me not even five minutes ago about not knowing all the secrets. You may not know who all the players are, but you knew exactly what you were doing and what was going to happen. They're going to *kill* people. Maybe me or some of my people. They're going to get their revenge. People are going to die because of what you did."

"I didn't know. I didn't know!" she insisted, sobbing.

"Wrong," Mina spat. "But lucky you, you get to spend a lot of quality time in a box thinking about what you did and what it means." She crouched low, a few centimeters away. "Give us everything inside your brain, and I mean *everything,* and I'll make sure you get a plant or two inside your box. That's the only deal you're ever going to get."

"I'll help," she moaned. "But there's not much there."

"You can say that again," Agent Darian muttered.

Mina stood as McAllister said, "A drone just touched down on the roof. Two teams have been deployed. I'm sending another tech team now. We need to make sure nothing blows up, to be on the safe side in case Lee's cancellation of deadly protocol didn't apply in the gardens."

"Doreen, is there anything in here that can harm us?" Mina asked. "Not just gas, but any booby traps?"

"Of course not." She went back to wailing. "Frankie wouldn't hurt me! I'm his morning glory. His sweet pea. He would never place me in harm's way."

Mina refrained from gagging. The shut-off reflex was in full effect today. "Exactly how long were you and Frankie together?"

"Four months, three days, six hours, and forty-two seconds. Then he was taken away from me! Oh, my Frankie, my baby, my love. He's gone! He's all gone," she wept.

Mina glanced at her director's still-hovering image. "I would predict Frankie put in some fail-safes she doesn't know about. Make sure the tech team treads softly." To Doreen, she said, "He used you. You were convenient. You were malleable. Did you meet on the tiers? Did he come up and compliment your annuals or your gardening prowess?"

"Yes! He said they were divine, like the sunlight in my eyes. He said it was love at first sight!"

"You believed him? That's such a shame, Doreen." Mina hauled her off the ground, commanding her with her eyes to stop weeping. Mina was not role-playing. Doreen understood. She quieted.

"If anyone dies because you know something and didn't tell me," Mina said, "you'll never, ever leave your box. Are we clear? You need to start talking. Now."

———

"It's been two hours," Mina commented to her partner. It was good to see the light of day. The secret room was dark and uninviting. Mina blinked a few times. "I don't think we're getting any more out of her. At least for today."

The delivery area was crawling with agents. The tech crew had taken apart the room and found no threats.

"Doreen knew more than she thought, but it still wasn't a lot," Lee replied.

"She had no names, no faces, and no way to find any of them. Frankie didn't even give her contact info other than his. The only thing inside that secret room were monitors and an alert button. Feels more like a safe room than anything else. I picture Frankie holing up in there if things went bad. A place to hide, nothing more. Tedesco, according to her, didn't even know it existed. Frankie had it set up when he did the recent security upgrades. This is all Frankie, so Tedesco wouldn't keep anything in there.

That means we still haven't found what we've been searching for." Mina felt more than frustrated. "We need names. We need locations. We need more."

McAllister walked up. He'd arrived on scene twenty minutes ago. "I'm having Doreen Beltrami moved to Government Three. I don't want her in the same vicinity as Tedesco. We have enough to hold her for now. Her DNA is all over this place, including on the red button. Once the tech unit figures out where that call goes and puts a trace on it, we'll have more to work with."

"Frankie did a number on her," Lee said.

"Don't go feeling sorry for her," Mina ordered. "She's a forty-seven-year-old woman who can think for herself. She chose wrong, and she'll pay the price. That cost will be even higher if something happens to any of us. Don't forget, she was the one who alerted Tedesco's followers about what was happening. She is culpable and undeserving of your pity."

"It's getting late," Director McAllister said as he glanced at his cuff.

Mina took a second to mourn the loss of hers. Her whole life had been on that thing. She'd have a new one soon. The order was already in. But still.

"You two are excused for the night," McAllister said. "I want you well rested and ready for tomorrow. The tech team will stay on, searching for any clues and going over the safe room. We will resume our investigations here in the morning. Remain on high alert. We now know for sure that Veritus has sensitive information about us. We just don't know what they're going to do with it, or how easy it will be for them to find what they're looking for." He turned to Lee. "What's happening with the Cupid's Bow?"

Lee hadn't reported yet because of all the Doreen craziness. "I'm getting close," he answered. "I haven't found a message, but I've found a possible location here in the city. Not far from where I live, actually."

McAllister looked pensive for a moment. "If he's here in the city, that means something. Keep at it, Agent Adams. If you don't finish it before morning, report in. I'm moving this priority up." To Mina, he asked, "What are your thoughts?"

"I'm not sure. I haven't had much time to process. Vince gave no indication at dinner that he knew I was an agent, although I would allow that when he was questioning my job as a linguist, he did so lightly and with a smile. But from the kid I knew a long time ago, there has to be a reason for all this." She hoped a good one. "I don't think he's trying to waste our time. He could be in danger, or he's trying to tell us something. Hopefully, we'll uncover what it is soon."

"You're both excused. Veritus will need time to set up a plan and put it in motion. My hope is we stay one step ahead of them while they do it. Reports are coming in from abroad. The more members we pick up, the more intel we'll have." Someone shouted for his attention, and he nodded as he walked away.

Mina and Lee headed to the landing pad. A government drone was waiting.

Once in the air, Lee commented, "That was completely

wild. Did you ever for a moment think Doreen would be involved?"

Mina took a breath and settled her head back on the rest, closing her eyes. "No. And that's the problem. I should have."

Lee made a gurgling noise. "No way! *She* didn't even know she was in on it. It's been what, four months? I bet she didn't even believe it herself most of the time. She's clearly not cut out for that kind of work. She wanted to make Frankie happy and was excited to be in what she assumed was love. But it wasn't anything. Frankie saw a sucker and took the opportunity."

"Well, that sucker has put our lives in direct jeopardy. Don't forget it for a second. And take what McAllister said seriously. High alert from now on. We don't know what was sent from that room or what the *signal* meant. Even though Doreen acted like she was cooperating, I didn't get the vibe she was fully honest with us. She's scared for her life. Fear makes people irrational. She wouldn't agree to say anything until McAllister allowed her to come in under an alias. It was the only way to get her to stop wailing." Mina blew out a breath. "So much for us getting time off."

Lee chuckled. "I didn't really expect it to last very long. It was a nice idea, though."

"We started the day with bacon. At least that was something."

"Yeah, I guess it was."

A few moments later, they touched down near Lee's place. Mina peered out the window. The neighborhood was not aging well, and the buildings were all in need of repair. "Have you been contacted by headquarters about a new place?"

Lee brightened. "No. But I'm hoping they'll reach out soon. I still can't believe it. I left a message for my mom. She hasn't gotten back to me. She's going to be amazed." The passenger door began to rise. "I'll see you tomorrow. Thanks again for letting me stay at your place last night. It was really nice of you."

"No problem. My breakfast tomorrow is bound to be bland and boring. Stay alert, Lee." She gave him a three-finger salute as the door began to close.

The sim intoned, "Next stop, The Spire, hub level twenty. Do you wish to make any changes?"

"Yes, in fact, I do."

Chapter 10

"Damn, that really blows," Kaylee said. "Like, hard. It blows like a big, stinky, gas-bagging killer wind blast."

"I know." Mina petted Dag, who was curled around her legs like a giant teddy bear. His snoring was epic.

"Do you think whoever got this red alert from Doreen the Gas-Bagger knows who you really are?" Kaylee rearranged herself on the floor. She sat across from Mina, her back resting against her lounger. Kaylee's home was comfortable and stylish, with a touch of sass. It was a perfect reflection of her. "If they run facial, they'd just get an old pic of Wilhelmina Kandy Kane."

Mina winced. Being reminded of her surname, which she gave herself at the age of three, was always kind of a shock.

"That doesn't necessarily mean they'll be able to track you down," Kaylee added.

"The Spire has my birth name on record. If they have

good hackers, like I assume they do, they'll find me eventually."

"'Eventually' is the key, right? If we track them down first, it won't be an issue."

"That's the hope." Mina stretched. It had already been late when she arrived, now it was later.

"You can crash here for the night. My lounger is pretty comfortable." Kaylee reached back and patted the orange, well-loved lounger with its assortment of vibrant throw pillows in all colors of the rainbow. Somehow, it all worked.

"Nah," Mina replied. "My platform is amazingly comfortable, and it's calling to me right now." She yawned. It was edging toward midnight. "I just needed some girl time. Being able to talk this through was a good debrief. Man, Doreen's a real head case. I can't believe someone would ever fall for a guy like Frankie the Manipulator. It defies logic."

"I don't find it surprising at all." Kaylee stood, helping Mina disengage herself from her lovable pile of fur. Dag barely woke up, rolling onto his belly, snoring louder. "Love is a powerful tool. Speaking of love, what's been happening in Love Town?" She giggled. Dag's ears perked, but he stayed mostly comatose.

Mina had been so busy filling her friend in about what was going on with Tedesco, she'd completely forgotten to tell Kaylee about the Cupid's Bow. "Lee is getting close to finding a location, and get this, it's in the city."

Kaylee gasped. "Are you kidding? Why would he be here?"

"That's the question of the hour, or rather, the question of the...how many days have we been at this?" Mina yawned.

"If I remember correctly, Vince had a bruise under one eye. Do you think he's in actual duress? I find it hard to believe that a colonel in the Protectorate would be in trouble like that and wouldn't enlist the hundreds of troops at his command, but I guess it's possible?"

"Lee thinks he might've gone to these lengths to get a message to me, but couldn't do it the regular way because he was being monitored. That makes the most sense, honestly. Once Lee hacks the location, we'll see where it is and go from there."

"That's very logical. Well done."

"We'll see." Mina turned at her pal's door. "Thanks for calling a ride for me. I should have a new cuff by tomorrow. It was late in the day when mine got ruined, and McAllister has requested a specific model as a replacement, so I have to wait a bit. It sucks to be without. I liked that one. It was free of any kinks. It's a good thing my new residence has a smudger and a retinal scanner, or I wouldn't be able to get inside. I'd have to call Suzanne, my mega rep." Mina chortled. "She'd love that. She'd want an immediate update on everything Vincent Kramer."

Kaylee snorted. "Those reps have to work hard to earn those credits. Not a problem calling you a ride. My craft barely gets any use these days. Don't go anywhere else either. Go straight home. Doreen the Gas-Bagger wrecked your social life for a while. Keep me posted about Vince. I'm completely intrigued."

She started snapping her fingers, and Mina buzzed out the door. "Do *not* start singing."

"Can't stop meh."

Mina darted into the tube to the sound of, "He's gonna win, not gonna throw a dumb lob, cuz he's an international heart-*thrroob*."

"Those aren't the words," Mina called as the tube doors shut.

"They are now!"

Being with Kaylee always cheered her up. Minus the singing. Or because of it?

The ride home took less than five minutes.

Mina was inside her residence within two more. After Veronica's greeting, Mina realized she was hungry. "Eggie, make me a bowl of tomato soup and a grilled cheese on sourdough."

"Processing your order. Would you like pepper jack? It gives a rather bland sandwich a nice kick."

She chuckled. "No. Cheddar is fine." She and her meal printer were at a bantering point now. She didn't hate it. Her last meal printer had been boring by comparison. There were a lot of benefits to living lux.

As Eggie was preparing her meal, Mina ordered, "Veronica, turn on screen in living area." A moment later, it popped on. Mina's data on Geoff Ramsey flashed. The search had been completed while she was gone.

She noticed something and moved forward. "Computer, enhance left quadrant by thirty. Bring it front and center." It enlarged and floated to the center. She peered at the name and the job description following it.

It was a different spelling than his birth name—he'd used Jeffrey Ramsey—but the job was intriguing.

Eggie beeped, announcing her order was ready, and she went to retrieve it.

"Why would he be working under an alternative spelling of his name at a Pleasure Emporium in Vegas?" There was a chance it wasn't him, but the timing conveniently corresponded with a gap in employment for Geoffrey Ramsey. He'd held the Vegas job right before he moved to the city.

"Would you like me to try and answer that?" Veronica asked.

"No, just speaking out loud." The perils of having voice command as part of your daily lifestyle.

"Veronica, put a call into Harri Hampburg, home address, contact on file. Put in a request for a vid chat, but offer audio only as well. No formal message if he doesn't answer." It was late after all. There was less than a twenty percent chance Harri would pick up, but Mina wanted to know a little more about Geoff's Vegas life before she explored this line more.

A full minute later, Harri popped on her screen, the data sliding automatically to the side. He was a wreck, his hair all mussed and circles under his eyes.

"Harri, what's going on?" Mina asked. "You look like hell."

He ran both hands through his hair, leaving it even more messy and wild. "I got fired."

She set down her spoon. "Seriously?" That wasn't good.

"They said it was because of a performance issue, but it's not a coincidence. They called me into the office not even ten minutes after you left. They had to have been listening. There's no other answer. Now I'm just waiting for the other ecoboot to drop. What are they going to do to me?" Anguish poured out. "They could evict me from my residence. They could blacklist me from ever getting other employment. My borrows won't hold. I'm going to end up in the outskirts!"

"No, you're not. I swear. I can help get to the bottom of this. We'll solve it together."

"Don't you see? There's no bottom. It's a dark, horrible abyss. What they do to me will be never ending." He shook his head. "I told you this would happen. I *told* you. I don't know what to do. It's a nightmare come true."

"I can fix this," Mina promised.

"There's nothing to fix. Corporations like Bliss Corp rule the world. How can you not know that by now?" He was angry. He had every right to be angry. Mina had insisted on that meeting, and it'd cost him his job, his livelihood, and his well-being.

"This is my fault. I told you I'm going to fix it."

"I appreciate that. But I'm already in their sights. There's nothing you can do."

The hell there was. "I'm not giving up on you, Harri. I made you a promise. All is not lost. I just need to call in a favor or two. Stay where you are. Someone should be contacting you within the hour."

"I'm not going anywhere, because I have nowhere to go."

Mina winced. Asking him for more information at this moment was going to be awkward, but in order to solve this case—should be an *official* case soon, if she was lucky—she had to search for answers. Harri had information in his brain that she needed. "I found out something about Geoff. I need to ask you a few more questions."

He gaped. "Answering your questions is what got me here in the first place!"

"I understand. I'm sorry." Another wince. "If it's any consolation, it's a tactical mistake on their part to fire you. Now there's no harm in sharing it all, not to mention you're a sworn, protected government witness."

"What do you mean 'no harm'? They could kill me. They're probably monitoring me right now."

"Killing you would not be to their advantage. They want to keep a very low profile. We're speaking on a secure line. I reached out to you. My security is embedded both ways. But even if they are monitoring you, they know I'm a federal agent. If they harm you, I will prove it. They wouldn't dare risk exposure like that. Everything they do is to benefit their bottom line, which is amassing currency." She said it loud and confidently, just in case they *were* listening. The chance they could infiltrate a highly secure line wasn't likely, but it wasn't zero either. "Please answer one question. Then I'll let you go."

He looked at her intently but said nothing.

She took that as a yes. "Did Geoff used to work in Vegas? That's all I need to know."

"Not that I'm aware of. He's never mentioned anything about Vegas."

"He never mentioned that he worked in your same industry? Never let it slip?"

Harri's eyebrows shot up. "No." He hesitated. "But..."

"Come on, Harri," Mina encouraged. "The only thing left to do now is bring Bliss Corp to its knees. That's how we win this."

"It's just...he seemed to know a lot of the jargon we use. Not sex jargon, obviously. But words we use behind the scenes. Things that we would never say to a client. I thought it was a little odd at first and told him so. He just chuckled and chuffed it off. He said he's been going to Pleasure Emporiums since they opened, and he must've picked up on some of the phrasing. I let it go."

"That's what I thought. Thank you. Answer any calls that come through in the next hour. If something else happens, contact me right away. And for what it's worth, I'm really sorry. I'm making a pledge to you that you will remain safe. That's a promise."

"Thanks. I appreciate that. At least I have a subscription to Holo Interactive. They haven't taken that away yet. I can jump into a game. That always helps."

"Good idea. I'll be in touch." She signed off.

Mina glanced down at her soup. She wasn't hungry anymore. She pushed it away. Until she could get a hold of Geoffrey Ramsey and interview him to confirm all the details Harri had provided, an official investigation wouldn't be opened.

So, in order to help Harri now, since she'd gotten him fired and it was clear Bliss Corp knew she was investigating, she had to resort to something unconventional.

She knew it was late, but he was probably up. "Veronica, put a call in to Norman Webb, request vid chat, but if it goes to message, send this: Hi, Norm, it's Mina. Calling in a favor. I have a chance for you to get your fingers sticky, just the way you like. Tag me back as soon as you can."

Chapter 11

"Damn right I like to get my golden fingers sticky." It was unsurprising that Norman Webb was up late and even more unsurprising that he'd taken Mina's call. "You're looking well." He squinted, leaning toward the screen. "Haven't heard from you in so long, I figured you moved out of the country." He gave a snort along with a short, barking laugh as he tossed his head back. What Norm didn't carry in stature, he made up for in enhanced sharpness. His age was ambiguous to any onlooker. He appeared like any typical middle-aged gentleman, standing a little shorter than average, lines at the corners of his eyes, neatly shorn iron-gray hair, perfectly enameled teeth, no sagging skin.

"You know why I haven't reached out, Norm. I have to use those golden fingers sparingly. Ex-marshal turned PI turned unlicensed can get a girl like me in a bunch of trouble. How are you, by the way? You're looking good. Still spry and healthy, I see."

"Not doing too bad. Got myself an exercise membership at one of those dome centers. I can keep up with the young ones just fine. Though, why they have to have the screens blasting all the time is beyond me. Screens are enormous, too, taking up two full stories. The noise is deafening. Quiet and contemplative can go a long way." He brought a bare arm into view and flexed. "But now the golden fingers have some muscle to back them up." He made a fist and rotated it outward.

Mina laughed. "Those muscles will come in handy, as my sticky situation is in need of a little heft."

His expression sobered, as it did when he talked business. Norman Webb could be a jokester, but he was all business when it came to the craft he had honed for thirty years, plus ten more on his own. He'd been a marshal with the federal High Crimes Unit, but his and Mina's paths had crossed more than a few times. His personality was infectious and hard to ignore. He was also intensely curious and wasn't afraid to get right up in anyone's face, which made him great at his job. He missed little and called out what he saw. He'd been the first and only agent to ever doubt Mina's cover story of working with Street Crime. She'd never officially come clean to him, but he knew she was with a secret department and didn't push.

She'd used his expertise in the past as an independent officer when her cases had needed that little extra boost. Director McAllister didn't necessarily condone it, but if it got the job done, he was okay with it. He was well acquainted with Norm Webb. But even so, Mina and

McAllister usually tiptoed around his involvement, never naming him outright.

But Mina owed it to Harri to bring in someone who could handle the job from the outside, and Norm Webb was that man.

"What's bothering you that these golden fingers can help with?" Norman asked, wiggling his fingers.

He'd solved more crimes for his unit than the next two agents combined. The joke was whatever he laid his hands on turned to gold. If Mina had a good sense of body language, Norm had one on super growth hormones. The agency he worked for had been sorry to see him go, but retirement was mandatory at age eighty.

"I'm going after a big, big fish, Norm. As in a multi-trillion-dollar fish, to be exact. This so-called grouper is allegedly testing a big-time pharma drug on unsuspecting humans, and I've personally seen the effects up close. I've got a civilian embroiled in it, and because it's not yet a federal case in my jurisdiction, this civilian needs a little extra protecting. I also could use help digging for that very elusive gold."

"Have I ever told you about that time I protected the president of a small country and his family for forty-three days on my own?" His eyes lit at the memory. Norm loved telling stories of his past escapades.

Mina chuckled. "You have. You fooled two different factions that were after them. Convinced them that they'd left the country and then ferried them to safety. And that's why you're the man for this job."

"I've got more credits than borrows these days. I'd

love to do anything I can to help a fellow agent."

Mina filled him in on the parameters. "The civilian has been informed and is aware you'll be contacting him. His protection is of utmost importance to me. We go back, and I got him involved. Since the company fired him, they know something's going on, but I'm not sure how much intel they have. They certainly know there's no open case yet. So they may be biding their time. We're also looking for like cases, either inside emporiums or out. We need on-record interviews with vics. I'll have to join you to make them official, but you can set them up. According to gleaned information, these adverse pharma reactions are happening quite a bit. Plush is a full-on craze, so it shouldn't be too hard to track a few people who've had it happen to them or a loved one."

"Pleasure is all anybody talks about these days," Norm half groused, half chortled. "I can start at that exercise dome. I've made quite a few contacts there already. If it's as prevalent as you seem to think, I bet these young body-conscious youths know something about it."

"I bet you're right. For now, we use this secure channel to communicate. I'm temporarily without a cuff. If big corporate gets wind of what you're doing, be prepared. They could come at you hard."

He made a swiping gesture with his hand, fingers wiggling. "*Pssh*. They don't scare me. There's nothing they can do to ol' Norm that hasn't been done already. They won't outright kill me. They don't want bad press. I'll leave a little vid testimonial and let it be known it will be automatically released if something happens to me.

That's standard these days anyway. Times have changed since I was a new marshal, flexing my wings in the jet stream." He shook his head sadly, his ice-blue diffracted eyes narrowing. "People had more integrity. Maybe that's because they were fearful about the new boxing rules our government had set up for the soon-to-be incarcerated. Those early boxes put the fear into people for some time. But, whatever the reason, there was less sneaking around. When the criminals did their business, they did it out in the open." He chuckled. "Which, honestly, made them easier to catch. That's not so these days."

"I hear you. I spend my life trying to track down the sneakers." She didn't elaborate on the work, and Norm didn't ask. "Check in with me tomorrow, or if you get a line on anything significant. I'm counting on you to keep the civilian safe."

"I will, there's no doubt about it. If you need me, get in touch. Go get 'em." He popped off the screen.

Mina yawned. It was beyond time to get some of that sleep everyone was talking about.

"I've got a location," Lee said excitedly as he climbed into the craft. "I was going to call you, but then we got the summons, so I thought I'd tell you in person."

"A Vince location?" Mina rubbed her tired eyes. McAllister had summoned them in. Something was up, but he hadn't said what, which was worrisome.

"Yes. And there was a message. It doesn't make much sense."

"What is it?" Mina tried to keep the antsy out of her voice, but this was big.

"It just said Princess Priscilla of the Poconos. It was embedded into the residence location that's less than a kilometer from my unit. The message was coded with that old-fashioned code you helped me with last time. From the looks of the residence, it's a shabby, run-down building like mine. Then McAllister called, so I had to go. I brought it with me." He patted his pants. "Does the Priscilla thing make any sense?"

So much sense. "Yes. Vince wants me to go there. Princess Priscilla was a game we played when we were young. He was the Servant of Seville." Lee looked worried. "Never mind. We just talked about it at dinner, so I'm one hundred percent certain that's why he chose it. He made sure it was fresh in my mind." Mina glanced out the window as they flew, thinking about their conversation. He'd found an opening when she'd brought up the term *knight,* and he'd tried to make sure she understood what was to come.

They were almost to Tedesco's penthouse. She suspected McAllister had never left.

"We need to get to that residence as soon as possible."

Lee looked intrigued. "Do you think he'll be there?"

"I'm not sure. But I do know that whatever he wants us to find will be. Depending on what's going on at Tedesco's will determine how soon we can check it out."

"Do you know why McAllister called us this early?" Lee yawned and rubbed his eyes. He'd likely been up all night, and it was a little before dawn.

"No. I received a recorded summons."

"Is that usual?"

She sat up. "Come to think of it, no." She glanced out the window again, relieved to see they were landing on the penthouse roof, where lots of other government craft were parked. It would've been highly unlikely that Veritus could've overtaken a government drone, but there wasn't a zero percent chance it could happen. With both Veritus and Bliss Corp, the calculations could never include a zero. That was getting old. "I suppose I should've called in a verification on this craft before I boarded. These are weird times, and we shouldn't take anything for granted. You know, with no zeros and all."

Lee gave her a strange look. "Oh, I checked before I got in. I always do."

Mina shot one of his own owl stares back at him. She needed some coffee. "What?"

"Every drone has a scan code on its belly. On the right channel, it broadcasts, to the second, a record of engine status, prop articulation, any hacking attempts, and numerous other safety precautions. I entered the image into my cuff and uploaded it as it landed. You should really start doing that." He looked a little scandalized that Mina hadn't taken A-grade precautions before she boarded.

"I was referring to verifying that this was in fact the craft McAllister had sent. As for commandeering, it's a high crime to interfere with a government drone. Plus, it's virtually impossible because of all the fail-safes installed in these things. Plus-plus, the craft gives an up-to-the-millisecond audio alert if any of those things you mentioned goes wrong. I've been doing this for a long time, Lee. The government takes the protection of their agents extremely seriously. You shouldn't be paranoid to go for a ride before checking the numbers first."

Lee snorted. He actually *snorted.* "I have software at home that can commandeer this thing remotely"—highly illegal—"so taking appropriate precautions isn't paranoid, it's smart."

It was too early in the morning for this, but she opted to teach. "Lee, if someone was interested in commandeering a government craft remotely, then the agents in question are likely to be *on* board when it happens. A villainous, hijacking cur wants us, not the craft. So, uploading data *before* you get on means very little. And if that very, very unlikely scenario were to happen—say, right at this exact moment—we have adequate means to resist it. Not only is there software to disengage or block the threat after it's received, but we have antiterrorist *hardware* on board. Jetties, floats, bubbles, guns, lasers, and more." She patted the panel beside her, indicating that there were ample things embedded on the inside to help them in such a scenario. "The likelihood of an event like that actually occurring is so minor it's not worth it to go to extremes before boarding. And honestly, it's ridiculously illegal to hack a government craft, so I'm going to forget you said something like that *out loud.*"

Lee looked sheepish. "I'm just saying," he mumbled, "safety is important. It never hurts to be prepared..." He trailed off.

"You're right, it never hurts to be prepared. But no use being paranoid either. And now you know." Thankfully, they had landed. Mina was anxious to talk to their director about everything Lee had uncovered.

The doors opened, and they disembarked. Agent Darian was there to greet them. It appeared as though she hadn't gone home the night before either. Her hair was escaping its customary knot, and she barely stifled a yawn.

"Hi, Anna," Mina said. "Looks like you had a rough night."

"Yeah. It's been a long one. Come this way," she instructed.

"What's going on?" Mina asked as they followed. "Why are you still here?"

"Doreen is dead."

Mina pulled up abruptly. "She was being transferred to Government Three when we left. What happened?" And why hadn't Mina heard about it before right now?

"Veritus happened. That's what we think, anyway. They somehow got to her remotely."

Lee shot Mina a look, as if to say, *See? Things* can *happen remotely.*

She ignored him like the professional she was. "How did she die?"

"She...keeled over. Medi-unit said she blew up on the inside. Something she ate, apparently. She made this strange face, gripped her belly, and fell over. No one knows how it happened. Intelligence is trying to figure it out. Best guess is that she ingested something."

Mina thought of all the candy wrappers she'd seen inside the bunker behind the waste room.

"It's possible Veritus sparked it remotely, or it was going to kill her at some point anyway," Agent Darian finished. "They aren't sure. Tech didn't pick up on anything else in the vanity. They think she ingested all of it, leaving no trace, and, you know, they weren't thinking about scanning her insides. We cleared out for a few hours just to be sure, then came back."

"That's intense." Mina made a face as they walked into the residence, which was crawling with agents. McAllister stood in the middle of the chaos. He waved them over.

"Follow me," he ordered. He was wearing a SWAT vest. Things were definitely serious.

"Why weren't we alerted when Doreen was killed?" Mina asked.

He didn't answer until they were well away from everyone. His face was streaked with exhaustion. "I didn't alert you because if Veritus knew what Doreen was doing as she was doing it, they know who she was talking to. The tech team found sensory cams and audio links throughout the hidey-hole safe room and inside the delivery area. Having you and Agent Adams come here now is a risk, but since we've been over every fiber of this place, including the gardens, and have redirected all the satellites out of the area, this is the best cloaking we have at the moment. What I need to discuss is too sensitive to discuss over the airwaves, even on a secure line, so that's why you're here."

Doreen was dead. Poor, gullible Doreen. Even though she'd made some very bad choices, Mina hadn't wished her harmed or dead.

"Poor Doreen," Lee muttered.

"Yeah, that's too bad," Mina said. "She was certain they'd kill her if she cooperated, and they did." Except nobody had expected it to happen quite so quickly. "She made bad choices, but she didn't deserve to die."

"Neither do either of you. That's why I'm sending you into lockdown." Which was basically a safe house on steroids. No communication in or out. It was the equivalent of being boxed up. McAllister wasn't fooling around.

Mina said, "What—"

Lee followed with, "Huh?"

Mina began again. "Wait a minute. We can't go into lockdown. This is our case. It's our op." She motioned between her and Lee. "We can't help bring the rest of Veritus down if we're stuck in a box somewhere with no resources in or out."

"Not your call," McAllister stated firmly. "We believe Veritus has had eyes and ears on this residence the entire time. They have facial rec on all of us. They are proving to be very smart and very aggressive. They took out a wit right in front of us, and we still don't know exactly how they did it. These people will stop at nothing to get what they want, and that's death by way of revenge. Your deaths." He glanced between the two of them, daring them to argue.

"Maybe a safe house isn't so bad?" Lee offered.

Mina shot him a look—less owl, more scrappy pigeon. "While I understand your reasonings, and they are sound, and I will follow your orders, I deeply dislike the idea of rabbiting down a hole," Mina argued lightly. Heavy on the light. "We haven't had a chance to update you on what Lee recently discovered about the hacked Cupid's Bow. Investigating that lead might provide a safe option for us. It's a place no one would think to search for us." The key to a successful location for a safe house was to choose a place that neither she nor Lee, nor the federal government, had any affiliation with. This location was exactly that. Then, for Veritus, it would be like trying to find a quark in an electrical storm.

McAllister turned his attention to Lee. "Report, Agent Adams."

"I was able to hack the Cupid's Bow and found the encrypted location. It's a residence near mine. Along with the formal drop point came a five-word coded message. The code was old-fashioned. Agent Kane recently used it with me, so I was able to break it quicker. It read 'Princess Priscilla of the Poconos,' which meant nothing to me, but it seems to have meaning for Agent Kane."

McAllister turned to Mina, who nodded in agreement. "It's a game Vince and I used to play as children. I feel Vince is directing me to investigate this location personally. In fact, just so I fully remembered the reference"—Mina would've known it was from him in a heartbeat anyway—"he brought it up at dinner. This was a carefully chosen reference. It's not an accident."

Their director was quiet for a few seconds. "Do you think he's at this particular location?"

"I do not," Mina replied. "If he was, I think he would have used Servant of Seville as the message instead."

McAllister's brows arched up. "Another game?"

"Same one, but his role, not mine. Instead, I think there's something there he wants me to find—"

Lee offered, "I actually think a hacker lives in that unit...one I might know. Well, loosely, like on the boards and stuff."

Mina shot him a look. "That would've been helpful information to have beforehand."

He shrugged. "It was a short flight."

"You think Vince is leading you to a hacker?" McAllister asked.

"I'm not sure," Lee said as he scratched the back of his neck. "I only know that a hacker occupies that unit."

"Sir, there's no way to know much before we go in to investigate," Mina said, trying to keep her voice even and not veer toward pleading like her heart wanted. "This location is unknown to anyone in our organization. It can provide us with temporary cover while we're there. It's not even dawn. That would give us an element of surprise," Mina continued. "Most people are asleep for hours yet." Then she hedged, "And, um..." She wasn't ready to admit to Norm's involvement, but she couldn't lie to her boss either. That's not how she operated. Best to just come out with it. "It just so happens I was in contact with a familiar spider last night."

Former agents who were still in the game were called spiders. Though, since Norm couldn't qualify for licensing because of his advanced age, he was more like an old crab. Even better. Veritus would likely overlook someone like him.

"The civilian I spoke with yesterday is having some issues," she went on. "He was fired from his job." McAllister's eyebrows shot up. "So, I set this particular spider on that web." Play on words. Tricky. "But I can easily redirect him toward providing physical support for us." After he placed Harri somewhere safe. "He's remarkable at blending. His interest is piqued, and he's all in, and most importantly, he's unknown to Veritus. He wasn't anywhere near this last night."

McAllister knew exactly to whom Mina was referring, without the fantastic wordplay. But Mina had to be vague, because even though they were standing at a distance from others, there were lots of agents she didn't recognize milling around and didn't want anyone to know this particular business.

That, and she and her director never talked outright about Norm. The former marshal could be a liability if involved. Something the government would frown upon. Officially, he was never involved in any case.

So more ghost crab than old crab or, quite possibly, old ghost crab.

Lee nodded along.

McAllister crossed his arms, turning to Lee. "Who is this hacker? And specifically, how did you uncover it was their residence? Hackers are notorious for altering data."

"They are." Lee knew that tidbit firsthand. "Their hacker tag is HarHarBiggins12. That's all I really know. It was by chance that I spotted the connection to the Cupid's Bow. One time, a few years ago, that particular hacker posted some unusual code. They needed help decoding it. I was the one who figured it out. It was strange, a coded language that ended up being a mix of three different types of tangine. Super ingenious. Anyway, once I sorted it out, I realized this hacker had accidently attached their physical location to some data points. I let them know, and they thanked me and removed it. It wasn't concerning at the time because this interaction happened on a very tightly enclosed, super-encrypted board with limited access to only four other hackers. All of us have taken the hacking oath, and none of us would ever betray a location to just anyone. I kept that code, mostly because it was interesting, and when I ran a full compucheck on the message Vince attached, my comp referenced it. I compared the location points. They are identical. I'm one hundred percent certain it's the same location."

"I see. But even so, we can't rule out the possibility that this is a trap to lure you to this specific location," McAllister said. "We don't understand fully why the colonel has sent this encryption device to Agent Kane in the first place."

"If I thought for a moment this was a ruse, I would agree with you," Mina said. "But Vince chose his words carefully. If someone was tampering with this device, they wouldn't know to use Princess Priscilla of the Poconos. If Vince was in trouble, and he'd been forced to send me this, he would've used Poppy Misfit or Dangareen Dog as a warning not to enter this location without force. Those were the villainous characters from our childhood make-believe games. No one would know the difference between any of these characters except Vince and me. Vince understands that I'm competent at deciphering clues. Princess Priscilla is a direct reference to me, in a nonthreatening way. Using further elements of surprise can and will help. That, along with unmarked backup, should make investigating it safe."

McAllister grunted. "And what do you propose is a *further* element of surprise?"

Mina shrugged. "We can obtain a warrant. That would allow us to enter secretly without having to expose ourselves."

"On what grounds?"

"Broadly, we could use the Foreign Government Aid Act of 2099. If we believe a foreign agent is in trouble, we have grounds to investigate all leads, including search and seizure, for up to forty-eight hours. We can leave my interpretation of the coded message out, as it's just that—my interpretation. We go with the concrete evidence we've gleaned so far, which is more than enough to secure a warrant. Vincent Kramer has led us to believe he's in trouble. Going in without alerting this hacker is the right option, because as you've already stated, we don't exactly know what's waiting for us there.

I'm not interested in putting myself or my partner in danger. But I'm also not interested in boxing up. We can continue to be assets on this case. In that location, there is a possibility we could keep working. If Lee is familiar with this hacker, and everything is on the up-and-up, it's likely we can stay there, at least for a while."

McAllister appeared skeptical, but tapped his cuff. Everything they said now would be on record.

He addressed Lee in a formal tone, "How certain are you that the signal from the encryption device—given to Agent Kane by the colonel-in-arms himself of the French Protectorate—originated from a residential location in this city?"

"One hundred percent. There's no question."

McAllister shifted back to Mina. "What were your instructions per this encrypted device once it landed in your possession?"

"If I did not hear from Vincent Kramer, the colonel-in-arms of the French Protectorate, within one full day, I was to take the encrypted locator delivered to my personal residence to Chaz Burquist, the head of the International Judicial Committee, wherein a formal investigation into Vincent's whereabouts would be taken up."

"This request was made to you in a personal plea by Vincent Kramer via a residential vid chat, is that correct?"

"Yes, that's correct."

"Was your impression that the colonel-in-arms was in danger?"

"It was. He was agitated. He was worried. He had a hint of discoloring under one eye. He feared something might happen to him and that no one would be able to find him."

"You have vid documentation to back this up?"

"I do."

"Has it been formally delivered to the federal government?"

"It has."

"I have reviewed this vid interaction personally," McAllister continued for the benefit of the cuff recording, "and it's of my opinion that the colonel-in-arms of the French Protectorate might be in trouble. Therefore, I'm invoking the Foreign Government Aid Act of 2099. I am hereby submitting an official request for a forty-eight-hour search-and-seize warrant to investigate a private residential location from which this signal is emitting in order to track down the colonel-in-arms of the French Protectorate." He tapped his cuff. "You have exactly thirty minutes to investigate this location, talk to this hacker, and see if the situation there will sufficiently keep you cloaked from Veritus. The warrant will be ready in less than ten minutes. If there's a glitch or the magistrate wants a face-to-face, I'll alert you." After a prolonged sigh, he continued, "The only reason—and I mean the *only* reason—I'm allowing you to do this, is that I agree that sending you to a government-known safe house could hinder this investigation. Innocent lives are at stake. Having you in a location that is unknown to anyone is optimal. Your instructions are as follows. You will take a craft to Government One, where you will arm yourselves and suit up. You will alter your appearances temporarily.

You will contact your backup." That came out as a growl. "Then you will take a secure mag-lev near that location. This is the only way we can be sure you're not tailed, as the tunnels have no signals in or out. You will approach the residence stealthily, and you will enter by surprise. That's an order. This hacker is not to be alerted to your presence ahead of time. We must minimize bodily threat and their ability to contact anyone. You will report back to me within ten minutes of entry. Is this all clear?"

"Clear," Mina hurriedly responded. "Very, very clear."

Lee nodded. "We will follow your orders completely. We don't want to, um, die."

Lee was right. They, um, didn't.

Chapter 12

ONCE THEY WERE on the roof, an agent in full tactical waved them over. "Agent Kane, Agent Adams, follow me."

"Is that a combat drone?" Lee asked incredulously.

The agent nodded to confirm. It was matte black and looked like it was made of six-centimeter-thick titanium. It had black skeleton covers, and the windows were coated in carbon film. It shouted *combat.* There were several places that would allow passengers to mount and fire barrel lasers.

Overkill for the current mission, but okay.

Well, maybe not, since Doreen had blown up from the inside.

Once they were both secured, the agent got in to pilot the craft. It wasn't typical for a drone pilot to wear tactical gear, but nothing about this situation was typical.

They set down at Government One in less than two minutes.

Another agent, this one without tactical, led them down to enhancements, where they grabbed a couple of hats with built-in hair extensions. They weren't planning on mixing with the public for very long, so an extremely temp disguise would work.

Honestly, Mina wanted something she could rip off at the first convenience.

She also grabbed a pair of shades, and Lee took a pair of clear, blue-tinted glasses. They made his eyes look even bigger and weirdly green. They both changed into micro-weave carbon-mesh undershirts, which would protect them from a long-range bullet or a short blast from a laser. Anything up close, though, and they would feel it.

Mina and Lee headed to tech. She wanted her new cuff. She knocked on the outer door of the lab. No one answered. "I don't think anyone's here," she said, glancing around the quiet hallway. It was super early, not even five a.m., and the tech staff was specialized.

"I think you're right," Lee said, stifling a yawn. "Maybe they can courier it over when it's ready."

Mina gave him a look. "We aren't having a cuff delivered to a secret hideout. I'll just go without." It might be better if she didn't have one at the moment, even though it was inconvenient. She nodded down at Lee's cuff. "Power yours off until we arrive. You can turn it back on once we see how secure this place is."

Lee nodded. "Good idea." He touched the side of the screen, and it went dark. "Though, I've added some extra"—he cleared his throat nervously—"security programs I wrote myself. You know, to be extra sure no one can track it or hack it."

Instead of launching into another paranoia diatribe like maybe Lee was expecting, Mina grinned. "That's excellent thinking. Covering your tech as a Level XIII is genius. You can add the programs to mine once it arrives." Then she would be Lee-safe.

Lee blushed. "Okay."

They paid a visit to the weapons room next.

A government agent with an unknown affiliation sat behind the counter. He wasn't name-badged and didn't offer up a moniker. "Are you the ones everybody's talking about?" he drawled, barely moving from his place behind the counter. "There's been quite a flurry of action on the gossip comet. My cuff's lighting up left and right. Y'all got me up out of bed early today, too. Was told I had to get here as soon as my ass could deliver me and just made it in a few minutes ago."

Before Lee answered with a resounding yes, Mina answered, "We're not here to discuss that."

The agent gave them both critical once-overs, but didn't press. "What can I help you with?" He unraveled himself from the gel-cush he'd been reclining on.

"Something we can conceal easily," Mina answered. "We'll be mixing with civilians."

"You want something that can stun, kill, or maim?" he inquired. "We got anything your little heart desires. An assortment of danger in the form of stickers, hots, and holes, all things that say, 'Don't mess with me.'" He tugged open two cases, exposing a wide range of weapons, from microstunners to blasters as big as Mina's forearm. The blaster wouldn't work. Too cumbersome. They shot scrap metal and hurt quite a bit. Hard to get all the bits out.

"Cool. Is that a regulator pick?" Lee said, excitement clear in his voice. "I've never seen one before." He picked up a long sharp object coated in dark carbon that had an electrically charged core. It was called a regulator pick because it was sharp and kept people in place, not only by causing an awful lot of bodily fluids to leak, but also knocking them out with an electric pulse at the same time.

It was a bloody pick. *Literally.*

The agent behind the counter gave Lee a look. Kind of a quirked eyebrow coupled with a frown. He'd picked up on what Lee shouldn't be broadcasting—that he was a very green, very young rookie. So green he was a walking, talking ball of moss.

All agents were required to go through weapons training. This agent might not let them check out stuff that could kill someone if he felt they weren't trained. "What he means is," Mina started, using her carefully modulated explaining voice, "he hasn't seen one of these *since* his cadet training." She emphasized the event like it'd been a long time ago, even though the rookie looked twelve. "He hasn't touched one up close and personal." She shot Lee a smile, showing teeth. "Isn't that right, *Agent* Adams?"

"Yes, of course," Lee replied smoothly. Or as smooth as Lee could manage, which meant he hadn't coughed or choked, shifted his eyes downward, or looked guilty in general. *Go, Lee.* "That's exactly what I meant." He carefully put the regulator pick down and chose a maxistunner, something he was familiar with. "I think I'll just take this."

The agent gave him a curt nod, but thankfully didn't interrogate him on the proper usages of a stunner.

Then the agent turned to Mina. She picked up a hot laser the size and shape of an egg. Not exactly as potent as the Sunray Doreen had waved around, nor was it a gun exactly. It shot a mildly concentrated beam out of the top once the cover was opened. They had to assume if Veritus came after them, it would be an up-close attack. She could palm the egg on the mag-lev, no problem. "I'll take this."

"May I also suggest a few blades?" He picked up something that looked like a common stylus some used for convenience on personal boards. He depressed a switch on the side, and a dagger the length of Mina's index finger sprang out of the top. It was conical and needle-sharp. "You carry this in your pocket, like it's for everyday use. It's made of lightweight tiluminum, a mixture of titanium and aluminum. It's strong as hell. Then"—he jabbed it forward—"you stick it up between their ribs. It pierces the heart. *Bam*, that guy falls over dead. Comes in real handy."

"Um, thanks," Mina said, not meaning it. He retracted it and handed it to her. She inspected the side and saw a shallow groove.

"Won't work without a thumbprint. I'll DNA-match

you in a second." He grinned and turned toward Lee. "And for you, may I suggest a brander?" He picked up something that looked like a regular helix box, a DNA reader where you inserted your finger for a microskin scrape. Some people carried them around for convenience. Lots of places needed proof of who you were in order to charge you borrows. "It looks like a helix, but when you flick it open like this..." His thumbnail clicked against the top, and out shot a short two-sided blade. "You can plunge it right into that asshole's heart. Don't worry about going between the ribs, this'll go right through his chest plate. Then he's dead before he knows what happened."

This guy obviously had a thing for hearts. And death. No wonder he was stuck behind a weapons counter. Trigger-happy agents did not get to venture out into the field very often. They were considered a hazard, and rightly so.

"Yeah, sure," Lee said as the agent handed him the brander.

"It's called a 'brander' because you get branded by it. Get it?"

Not really.

Mina couldn't wait to get out of here. "Speaking of DNA," Mina said, hoping to speed up the process, "you need to get ours before we can leave with these, correct?"

They'd completed four DNA scans since they'd been in the building. But protocol was protocol.

"Yep." He motioned them over to a government box called a Lockit, because it locked your DNA in a stand-alone system with no connection to outside input. This tech would obtain a scan of their chipped identities and couldn't be manipulated like certain helix boxes in civilian sectors. Civilian boxes took their DNA matches from a database controlled by the government and, of course, the occasional hacker. This one was locked up tight. Lockit. The agent winked. "Put your pretty little finger in there. It'll only take a microsecond."

Mina did not give him the satisfaction of a reaction. She placed her *pretty little finger* in the helix so the kill-happy agent could read the scan. "Mina Kane. Street." He appraised her like he didn't believe the designation. Small world. Mina shrugged. That's all he was going to get. A shrug.

"You're next, bud," he drawled at Lee.

This guy had to have been born somewhere in the South. People down there still carried slight accents. Since business, schooling, socialization, almost everything people did outside their family units was done virtually, it made sense that people sounded similar. But the South clung to its roots, which was unsurprising to those born in the South. So Mina had been told.

Lee placed his finger inside the Lockit. Mina was happy he didn't request to use a hair-strand reader instead, which was his usual choice. Mina had never asked him why.

Once Lee was done, Southern Agent Guy glanced at the readout. "Lee Adams. Street." He gave them both penetrating gazes. He didn't get a response, so he gave up. "These toys are temporary, mind you. You're authorized for seventy-two. If you need them longer than that, you'll have to get approval from up top."

"Understood," Mina said. She turned to go. She was *so* done with this guy.

When they were almost to the door, he called, "By the way, my name is Agent Beau Harvey. It was a pleasure to meet the agents who took down Veritus. Hope y'all have a very nice day."

Mina simply lofted her hand behind her as they walked out the door, barely refraining from rolling up her middle finger.

Another agent in plainclothes was waiting for them. "Hello, I am Agent Larson. I'm here to accompany you down to the mag-lev departing area. Are you familiar with how the station works?"

Mina was, but she knew Lee wasn't. "If you could go over it with us, that would be great."

Lee flashed Mina a quick smile.

"Of course. We're going to take this tube right here down to sublevel V." They boarded the waiting tube. "The government mag-lev is designed to look and act exactly like public transpo. It's the prime way we deliver agents around the city when they go deep undercover. The tunnel is fortified with a twenty-centimeter fiber-alloy block. No signals in or out. The train looks exactly the same as all circulating trains, including wear and tear. We have seat fillers already installed, which is necessary so the civilians who board after you think everything is completely normal. The train you're boarding will pull into the 22nd Street Station, no prior stops. You'll get off, along with the other riders. From there, you'll head into the zoom tunnel and disembark to your destination. Four undercover agents, on board now, have been assigned to linger in that area to provide assistance if needed." The door slicked open, and Agent Larson inclined her head, meaning she had no intel about where they were going. They walked into the underground station. "The train will then complete a full route before emptying of riders and heading back here. If you need to use it again, all you have to do is contact HQ with a request. A transpo-specific number should be programmed into your cuff." Agent Larson glanced down at Mina's wrist and saw it was cuff-free. Her eyes widened.

Agents were not usually without their cuffs.

"Mine got into a little accident," Mina said. "Tech wasn't in yet this morning." Agent Larson still seemed concerned, so Mina added, "Agent Adams has one." She indicated the new, shiny cuff on Lee's wrist. He helpfully stuck it in the air, turning it toward his chest so she didn't see it was powered off. "So I'm sure we'll be fine." Mina didn't need to explain anything to this agent. She was being nice.

"No problem." Agent Larson waved away her concern after catching herself. "I understand." She gestured them through a door. "Here we are." They exited into a long, dark tunnel.

It resembled a typical zoom tunnel, domed at the top, tiled a clean white, but without the people conveyors, vid ads splashing color on the walls, sunlight ultras making it seem like daylight, and zillions of pedestrians moving to and fro. Other than one agent behind a plexan shield, looking bored, nobody else was around.

As they walked, Mina spied the train behind a vacuum-sealed clear barrier. At the mag-lev entry point, Agent Larson gestured in a sweeping motion. "From here, you enter the vac area. Then just proceed onto the train. Any questions?"

"Nope," Mina said. "Thanks for the rundown. We have it from here."

"Great, and good luck." She turned and left, walking purposefully back the way they'd come.

Lee looked around, wide-eyed, making small mewing noises. "It's amazing down here," he said. "I had no idea the government had their own mag-lev posing as public transpo. I wonder if I've ever ridden on it after it dropped an agent off. That would be cool."

"It's a possibility," Mina said.

Magnetic-levitating trains were supported, guided, and propelled by huge friction-free magnets. To further increase speed, the air in the tunnels was removed to eliminate wind resistance. In order for that to happen, the entire tunnel had to be vacuum sealed.

They stepped toward a long, enclosed entryway, and doors slicked open. Once inside, they passed through another door, this one a big turnstile with thick panes of plexan to keep the air contained as they passed through. Once in the next compartment, they stopped and waited.

A sim intoned, "Sealing compartment. Please remain where you are. This will only take a moment." Props sounded overhead as the air was sucked out, and new air from the vac'd train area replaced it. Upon competition, the sim said, "Please exit through doors and board the train. Thank you and have a nice day."

More doors opened, and they passed through a narrow space that led to the train. The train compartment automatically opened.

"This is cool," Lee said. "I've never ridden a mag-lev almost alone. I'm usually crammed inside the vac chamber with fifty other people."

That was the average number of passengers allowed to fill the space. Some stations had bigger trains and bigger vac chambers, but fifty at a time was norm.

"I can actually *see* what's going on," he continued. "The mechanisms are amazing. All that tubing to make those air exchanges that quickly. Do you know how much infrastructure there has to be to do that?"

So much?

Mina let the rookie have his geek-out. Passengers were scattered here and there. Only the tops of their heads were visible. Mag-levs had tall, cushioned seats that swiveled depending on whether the train was accelerating or decelerating, because the takeoffs and stops were hard on the back and neck. The other people on the train were agents, or agents in training.

Nobody made eye contact.

Mina and Lee took a seat, settling in. The train immediately took off. It was typical for mag-levs to have a jolty start, then smooth out quickly. Mina was pretty certain that speeds could get up to nine hundred kilometers per hour, making a cross-country mag-lev ride several times faster than anything that could fly.

"I contacted the spider after we changed," Mina told Lee. "I left a message. If he's available and can keep his other assignment safe while he's gone, he'll meet us there. If he's not there, we're going in anyway. McAllister will be impatient right about now. It's time to figure out more about who this hacker is."

"One thing I know for sure is that they're honest. You can tell those kinds of things by the language they use and how they conduct themselves on the boards. Hackers are sneaky by nature. But you notice the ones who are quality, and HarHarBiggins12 is the real deal."

"There's a chance you might be a teensy bit biased."

"I'm not."

"I'll be the judge of that," Mina said.

CHAPTER 13

MINA IMMEDIATELY SPOTTED Norm where he stood in the shadows between two buildings. Lee hadn't been lying—the area was shabby, with lots of junk piled up.

Norm stuck out a bit. So did Mina and Lee. Even with downgraded enhancements, they looked too clean and upscale for the area. Most people around here were down on their luck and had little to no borrowing power. That meant repurposed clothing, no enhancements, no shiny cuffs, no trendy footwear.

Mina checked behind them for the twelfth time since exiting the zoom tunnels to make sure no one was following. She didn't see any of the agents assigned to look out for them either, so they were doing a good job. Then she nudged Lee across the street.

There wasn't much pedestrian traffic this time of morning, just an occasional airchair puttering in the distance. One person flew above them in a jetty that sputtered loudly. As she and Lee waited for them to pass,

Mina hoped they had enough power to get them where they were going.

"I need to signal Norm," she whispered. "Are you sure the building will have minimal security? Entering by surprise is important."

"I'm not absolutely certain. But if it's anything like mine, it shouldn't be a problem. I have tools with me, including a mini airmeld system that will allow me to hack whatever alarm is in place. Unless it's been seriously upgraded, which I doubt."

"If a hacker lives there, shouldn't we expect it to be more fortified?"

"Not the building itself. That would take too much energy to maintain, but their specific unit will likely have more. We'll see when we get there."

As they approached Norm, who was reading something on a handheld board, he gave a slow nod without looking up.

Mina and Lee continued on. It was still super early. Most people weren't up yet. Since many people worked remotely, or didn't work at all, life tended to start only once the sun was fully up.

They stopped in front of the building. Mina glanced up. It was tall and skinny, at least twelve stories. Most of the windows were covered. They weren't solar-catch, and it had to get cold, especially with winter creeping in on them. Mina tested the front door. It swung wide. She raised a single eyebrow at Lee. It should've been secured.

It'd been a while since Mina had visited a neighborhood like this. She didn't remember encountering unlocked entryways and wondered briefly if this could be a trap.

If someone tried to get to Mina at The Spire, they'd have to give DNA, go through a few security protocols, possibly talk to a person, for sure a bot. That was just to get *inside* the building.

Lee said, "It's not uncommon around here." He squeezed inside ahead of her. Mina had her laser egg out, feeling a little ridiculous holding it. Lee got busy at the main command center of the building, which consisted of a wall full of palm plates, smudgers, and other gadgetry that looked like it was never, ever used. At least when the building was built, it had some kind of security plan. Not so much anymore.

Lee's mini airmeld hacker system was comprised of parts no bigger than a few centimeters each. It was interesting to watch him work, connecting all the pieces and clicking together a mini keyboard. Mina glanced outside, spotting Norm. He had eyes on the building, even though he was sticking to the shadows. He would enter after they went through the interior door, which popped a few seconds later.

"That was fast," Mina whispered.

Lee simply nodded like it was all in a day's work. Except it'd taken only thirty seconds. Lee motioned for her to follow. They jogged up two flights of stairs. The place, tiny and cramped, had only four units per floor, two on each side.

At the third-floor landing, Lee raised his hand. Mina stopped. She followed his gaze to see a sensicam mounted in plain view over the first door on the right. The hacker wanted visitors to see it.

They could either rush past it and hope they gained entry before the hacker knew what was happening, or find a way to turn it off. Judging by the fact Lee was pulling things out of his pockets, he was opting to shut it down. That was probably the smarter idea, since neither of them knew what alarm features were connected to this particular cam. If the French Protectorate had anything to do with it, they could be advanced. Some emitted shrieking noises, beta rays that hurt your eyes, or an electric pulse. Anything lethal was against the law.

Mina glanced around the hallway. This was definitely a place to go if you wanted to keep a low profile.

A small creaking sound came from the stairway. Norm was keeping his distance, listening for any kind of tail. Mina was glad he was there. She tried not to be overly antsy. Their director wasn't going to wait very much longer to hear from them, especially now that he'd know they'd been delivered to the scene. McAllister wouldn't hesitate to send in backup, which would light up the neighborhood and draw attention to everything and everyone around them.

In front of her, Lee nodded to himself. Apparently, things were going well. Mina still clutched the egg. She was pretty sure Agent Harvey had been messing with her when he'd given it to her. This thing probably couldn't even light an old-fashioned candle.

Lee took a step forward, then another. They hadn't really discussed a plan of entry. He peered over his shoulder. Mina pulled a lock disengager out of her pocket, but she knew it would be of little help. A hacker would have digitally fortified locks. But she could try.

While she was sleuthing out how to disengage the locks remotely, Lee pulled a small NeuDAR wand out of his pocket. He scanned the doorframe, along with the side walls, looking for electronics and palm plates. He pocketed the wand and held up two fingers, then gestured above the handle and below, indicating there were two locks. He pinched his fingers together to show they were roughly a centimeter and a half deep. Then he made an X with his hands and swept them down to indicate—she guessed—that there were no booby traps. At least not of the electronic or bomb variety.

Mina stuffed the disengager back into her pocket. The laser egg wouldn't be strong enough to melt through the mechanisms quickly without detection, and they didn't have any mini hydro-bombs on them.

So Mina would have to do this how they did it in the olden days. She was going to kick the door down. It was the only logical way to gain access without alerting the hacker ahead of time.

Mina paced quietly to the door and focused all of her momentum in front of her, then rammed her foot next to the handle. The door splintered loudly and crashed open like a crate lid being ripped off. They'd been lucky it was a shitty, old door.

Lee rushed in first. Before Mina followed, she caught Norm's eye as he made it to the landing. She indicated with her head that he should check on the neighbors in case the noise had been an issue. In this neighborhood, they were likely used to loud bangs and probably wouldn't alert the PPF right away, but it was better to be sure. Mina moved forward and almost crashed into Lee's back, because her partner had surprisingly come to a full stop.

She peered over his shoulder and caught a glimpse of a young woman sitting in front of a giant tech screen. She had long, curly, red hair, wore large capacitor headphones, and was looking at them like they were both crazy.

No one spoke.

The girl slid off her headphones. "You coulda knocked first."

Nobody said anything.

"Um…sorry?" Lee squeaked.

Mina ducked around him, taking charge. "I need you to stand up and move away from your tech. We have a warrant. We're not here to do any further damage, and you're not in any trouble. We just have some questions for you, along with some requests. If you answer everything truthfully and give us your full cooperation, and we find you haven't committed any crimes, there won't be any issues."

"You're federal agents, aren't you?" The girl pushed back from her chair and stood. Mina had omitted that part. She shouldn't have. "At least you are," she said to Mina, then her gaze moved to Lee. "You, not so much."

She placed her hands on her hips. She was wearing comfort clothing, and her hair was tousled. She couldn't be more than twenty and seemed completely undaunted by the sudden intrusion of federal officers into her home. She cocked her head, squinting. "Does this have to do with the French government? Because I knew I shouldn't have taken that damn job."

She was relatively tall, her features delicate and not overly enhanced. Her nose was upturned, and she had a smattering of freckles that she had kept instead of micropeeling them off like most did.

Mina appraised the unit. It was neat and clean, with serviceable furniture, a few art pieces on the walls. It was instantly clear this hacker spent most of her borrows on her hack game. She had three screens surrounding her workstation. The one in the middle was massive, made of clear crystalline. There was another small screen on the wall. The workstation monitors flashed data, lots of it scrolling. Mina lowered her egg hand as she walked back toward the door they'd just crashed through, motioning Norm inside. She tried to shut the door, but it wouldn't latch because she'd busted the jamb.

They'd deal with that later. She turned back to the redhead. "What kind of surveillance do you have in here?" First things first.

"The typical," the hacker answered. "Sensicams, body-temp cams, motion, vid, audio, the works."

"Why didn't you fortify the door better?" Lee questioned in a disgruntled tone. "That looks like a Flow2000X." He gestured to her setup and the big compubase sitting at the end. "Those are spec and go for a huge amount of borrows. Only the hacking elite can afford them." More disgruntled issued out. Lee was having a moment.

The girl glanced at her setup like she was seeing the

Flow for the first time. "Why do you think I agreed to work with the French government?" She shrugged. "They bought me all this stuff." She swept her hand around, indicating most of it. "I haven't had time to fortify the damn door. I may be a Level XIV hacker, but I'm not exactly handy when it comes to installing hardware."

Mina had thought that after Level XIII, hackers just morphed into *superhackers*.

"It doesn't matter," the superhacker went on. "Even if I *did* fortify it, somebody who wants to get in here can. You did. This building sucks."

That made sense, at least to Mina.

"We need to discuss sensitive intel, so I'd like you to disable your recording systems. All of them," Mina said.

The girl sputtered. "No way. I'm not doing that. I know my rights." She tapped her foot. "You can't just kick my door down, come in here, and expect me to roll over and comply. Recording you is all I have to prove my innocence."

"I told you we have a warrant. And you don't need to prove your innocence," Mina argued. She wasn't ready to divulge just yet that Vincent Kramer had guided them here. She first wanted to hear what this superhacker had to say. "Your recording devices aren't secure enough, and they're unnecessary. Everything we say from here on out is being recorded on my partner's cuff." She gestured at Lee, who raised his arm, tapping on his cuff.

The girl put her hands on her hips again, expression pissed. "Are you saying I don't know how to encrypt my own gear? That's insulting. Nobody's getting through that stuff, not even the French government."

Mina gave up. If they had to, they could confiscate her security tech later, under the rules of the warrant. This was the second time the superhacker had brought up the French government. "We need to know who hired you within the French government and why."

"Should I have a barrister present?" She addressed Lee, ignoring Mina altogether. She must sense Lee was a kindred soul. "I'm pretty sure I'm not supposed to answer questions without some kind of representation."

"You don't need counsel," Mina assured her before Lee could answer. "We're not charging you with anything. We just need information." It was hard not to be huffy, but Mina was trying.

The girl narrowed her eyes. "I'm not talking about you *charging* me. I'm talking about protecting myself from whatever all this is." She gave an indiscriminate wave around the room that included Norm, who was standing quietly by the broken door. "I'm pretty sure you can't come into a civilian's home after kicking down the door, wreak havoc, and just leave."

Actually, they could, as previously stated. Mina had a warrant that said so.

"You don't need a lawyer," Mina repeated. "The federal government will pay to install a new, better door with quality locks. I'll also throw in a titanium triple bar as well. Looks like you could use it. I'll give you unofficially stamped data confirmation before we leave." Mina glanced over her shoulder at the door. "That should keep anyone else from kicking it in. That's more than others in this same situation have received."

"I want to see some badges." She crossed her arms. "I'm not cooperating until I authenticate. I authenticated the French government, and I would expect no less from my own." When Mina and Lee failed to move, she curled a finger in their direction to speed things up. "Pop 'em up. I want to see badges in holo."

Lee triggered his as Mina cleared her throat. "I...don't have my cuff on me right now."

The girl gave her a look. "You're a federal *freaking agent* and don't have a badge handy? What kind of shitshow is this?"

It was admittedly a little embarrassing. How did this go off the mag-lev magnets so quickly? HarHarBiggins12 was completely running the show. "My cuff ran into an unfortunate accident yesterday evening. I haven't gotten a replacement." Mina didn't go into the reasons. "But go ahead and authenticate his. If you still want mine, we can figure it out."

This girl, with serious spunk, gestured for Lee to move over to her setup. She picked up a scanner the size of a flower—and was actually shaped like a flower—and ran it over the holo image. Lee's face popped up on her screen. "Agent Lee Adams. *Hmm.* Why do you seem familiar to me?" She peered at Lee. "Do we know each other?"

Before Lee could spill sensitive information, Mina announced, "I think it's time we all sit down and discuss this."

Chapter 14

"Uh-uh." The girl shook her head, defying Mina for at least the fifth time. Maybe the sixth? "We're not sitting down and discussing anything until I check everybody out. Yo, old spooky dude by the door, you're next." She waved Norm forward with a swipe of her wrist.

Norm chuckled as he moved past Mina. "You got a hot one here." Norm's holo badge didn't look like Lee's. Instead, it showed only his face.

The girl scanned it, then leaned toward her screen. "Is this a medical ID?" She tossed a glance over her shoulder. "Are you serious? Why would I need to see your medical ID?"

Norm gestured at the screen. "Check out occupation. It's right there under the recent procedures. Ignore the age. It's only a number."

She read it out loud. "Former federal marshal. Thirty years with the federal government. Ten as a private investigator." She stood, giving him a perplexed look. "So? That's what you *used* to do. What do you do *now*?"

Norm spread his arms wide. "I do this. I happen to be providing backup. You live in a pretty shitty area, so you should be thankful I'm here."

"You guys just busted in like a comet blasting a crater-sized hole into a goddamn hilltop, and I'm supposed to be *thankful?*" She marched up to Lee, undeterred, placing a finger on his chest and poking him once. "How do we know each other? And don't lie to me. I have about six different devices rolling right now, and four of them detect fluctuations in speech. I'll know if you're lying. And I can run your speech patterns against the boards. I can face-rec you. I literally have myriad ways to find out who you are."

Before Mina could stop him—not that it would do her any good—Lee responded, "I'm Karmaseeker243."

The girl looked stunned for a second, then gathered herself. "No way. Karmaseeker243 is a federal agent? Mind blown." She brought her hands up to the sides of her head and extended them outward. "We've been on the boards together for years. You're the one who helped me with that trisplice code! I left my location embedded like a dummy. That was a few years ago, when I was sloppier before I became a Level XIV. Is that how you found me? You stole my code?" Lee started to sputter a denial, but she didn't give him a chance to respond. "You've always been quiet. Always watching. But honestly, you have an excellent hack game. But I never—and I mean *never*—caught the vibe you were an agent. I'm pretty sure it's illegal under our hacker oath not to admit something like that."

Lee shuffled his feet, looking wildly uncomfortable, still sputtering. "I didn't steal your code. I forgot it was in my computer. I haven't been on any boards in a while for that reason. The federal agent thing is...a recent development. I haven't had time...to sort it all out."

It was more than time for a redirection "What's your name?" Mina asked. "How about we start there?"

"Harmony Biggins," she answered. Well, that explained her hacker name. "What's yours? The Badgeless Avenger?"

Oof. "Agent Kane. I told you I can pull the badge up if you want, but I'll have to do it on your fully secured comp."

This girl was taking no prisoners. Honestly, it was pretty impressive.

Before Mina could respond further, Lee's cuff sent up a red star.

Red meant *answer or else.*

Lee tapped his cuff. Duncan McAllister's face took the place of his badge.

"Report immediately." McAllister was not happy they'd taken so long.

"Holy *shit,*" Harmony breathed. "That's...that's the guy from all the screencasts last night." She waved her hands around. "He took down Veritus. Wait..." Her gaze bounced around as she tried to figure out why these two agents, suddenly in her home, were in contact with the same man who had proclaimed to have taken down Veritus.

Mina knew it wouldn't take her long.

She didn't dare smile. "Director McAllister, please meet Harmony Biggins. So far, she's admitted to taking a job with the French government. She seems willing to cooperate, but we haven't gotten further than that. She has no intel yet on why we're here."

"Is the residence secure?" McAllister growled.

Mina glanced over to see Norm fortifying the door. He'd gotten it closed and was rigging up a blockade with one of Harmony's chairs.

As she watched, Norm banged the chair against the wall, breaking it apart.

"Hey!" Harmony called, moving toward him. "You can't just destroy my stuff like that. Put that down!"

"The residence is being secured at the moment," Mina commented without even a whiff of a grin. "I can honestly say nobody's going to look for us here. But I'm not sure how long it will be feasible to stay."

Harmony's quarters were cramped, to say the least.

McAllister announced, "We've just received intel from a few of the Veritus members we've tracked down. They've been given Babble."

That was huge. Babble had been restricted as a truth serum because it caused whoever received it to spill every single dark secret they had, not just what they were asked about. McAllister had to have gotten special permission from the higher-ups to use it. "They've admitted to getting the signal from Doreen. They're saying that something is planned to happen in the next twenty-four. I'm sending another team to monitor your location from outside. They'll serve as backup for the four agents who accompanied you there. I'm not taking any chances."

"Hey, wait, *what?*" Harmony had picked up on the last bits of McAllister's statement. "Did he just say something about Veritus and that something is going down in the next twenty-four?" Her eyes bounced back and forth between her and Lee. "Holy solar flares! You're the ones who took that old guy down last night! The Tedesco guy? You blew him up." She paused for a second, taking in a much-needed breath. "That's totally wicked. I can't believe this. You're standing right here. In my shitty little unit."

Harmony was only guessing, as there was no way she could know anything for sure. Mina kept her face stoic. She was relieved to see Lee wasn't giving anything away either.

McAllister was agitated. This wasn't going exactly according to plan. "Lee, hand me your cuff and take Harmony to the eating area and get some water." Mina held out her hand. It sucked not having her own way to communicate. Lee slid it off his wrist and handed it to her. McAllister's face wobbled as Mina took it and walked away. She was able to go only a few meters before she was stopped by a wall. She leaned her shoulder against it. "We should be safe here. I didn't spot a tail. Harmony has admitted to taking a job for the French government. She knows nothing about why we're here. She hasn't mentioned the Servant of Seville." Mina chose to use Vince's make-believe name, as she didn't want Harmony to have any clues. "She has an elaborate tech setup.

We can use one of her secure channels to set up a communication link between us."

"Do it quickly. I want you in immediate communication until we figure out what's going down in the next twenty-four hours. Apparently, the members we have in custody are low ranking, and Veritus covers itself by only allowing a few of the members to have complete orders at any one time. But we're working on it."

"I plan to immediately get to the bottom of why I was directed to this location, which is inhabited by a twenty-year-old female hacker."

"I'm twenty-one and a half," Harmony piped up from behind her.

"Do it soon," McAllister ordered.

"Oh, and I promised her a new door and some secure locks, on the federal government. And she'll probably need a stool replacement."

"That's not all I want!" Harmony called. "I'm honing my list of demands in my mind at the moment."

"This is not a production vid about federal agents," Mina tossed back. "That's not how this works."

"Then I'll just withhold the information you need, and you'll be forced to deal. I'm pretty sure that's how it works," she answered, smirking.

"Whatever she wants," McAllister grumbled. "Just get it done. I'll be expecting that communication link shortly. Make sure it's hack-proof." He snapped off.

Mina turned. Harmony and Lee were staring at her from less than two meters away.

"What?" Harmony shrugged. "My residence is insect-sized. Where would you have me go? And I shouldn't have to remind you, kicking me out wouldn't exactly help you achieve your goals."

Mina moved forward with purpose, handing Lee's cuff back to him. "This isn't a game. By your own admission, you were hired by the French government, and we need to know why. What we're investigating is very serious."

Harmony crossed her arms. "I heard what that guy said. He said 'whatever she wants.' Before I start spilling my guts, I need something."

"That was federal agent-speak for 'get the job done,'" Mina said. "I have other options available to me if we can't work this out here, including taking you in to Government One for a formal interview."

"Not until the threat of Veritus is out of the way," she countered. "You can't go anywhere for at least twenty-four. I heard your orders. And by the way, are you honestly bringing that killing ring Veritus to my door? A door that won't keep out a rat looking for printed crumbs, thanks to you. I'm pretty sure if this ever goes to trial, my peers are not going to be too happy with you." She tossed her arms out with dramatic flair. "I am but a lone, fragile girl in this big harsh world"—she blinked a few times, playing up the innocent—"and...and... these brutish federal agents kicked my door in. They commandeered my tech, broke my furniture, and tried to take away my constitutional right to record them. Then...wait for it, wait for it...they led a pack of *killers* to my home. It was so, so scary. I feared for my life." A single tear actually trailed down her cheek like she'd called it up for duty. Oh, she was good. After the rehearsals for the vid production were over, she cocked a hip. "I mean, your boss did a media blitz last night and claimed Veritus was over and done with. Yet, here you are, hiding out at my house. It would make for a very interesting defense. I'm pretty sure they'd give me whatever I want. And I'd probably ask for a lot. I mean, wouldn't you? You've pretty much burned my entire life to the ground."

Mina let out a long, exasperated sigh. Norm couldn't stop chuckling, which wasn't helpful. "Okay, you win. What do you want? It better be within reason. And after we agree on terms, you're going to give us every single detail, show us every single document, every mode of communication, and explain to the smallest quark what went down between you and the French government." Mina glanced around the room. "I guess it's a good thing you're recording everything, even though it's within my power to have you shut it down. We'll need those recordings as federal evidence once we leave. They'll also stand as proof of the deal we strike. Whatever we agree on will hold up in a court of law, since you like to talk so much about going to court."

Harmony was positively gleeful. If Mina had almost thrown her hands up in defeat, this girl was barely refraining from eagerly rubbing hers together.

"*If* you leave, right?" Harmony said. "Because, potentially, killers could burst in here at any moment and spray gas everywhere. Then none of us gets to leave. We'd all be choked out and super dead."

"Go ahead," Mina encouraged, using Harmony's own

gesture, curling her fingers. "Get it all out for the cameras. Say anything you want. Do a tap dance. Orate a sonnet. I couldn't care less. Once you're finished, we can get down to making a deal. I mean, if that's okay with you?" The irony was not lost on Mina that Tedesco wanted a deal and wasn't getting one, but Mina was doing business with this cunning twenty-one-year-old superhacker.

"What I want is easy. I want a job. That's it."

"A job?" Mina tried not to show her surprise. She failed. "Are you serious?"

"I'm totally serious. If this hacker"—she jacked a thumb in Lee's direction—"can be a federal agent, I want in. You've seen this rodent hole. I want a better life. What could be better than being a federal agent? You have the power to kick in people's doors. Seems pretty spec to me."

"You're a superhacker," Mina sputtered. "That pays much...much more than what you'd get being an agent."

"I don't take currency for my jobs." She stuck out her chin, daring Mina to challenge her on that.

Mina shot a glance Lee's way. How in the world could there be two high-level hackers with hearts of gold? Lee shrugged, as if to say, *I don't know. Makes sense to me.*

Honestly, before she'd met Lee, Mina had thought every hacker made a kiloton of currency.

"Why don't you take coin?" Mina asked. "It's not illegal for hackers to take jobs from civilians who work in IT. People hire hackers every day to tighten their digital security, to retrieve lost files, to create blockades to prevent other hackers from getting in."

Harmony made a face that shouted Mina was completely out of touch. Lee nodded along next to her. They looked like conspiring twins.

"You gotta be kidding me," Harmony insisted. "What kind of jobs do you think I'm offered on a daily basis? Take a wild guess. Do you really think they're on the up-and-up? If you do, you're crazy-wrong. Ninety-nine percent of them require me to break the law. If I accepted *actual* currency for those jobs, I'd be thrown in a box like that." She snapped her fingers. "It's not worth it to me. My father's been boxed up for years, and with my mom losing her mind and strung out most of the time, I promised myself that wasn't going to be *my* life." She clapped her chest. "But I've kept up with hacking, improving my game, because I don't have any other skills, and no opportunities have presented themselves. Until today."

She had many skills, Mina thought. She was fearless, brave, and smart. She'd actually make a very good agent.

Mina took a seat on the only remaining stool in the room. There wasn't much cush left to the gel. It was hard and flat. "I can't promise you a job. Being a federal agent isn't as easy as snapping your fingers." She watched Harmony's face drop at the news. It gave Mina a little pang right in the heart area. "But if my director agrees, we can fast-track you to the vetting process. Once there, you take a series of tests, both knowledge-based and to measure how physically fit you are. If you pass the first round—on your own—you move forward. If you complete everything to a high standard, you go through to formal training, which takes at least a year. Then, once you're an agent, you start at the bottom and work your way up. That usually means being at headquarters for a few years at a desk job. Honestly, the federal government would be giddy to have an excellent hacker like you on staff. Your chances are very, very good. Once we get you on the inside, it's all up to you. But it's not something I can guarantee right here and now."

"Is that how Karmaseeker243 here got in?" She jabbed another thumb in Lee's direction without looking at him. "He's not doing a desk job."

Lee cleared his throat as Mina answered, "Not exactly."

"How old are you?" She turned to Lee.

Lee visibly twitched under the scrutiny. "Twenty-two."

Harmony buzzed a hot look back at Mina, her eyes narrowing. "He's six months older than me, if that. I want the same deal he got, or it's a no-go. I don't have to tell you anything. I know my rights. I was offered a job by the French government, and I accepted. They didn't pay me in currency. They gifted me some tech equipment. By law, what I do is not considered gainful employment. Some would call it a favor. Not only did they *not* pay me in actual currency, but what I did for them wouldn't even be considered hacking. I've broken no laws."

It was Mina's turn to cross her arms. "Let me guess, they gave you a Cupid's Bow, had you ping the location all over the place, finally anchoring it in the Pacific Ocean.

Then they *didn't* pay you to watch and see who hacked it. Am I close?"

"Maybe. So what?"

"I was the person who received the Cupid's Bow, and it came from the colonel-in-arms of the French Protectorate."

Harmony looked uncomfortable for the first time. "No, it actually didn't. I had a bot make the delivery once I was sent an address. And it wasn't the Protectorate, it was some low-ranking French government official. He described it as a prank on a friend." She waved her hand. "Before you chastise me for being gullible, I never believe anyone's excuses. I always *think* it's something else. I figured, because he gave me a Cupid's Bow, he was trying to track some disgruntled lover."

There was that *love* word again.

Mina confirmed, "It wasn't a low-ranking French official. It was Vincent Kramer. I'm trying to figure out why, and that's why you're going to help me. I need to know how he contacted you, how the information was transferred, so I can figure out what is going on."

Harmony's face brightened. "Kinda like being a secret agent." More than she knew. "If I do a good job, will it count toward my agentship application or whatever?"

"I'll certainly give you a recommendation based on how this goes. So will Agent Adams." Mina gestured to Lee.

"I will, too," Norman added. "My name still carries weight inside those hallowed walls. It's not just the bulk around my stomach." He chuckled.

"So, do we have an agreement?" Mina asked.

Harmony nodded. "We do. But if you screw me over, I'll make sure your tech never works properly again. That's a flaming comet streak of a guarantee."

Chapter 16

"Are you sure?" Mina stood behind Harmony, who was working at the tech table. They'd been trying to figure out for a while where the Cupid's Bow had been purchased. It was only seven thirty in the morning.

"Quit asking me that," the young superhacker snapped. "Your interruptions are getting older than your grandma's printer."

Mina pointed out, "If you want to be a good agent, you have to check, double-check, and triple-check your information." To Mina's ears, it sounded like she was mentoring again. What was happening? "Especially if the information sounds completely wrong, which this does."

"Everything that comes out of my mouth is a for-sure statement. I don't lie, I don't interpret data wrong, and I don't get shit confused. If I say the Cupid's Bow was purchased a week ago in this city, it was purchased a week ago in this city. It was sold by a specialty shop called Tech, Trinkets, and Trash, which happens to be one of my favorites. I go in when I have a few extra borrows to spend. They've got unique tech, along with all the trashy stuff. Like sensors that look like enhancement wands. You give it to a friend, and he or she will put it somewhere in their residence, then you can listen in, and they'll never know. I mean, if you were a total bitch or something. I wouldn't do that." Of course not.

The actual Cupid's Bow sat on her worktable. Lee had brought it with him. Harmony had plugged it into its coded receiver, since she'd been the one to code it in the first place, which was handy.

Both she and Lee had their heads together, working on figuring out where the Bow had originated.

"She's right," Lee confirmed, pulling his shaggy mop out of the huddle. "It was purchased at that store approximately a week ago. It cost over six thousand world currency, and it's listed here that it wasn't attached to any borrows at any bank. That means the person paid for it with physical coin and thus was able to keep their identity cloaked. The location and index ID are completely matched. It's a hundred percent accurate."

Harmony smirked, giving Lee a pat on the shoulder. Weren't they just a pair of hackers snuggled tightly inside a single piece of circuitry? Mina didn't have the patience right now to figure out if they were cute or nauseating.

Mina hoped that if they figured out where the Bow had originated from, they could discover why Vince had chosen Harmony, which was still unclear. Harmony was still insisting the Bow had not come from Vince, but from someone inside the French government. They hadn't been able to convince her otherwise.

"Let's circle back to the guy who you think hired you."

"Did hire me."

"This Louis Champlain guy," Mina continued. "You said you thoroughly checked him out. You had a confirmed address, performed an identity lifecheck, and had his job description. He works in the French government as an assistant minister in the Department of Goods and Services. Or the equivalent of that department in France."

"Yep," Harmony replied. "I did my due diligence. I'm manic about it. That way, I don't end up working for serial killers and overall bad people. As I told you, I'm not interested in landing in a box. He checked out. The only thing strange was there wasn't an image of him on the government site. Most of the other officials had their pictures up, but not all. But I cross-checked and found this one." She typed in a few things, and the image of a man popped on her screen. He looked run-of-the-mill with nondescript dark hair, nose a little on the long side, a bland-looking gaze. Underneath his picture were stats, including the name Louis Champlain and the correct job affiliation to the French government.

Norm came up behind Mina to inspect the image. "That's Felix Bouchard. I'd swear it on my mother's ashes orbiting around up there somewhere. He looks a little different, definitely enhanced. The eye color is diffracted, but you can't argue with that nose and those ears. I mean, he could've changed them, but he didn't. You see how that one ear on the right sticks out a little farther than the one on the left? I'd know that ear anywhere."

"You're ID'ing him based on the reach of his right ear?" Mina questioned as she squinted at the screen.

"I'm a detail guy. What'd you expect? I already told you I would swear it on my mother, may she rest in the eternal cosmos, and I don't ever do that lightly. It's him. I've had enough run-ins with the guy over the years to know what I see. He kept his chin, too. Silly thing to do. If you magnify it, you're going to find a freckle on the bottom. It's in the shape of a three-quarter moon. It's faint, but it's there. Details. You can't live without them."

No, you really couldn't.

Before Mina could order Harmony to do it, the hacker had already enlarged his face, using her fingers to tilt it up for a 3-D look. Sure enough, there was a very faint smudge in the shape of a three-quarter moon.

"I'll be damned. It's Felix Bouchard," Harmony said.

Mina tried not to overreact at the news. Since her mouth was closed, she figured she was doing pretty well.

"Who's Felix Bouchard?" Lee asked as Harmony pulled up Felix's data, flashing it on the screen next to the picture of who she'd just thought was a guy named Louis Champlain.

"He's an international spy and a notorious weapons dealer," Mina murmured, reading through the stats.

"Man, I guess when I'm wrong, I'm Jupiter-sized wrong. It just happens so rarely, I forgot how it feels. The burn is blistery," Harmony said. "Jeez, there's a lot here about his past, but not who he's affiliated with." She was asking the right questions and had readily admitted her mistake.

Mina was pleased. Recommending her to the agency would be an easy decision.

Norm snorted. "He's affiliated with whoever lines his pockets at the very moment his pockets need lining. He's of French descent, but he has residences in just about any country you can think of. The question is, why would Vincent Kramer hire Felix Bouchard to be his runner? He could've found somebody low ranking, or even just a friend of his to get in touch with Harmony. It makes no sense."

"Maybe they're friends?" Lee suggested. "Maybe Felix is doing Vincent a favor?"

"Not on your life, kid," Norm answered, so Mina didn't have to. "Felix looks out for Felix. He wouldn't mess around with the US federal government for nothing less than big currency." Norm ran his thumb back and forth over his fingertips. "You hire Felix so you don't get your fingers sticky from whatever you're involved with."

"This is still not making sense." Mina began to pace the tiny room, thinking. "With all this research, we still don't know why Vincent Kramer chose to have Harmony encrypt the Cupid's Bow and arrange for her to have it delivered to my residence. He directed me to this location himself. I'm supposed to discover something here." Mina knew she wasn't wrong.

"Kramer didn't direct you here." Harmony thumbed her hand at Lee. She was a thumber. "Karmaseeker here figured out where I lived based on some splice code."

Mina shook her head. Before she could reply, Lee explained, "I did find your location via splice code—coding you freely gave to me—but there was an encrypted message included with the Bow. At the very end."

Harmony looked stunned. "No, there wasn't. I would've known. I encoded the damn thing."

Finally, they were getting somewhere.

"Is there a way Kramer could've coded the Bow, or had Felix do it, before it got to you?" Mina asked.

"Of course not." But Mina saw Harmony's uncertainty.

"The code was old-fashioned and spread out," Lee said gently. "Almost undetectable until you pushed all the pieces together."

Harmony shot him a look. "You deciphered it?"

"Yes."

Harmony shrugged. "Then it had to be there. I must've missed it. What's bigger than Jupiter? Two Jupiters? Man, the frost is nipping all the way up my legs. It's not my day. You guys are ruining my carefully crafted never-wrong image. Well, what did the message say?"

Lee cleared his throat. "Princess Priscilla of the Poconos."

The young superhacker burst out laughing. "You're kidding me. If I'd uncovered it myself, I probably would've just left it in there, because that's hilarious."

"It was from a game we used to play as kids." Mina wasn't going to go into it further. "It's a direct reference. He wanted me to come here and find you. The question is why. Once we answer that, the meteor shower hits." As she began to pace again, Mina mumbled, half to herself, half to the room, "He knew I wouldn't go directly to Chaz without verifying the Bow—or at least trying to. He knew once I broke the encryption, I'd follow the message. That means whatever he wants me to find is here." She stared at Harmony. "That's why he picked you. He could've picked anyone, but he chose you."

"Thanks a lot," Harmony groused. "I'd like to think he picked me because I'm super frackaliously awesome and have a supreme hack game."

Mina shook her head distractedly. "Yes, that. But also because you're a part of this. Maybe you live in a location that's important to his plan, or maybe there's another reason he sought you out. Have you ever met him in person?"

"Hell no. If I had seen that hunk of an international heartthrob in the flesh, it would be scorched across my brain from his hot-laser brand. We've never met."

Lee made an incoherent sound, and Mina rolled her eyes. The international-heartthrob-brand thing was so over the top. "Are you sure?"

"Stop asking me that. Of course I'm sure." Then she huffed. "Well, I was sure of most things until you showed up, so maybe I've met him, but didn't know it was him. I mean, hello, my drool would've been activated, and that's hard to miss."

Mina resisted taking Harmony by the shoulders and shaking her. This was important. She focused on the young, smart-mouthed superhacker. "When I say, 'Are you sure,' I'm asking you to think. Vincent Kramer has the resources to hire people like Felix to do the work for him. I need you to explore your memory for any unusual back-

and-forth you've had with anyone recently. Something that doesn't happen every day. Something or someone who was different. Maybe it was a new neighbor greeting you for the first time. Maybe it was somebody who bumped your shoulder on the street, or someone who struck up a conversation with you on public transpo. If you want to be a good agent, this is your first lesson." She was a mentoring maven. *Booyah!* "We're looking for something out of the ordinary here. Something to indicate you had some communication with him, or someone he sent, before Felix contacted you."

Harmony took Mina's suggestion seriously. Mina could see her brain heating up as she filed through her recent memories to try to come up with something plausible.

Suddenly, Harmony stood, snapping her fingers. "There *was* something. Great gracious gnomes. I was out and about a day or two before this Felix guy contacted me. I was down by the sea, at the new Atlas Park, a place I don't go very often. It was a contemplation day. I won't go over everything that happens, but on contemplation days, I do a lot of contemplating. A lot. Anyway, a guy came and sat with me on a park bench. He was super old, with a kiloton of wrinkles. I remember thinking, why doesn't this dude help himself out? Nobody has to look that old these days. But then I took pity on him, thinking maybe he had no borrows."

"Yes, yes, but what did he say?" Mina encouraged. "Specifically."

"I'm getting to it. You can't hurry a good story. There we were, sitting on a bench in front of the water."

She made a horizontal gesture with both hands, setting the scene. Harmony had a flair for drama. Mina, oddly, didn't hate it. "He shuffled up. Come to think of it, he had a cane. It was pretty shiny. Probably made of titanium or aluminum. Something like that. Anyway, he kept tapping it on the ground. It was kind of irritating and kind of endearing at the same time."

"Did you get the feeling he knew who you were? Did he ask you random questions, or were they personal? Think hard," Mina instructed.

"He talked about the weather, which was boring. Why do old people always talk about the weather? Then..." Her face morphed into incredulous. "Then he talked about my father! I didn't even catch that at the time. He brought up my dad in a roundabout way, and all of a sudden we were talking about him. He got me to spill about my dad! Crafty bastard. He was good. Made me comfortable, like we were just shooting the shit. And then I was talking about lawbreaking and admitting I hadn't seen my father in several years."

"You said your father's doing time in a box. Why is he in a box?"

She shrugged. "Same reason I'd go in one if I took currency for jobs. He was a genius hacker who got obsessed with the grab. He took work and gladly broke the law. It caught up with him. He's doing ten to twenty. He went in when I was eight. Messed my mom up nice and tight."

"What's your father's name?" Mina asked. She held her breath. It all had to fit somehow.

"Strum Littlefield."

Chapter 16

LEE IMMEDIATELY LAUNCHED into a coughing fit. Mina walked over and drummed his back. "Take it easy there, Agent Adams," she said. "It's going to be okay. Get it all out. There, there."

Norm was shaking his head, muttering things like *good gods* and *no frickin' way.*

Harmony shook her head. "Last time I checked, you don't get to pick who your parents are. It was just my stupid luck. I often wonder if the cosmos was playing a joke on me by assigning them as Mom and Dad."

"Your dad is not only a genius hacker"—Mina knew she was telling Harmony what she already knew—"but he's also a criminal mastermind. He's all anybody could talk about for years after the bank crash of '94."

It wasn't just any bank crash either. The banks lost all their data for two full weeks. When they finally got back online, hundreds of thousands of people had had their borrows zeroed out. It took them a full year to track down Strum Littlefield as the originator. And another full year to make the charges stick. They had to call in renowned hackers from all over the world, and even they had issues figuring out how he did it. As far as Mina knew, they never fully figured it out. The entire banking industry had changed the way they processed information after that.

"He's legendary." *Cough, cough.* "A modern-day Robin Hood," Lee all but croaked.

Harmony morphed to angry. She stood with balled fists. "He's in no way any type of Robin Hood character of the past. He broke the law. He broke it so bad he had to leave us. He broke it so bad he drove my mom toward a mental break she never recovered from. Nothing's worth that. That's not brilliance. It's pure selfishness. My dad has only ever cared about one thing his whole life— amassing as much currency as he could. The federal government was on to him in the early days, so he could never spend it. They knew he was breaking the law. I have no idea where he stuffed it all away, and I don't want to know. I identity-chipped myself at thirteen and a half. I'm big, and he's little. That's the way it's going to stay."

Mina empathized with Harmony a great deal. The kid had gotten the rough end of the parental hacker deal, and she was clearly still in pain over her father deserting the family and her mother becoming ill. But the consoling would have to come later. Right now, they had to figure out how everything was connected.

Mina took Harmony's seat at the desk. Lee had set up

a secure connection to the government network. So far, there had been no alerts.

"Computer, send alert to Director McAllister via the channel route set up by Agent Adams," Mina ordered.

Harmony had authorized both Mina's and Lee's voice sigs. She hadn't wanted to at first, but eventually had given in. It was easier for Mina to do it herself rather than ask Harmony every time she needed to issue a command.

Mina continued, "Vid chat request, wall-screen engagement. Mark as urgent."

A second later, their director popped up on the shabby wall screen across from the tech station. Mina got up and positioned herself in front of the single camera.

When she was visible on his screen, her director said, "Report."

"We found the connection we were looking for," Mina said. "Vincent Kramer hired Felix Bouchard to deliver the Cupid's Bow to Strum Littlefield's daughter, identity-chipped Harmony Biggins. This is her residence. Either Vince made contact approximately seven days ago while he was in town, or someone else did, posing as an old man. They obviously know who she is and proceeded to prod her for information about her father, likely to confirm her identity. A few days after that, she was contacted via one of the hacking boards by Felix Bouchard, who posed as Louis Champlain, a member of the French government. Harmony checked him out, everything looked solid. The arrangement was for her to program a Cupid's Bow and keep an eye on it. Payment was made in tech. The Cupid's Bow was delivered to her about a day later. She received only my address, no personal information, and sent the device via a delivery bot commanding three levels of authentication. That's all I have so far. We are still looking for the reason why."

McAllister was alone in a dronecraft. His face was inscrutable as he took in the information. He would know all of the players without further explanation. "That's very interesting. Good work, Agent Kane. Consequently, it has just been brought to my attention that Ambrose Bernard has reported Vincent Kramer missing."

"Missing?" Mina's stomach sank. "Wait, he reported him missing through official channels?" That would be highly unusual. Governments did not admit to the general public that they'd lost track of one of their own.

Lee came to stand beside her. Norm was in the corner, paying close attention. Harmony looked a little lost, standing off to the side. Conducting business in front of a civilian was not the norm. But if Harmony had her way, she wouldn't be one for long. And in these cramped quarters, there was no getting away from it.

"No. Nothing official yet," McAllister commented. "I received this information through a trusted contact. Apparently, no one has seen Kramer in the last forty-eight. I have no intel on Strum Littlefield. Last I knew, he was boxed up. If I'm remembering correctly, his sentence was ten to twenty. He's been up for review in the past, but was denied release. As for Bouchard, I've had dealings with him in the past. The man is cunning, but levelheaded. Greed propels him. He's not known to be generally dangerous. For the right amount of currency, he'll do just about anything except kill. The man has his limits. He's also shrewd and smart. If he doesn't want to be found, it will take a lot of resources to track him down."

"If we can figure out why Vince chose Harmony, things should fall into place," Mina said. "I believe that her father is the answer." If Littlefield was still incarcerated, the connection wouldn't make a lot of sense, but they had somewhere to start. "Whatever Vincent Kramer is mixed up in, it's fairly clear that he doesn't want the French Protectorate to know about it. The Protectorate will likely not make his absence public until they are forced to. The colonel-in-arms doesn't just go missing. If the public finds out, it'll be a national security issue."

"Agreed. The fact that this is all happening at the same time that Veritus is plotting something does not feel like a coincidence, even though it very well could be. Determine if Strum Littlefield is still being detained. Once you know those answers, contact me." He popped off the screen.

Mina turned to Harmony. "Have you been in contact with your father since his incarceration?"

"I went to visit him a few times in the beginning. They allow kids under fifteen to send a personal message twice a year. All they did was show me a live feed of him from his box. It was creepy. He was just sitting there doing nothing. After that, there's been zero communication."

"Would he contact you if he got out?" Mina asked, taking a seat at the tech table.

Harmony took the main seat in front of the largest screen. Lee stood behind them. Norm went to check the front door and listen for the neighbors or possible intruders.

"If he could find me, maybe. He's got a big enough brain. But I've made it pretty difficult," she replied. "I haven't laid any crumbs. In fact, I sweep them up quite often. I value my privacy. Most hackers do. And this residence is not in a name he would recognize and is not in any way traceable to me." Mina raised her eyebrows. "Don't ask. It's not illegal. Just tricky."

"Vincent Kramer found you," Mina pointed out.

"True. But he or this Felix guy could've been watching for me, which is way unsettling." She rubbed her arms. "I go to visit my mother a couple times a month. Her location is public. There's no way my father could do the same from inside a box. Not that hard to follow me back here, especially if I wasn't looking for a tail. I have red hair just like my father's. Not exactly good for blending. I guess I should've changed it at some point, but it's also my grandmother Gertie's hair. I loved that woman. She died last year. The world lost a great dame with that one."

"I'm sure. Computer, access current location of one Strum Littlefield," Mina ordered. "Government access code Z73463-08."

"You don't need your code." Harmony smirked. "Anything not blocked by Level IV goes through this thing. Boxed criminals is Level II. She's a honey." She reached out to stroke the compubox the French government, or so she assumed, had purchased for her.

"I thought staying above the law was your sweet spot," Mina teased.

Harmony snorted. "It is. I don't do anything with the information I see. I just bottle it up nice and tight right here." She tapped her temple. "It's not against the law to look. It's against the law to share, profit, or exchange information." She recited that section of the law like she was doing it by rote.

Mina shook her head. So much to teach. "If you're hacking into the system and seeing things that aren't for your eyes to see, it's against the law. Guaranteed. You're reciting a section of the law from hard crimes, not privacy."

"Whatever. I know for a fact they don't enforce privacy laws. There are so many hackers out there, the government expects people are looking. You know that. I know that. Every little biddy on the planet knows that. It's what hackers *do*."

"Doesn't mean it's not a crime."

"I do the same thing," Lee interjected. "I mean, I did, before I became an agent, and it was legal and stuff. I never used the information in an advantageous way. It doesn't hurt to take a look. With a cross-check data breach inhibitor, the government never knows you're there anyway. Hard to track down something they have no record of."

"Not helpful," Mina murmured. "Not even close to being helpful. Hackers are dangerous creatures." A picture of Strum Littlefield appeared on screen. She remembered being interested in this case as a teenager. But she hadn't remembered what he looked like. The resemblance to Harmony was unmistakable. Same eyes, same cheekbones, and same hair. Strum was like an adult boy version of her.

Harmony gasped, covering her mouth as she pointed at the screen. "He's out! It says right there he's out. How did that happen? I check his status every month or so. Last time I looked, it said he still had eight and a half years. A hearing was coming up, but not for another three."

Mina read the details under the classification section.

Strum Littlefield had indeed been released eight days ago.

"There is no doubt in my mind your father is the connection we're looking for." Mina scrolled down. "Littlefield gets out and gives Vincent Kramer some important information. They must've known each other from before Strum was incarcerated. Maybe they were friends. Maybe they were colleagues. It's possible they forged some kind of a deal. Then Vince finds Harmony, confirms it's actually you, has Felix reach out via the boards, you two agree on a deal, Vince orders Felix to deliver the Cupid's Bow, the one he bought while he was in town. But before he gives it to Felix, he adds a quick coded message to me." Harmony was staring at her with some appreciation. "We have to find your father. If we can find him, then all of our questions will be solved." Mina's favorite part.

"How'd you do that? Put all that stuff together?" Harmony asked. "It was like your brain just unscrambled the scramble."

Mina chuckled. "That's the perfect definition of this

job. We unscramble the scramble. Then we bring the bad guys to their knees. It's very satisfying."

"I'll say."

"We need Strum to come to us," Lee said. "Because, you know, we can't leave and all."

Harmony switched from being impressed that Mina was sleuthing out the case, to looking downright panicked in a matter of seconds. She'd lost her father at an early age. Now Mina wanted her not only to contact him, but these federal agents wanted her to invite him into her home.

As a child, Harmony would've been angry at her father for what she would've considered abandonment, and that would have intensified as she became a teenager. Mina would've felt the exact same way. There's nothing more emotional than a teenage girl steeped in hormones. Something even advanced science couldn't contain. Mina wished she could give the girl a little more time, but they didn't have any to spare.

"I...don't know...if I can..." Harmony trailed off.

"You can," Mina stated firmly. "I know this is a hard ask. But if you want to be an agent, it involves making hard choices, sometimes on a daily basis. It never gets any easier to make a hard choice. Think about it this way—this is the perfect way to start your training."

Her face brightened, but she didn't respond.

"Your father will be happy to see you, kid," Norm added. "If I'd been separated from my daughter that long, I'd be overjoyed to see her face again. It won't be as hard as you think."

Harmony abruptly stood and walked toward the meal-prep area. "It's been so long. He left. It was really quick. I just—"

"I lost my dad, too," Lee said unexpectedly. "I was only three. I barely remember him. I just have these snippets here and there. I'd give anything to be able to talk to him again."

"How did you lose him?" Harmony asked. "Was he a hacker like you? Did he go to jail?"

"Veritus gassed him. He died a horrible death."

Harmony's mouth tumbled open. "Oh my goodness! I'm *so* sorry. I didn't know. I shouldn't have been so blasé about it."

Lee shook his head. "Don't worry. Nobody else knew until a few days ago. But I'm pretty sure you won't regret talking to your dad. After you meet, you can decide how much you want him back in your life, if at all. That's totally up to you. But don't be scared to set up a meeting."

Which had to be as soon as they could swing it.

"We'll be here with you," Norm said. "For moral support and all that."

How in the interplanetary solar system did they all become cohesive so quickly? It was a mystery. But Norm was right that they would support her. They were a unit. A bonified unity unit.

"Getting a hold of him is an absolute necessity," Mina pressed. "Vince wouldn't have gone to all this trouble if it wasn't important." She believed it was very important. "We do this job because we want to help. I need to contact my director in the next couple of minutes. I want to be able to tell him we're already on it and Strum is on his way."

Harmony straightened her shoulders. "Okay. Okay. Deep breath." She inhaled, then exhaled with a loud whooshing sound. "I can do this." She flexed her arms in front of her, rotating her wrists. "It's for the good of the world."

Not exactly *the world*. But maybe? It depended on what Vince Kramer was caught up in.

"Before my dad went in," Harmony said, "he gave me some codes to use if I ever wanted to get in touch. The old crappy compucase he left for me failed a long time ago, but I memorized them. I wasn't sure when he meant for me to use them, but it didn't matter because I wasn't gonna try. But now I'm gonna try." She began typing in earnest, head down.

Mina pulled Lee to the side, whispering, "Once we get Strum here and get the information we need, I might leave."

"But—"

"Keep your voice down. No buts. If Vince needs my help, I'm going. I'll slip out quietly. I believe in everything I just told Harmony. We protect those who can't protect themselves." Usually, that wouldn't be a guy like Vince. But it seemed today it could be. "Whatever this is, if I have a chance to help, I'm going to take it. Even if I have to drone over to France to do it. He trusted me for a reason. McAllister said there's a team outside keeping an eye on us. I'll slide out and make sure no one follows me."

"What am I going to tell the director when he asks to

talk to you? You don't have a cuff, so you can't communicate," Lee pointed out. "I can't lie to him."

"I'm not asking you to lie. When he asks, you'll tell him the truth. I might even tell him myself, depending on the information we get. Harmony has a spare cuff in that pile over there." Mina motioned to a heap of old tech. "Maybe I can use that. This isn't up for discussion, Lee. As agents, we make hard choices. This is one of them. My gut is telling me that if we don't act fast, something horrible will happen. I always listen to my gut."

"I got something!" Harmony called out excitedly. "I think it's him. He answered right away." They gathered around her. "I opened up the channel he gave me. I asked what his favorite color was, and he answered glitter. That was always our little joke. Then I asked him how he liked to sing, and he said in harmony. Which is how I got my name. It's him! I know it is."

"Request a meet," Mina said. "Ask him if he can make it to this address without being seen. Don't tell him you have company. Make it sound like you're looking for a father-daughter reunion."

Which, technically, it would be.

"Okay. Yes. This is cool. It's like we're on a secret mission," Harmony murmured, head back in the game.

A female sim with a cracking voice, the first Mina had heard in the residence, intoned, "Vid chat request coming from one Duncan McAllister. Do you wish to accept?"

Mina faced the wall. "Yes. Screen on."

CHAPTER 17

"WHAT'S TAKING SO long?" Harmony paced by Mina, who was sitting on the edge of a severely aged lounger. "He said he'd be here in an hour. That was two hours ago." Harmony checked her cuff again.

It was barely ten a.m., though Mina felt like they'd been here for years. In reality, it'd been a little under five hours.

Everyone was restless. McAllister had approved the meet with Strum, and Littlefield had agreed to come. Once she had the information he could provide, Mina was going to have to decide what to do. She wasn't kidding herself by thinking Strum was going to easily comply with their requests and instantly spill his secrets. But she was counting on Harmony to help convince him. They'd been over it a few times. The fearless superhacker knew what was expected of her, and she'd accepted the challenge with aplomb. If Harmony nailed this, Mina was going to fast-track her vetting process and do everything in her power to make sure this girl made it all the way through training. Harmony had what it took. After five hours together, Mina had zero doubt. She knew a potentially excellent agent when she saw one. Not only was Harmony motivated, she was determined, intelligent, had good instincts, and was asking all the right questions. It was hard to train for things like that.

"A male is entering the vicinity," Norm announced from his position by the lone window. "Approximate weight and height of Strum. Black hair instead of red."

Lee took a look. "Seems like he's trying to be careful to stay out of sight." He leaned farther. "Nope, must not be him. He kept walking past the building."

McAllister had alerted the team outside to be cautious, but to let a man of Strum's description through. But if they didn't think it was him, and he tried to access the building, there would be issues.

"He's not just going to walk up to the building," Harmony said. "He's craftier than that. At least I think he is from what I remember about him. He had a conniving side. One time when I was eight, he—"

A soft knock came at the door.

A millisecond later, a male voice murmured, "Glitter and sunshine."

The correct passwords.

Mina was up, heading toward the unsecured opening. She glanced at Norm, who shook his head. He hadn't seen anyone enter the building. He had a pretty good view, but not a three-sixty. Lee made his way over to the screen on the tech table. He leaned over, his voice low as he said,

"They were supposed to alert us when they spotted him. There's been no alert."

The team outside hadn't seen him approach, which was not a great sign.

Mina nodded to Harmony and mouthed, "You know what to do."

Harmony cleared her throat and proceeded to shake out both hands like she was trying to dry them. She closed her eyes, reciting some words of encouragement to herself. "How…" She cleared her throat. "How do you like to sing your songs?"

"In harmony," the man responded. "Are you in trouble, little one? You were so vague when you contacted me. I'm worried about you. Please let me in." He sounded like a father worried about his daughter.

"Um, okay. Just one minute." Harmony grabbed Mina by the arm, rushing her to the other side of the small space. "I don't know if I can open it," she whispered so close to Mina's ear that Mina could feel her hot breath. "I'm, you know, a little panicky. I think maybe you should do it."

Mina took a step back, settling both her hands on Harmony's shoulders.

Then she softly butted her forehead against the young girl's. "I need you to do this. If your father thinks you're in distress or that we're making you do something you don't want to do, the plan won't work. We've been over it. You can do this. You're just a little nervous. This is your first op. It's okay to be nervous on your first op. It comes with the territory."

"My first op," she murmured. "It's my first op! Yes, it's the first one." Her shoulders straightened, and Mina dropped her hands. "You're right. I can do this. Who cares if I have sweaty palms?" She ran her hands down the sides of her blue tuck pants. Mina had had her change into something more presentable. She didn't want Harmony to meet her dad for the first time in thirteen years in comfort clothing and uncombed hair. Harmony had to look the part to feel the part.

Harmony rushed over to the door. Norm was on one side, ready to disassemble the stool legs he'd used to reinforce it. He gave her an encouraging nod.

"Okay," Harmony said through the door. "I'm going to let you in now."

"Sounds good, darling. I can't wait to see you."

Norm removed what was holding the door together, and it creaked open and dropped downward at an angle like on overimbiber missing a crucial step.

"What in the hell happened here?" Strum moved into the room. He wore all black, along with a hood covering his hair. He tried to close the door behind him as best he could as he slid back his hood and took in everyone in the room in one glance. "You have visitors," he said to Harmony, looking neither surprised nor impressed. "Federal agents, in fact." He looked at his daughter, his gaze softening. "Are you in trouble?"

"No," Harmony replied softly, seemingly overwhelmed at the sight of her father.

Mina didn't blame her one bit.

Then Harmony remembered herself. "No." She cleared

her throat. "Um. These are my friends. We're involved in a big case. That's why I reached out to you." Harmony was trying hard not to betray her emotion.

Mina was impressed. Even though her father wasn't going to buy what she was trying to sell. Not even for a minute. The only thing Harmony was responsible for at this point was proving that she was acting on her own accord with no pressure from the federal government. Mina would take it from there.

Mina moved forward, extending her hand. "Hello. I'm Agent Kane, this is Agent Adams, and this is former marshal Webb. We're in need of your help."

Strum ignored Mina in favor of taking a step toward his daughter. "May I hug you? It's so good to see you. You look just like how I pictured. Strong, fierce, and beautiful. I've missed you so much."

"Oh. Okay." Harmony leaned into the embrace. Her eyes flittered closed for a brief moment. Then she broke contact, stepping back. "Nobody told me you were out. I'm...I'm happy to see you. I...I'm glad you're here."

Strum glanced warily at Mina and company. He clearly didn't want to say anything in front of an audience. It might be harder than Mina originally thought to get him to share anything of importance. "It was an unexpected decision on the government's behalf. I'm sorry I didn't contact you right away. I wanted to make sure everything stuck. If I saw your face and felt your hugs, and then they put me back in, I couldn't bear it. I didn't want to disappoint you either. It would be hard on both of us."

Why would he go back in? Once a prisoner was released, they were considered well and free. The federal government had done away with parole more than sixty years ago. If a prisoner didn't meet the qualifications to go free, including completing rigorous repopulation therapy, they were not allowed to leave.

The computer made a beeping noise, and Lee went to investigate. He sat down and began typing.

"Why don't you come and have a seat?" Mina gestured toward the lounger. "I'm not familiar with your case, but I can promise you I have no stake in seeing you incarcerated again. You did your time. Nothing you say to us right now will impact that."

The man with the red hair didn't move. He didn't even pretend like he was going to cooperate. "Since you have visitors, Harmony, I think it's best that I go. I'll be in touch." He turned to leave.

Harmony reached out and grabbed his shirtsleeve. "Please don't go," she pleaded. "This must feel like I tricked you. But I did it for a very good reason. I'm in a bit of trouble with the French government."

Mina studied Strum's face as Harmony began to explain her side of the story, starting with getting hired by Louis Champlain to encrypt a Cupid's Bow, not mentioning Felix Bouchard. Outwardly, nothing changed, but Mina saw Strum's eyes shift to the side more than once.

"In fact," Harmony ended, "it turns out in the end it really wasn't the French government at all. It was a notorious spy." She clasped her hands together like that was exciting news. Mina guessed it was. Harmony was told not to share too many specific details with her estranged father until they found out what he knew, which was standard procedure for an agent. She was playing it well. "And that spy was hired by somebody high up in the French Protectorate." Harmony then changed course, taking a cocky stance, crossing her arms, and sticking out her hip to bring down the final titanium rod, like Mina had coached her. "Maybe you know him? His name is Vincent Kramer."

"Vincent Kramer contacted you?" Strum's voice was tight.

It was the reaction Mina had been waiting for. Strum had definitely been in contact with Vincent Kramer.

"Not out in the open," Harmony replied. "He was sneaky about it. But something's going on. And now he's missing. We figured you might be friends or something. The time you got out matches when all this started happening."

The muscles in his face bulged, and Mina sensed they might lose him. She needed him to keep talking. "It might be best if you sat down," she said. "Can we get you something to drink?"

Through a clenched jaw, Strum asked his daughter, "Why did they kick your door down if you're not in trouble?" He gestured toward Mina.

Harmony seemed surprised by the question, but regrouped quickly. Atta girl.

She glanced at Mina. "Maybe you can answer that one." Harmony's voice held an edge. A small one, but it was there. She was still holding a grudge about that. Mina couldn't exactly blame her.

"We have a warrant. We had no idea this was Harmony's residence or that she had any connection to you at the time we entered the residence. I can't tell you everything, but I can promise your daughter is not in trouble with the federal government in any way. She's done nothing wrong. She took a job that she thought was offered by the French government. She was hired to ping an encrypted locator and have it delivered to a previously unknown address. No laws were broken."

Strum turned toward his daughter. "So, you're a hacker now?"

Harmony frowned. "It's not what you think. And it's not like I have many other choices. I was forced to survive after Mom had a bunch of breakdowns. It was hacking or nothing. So I got good at it. Really good. But it's not the job I want. Hopefully, that will be remedied soon."

Strum flashed her a genuine look of sympathy. "I heard about your mother. I'm sorry. There was no way for me to communicate. I would have if they would've allowed it."

"That's all well and good," Harmony said, "but what I'd really like you to do now is help us. I'm asking as your daughter. You can't take back what happened to Mom, you can't take back what you did and the time we lost, but you can do something good. I really want you to do something good."

Strum's expression turned pained before he could hide it. Harmony's words had struck him deeply. Without looking at Mina, Strum said, "I want full immunity. In writing. I'm not saying one thing without a guarantee I won't go back into a box. For any reason. It's non-negotiable. As much as I want to make my daughter happy, I cannot and will not go back inside one of those things. It is an inhumane way to live. The government should be ashamed of itself."

Mina replied, "That kind of arrangement has to be approved by my director. It's going to take some time. How about you share a few details that are in no way sticky while we work on it?" She addressed Lee behind her. "Get a message to McAllister. Let him know what Strum is looking for." She turned her attention back to Strum. "As I said before, we have no interest in placing you back in a box. The colonel-in-arms of the French Protectorate sent me a message personally. I believe I was led here to find you and to find out what you know. This is extremely important."

Strum crossed his arms. His daughter, who stood next to him with her arms still crossed, looked like his clone. "I'm not saying anything until I have that assurance."

Mina pressed, "Did you contact Vincent Kramer once you got out? It's a simple yes-or-no question, and the answer can in no way get you in trouble."

Strum said nothing.

"Do you know what or who he's involved with?"

Nothing.

"Is this linked in any way to Veritus and what they're up to?" A spark flared in his eyes. A small one, but Mina saw it.

Apparently, Harmony had, too.

The young superhacker reached out and flicked her hand against her father's shoulder, startling him. He dropped his arms. "You better not be involved with that horrible killing ring," she said. "If you are, I will *never* forgive you. And that's a promise!" She got close and poked a finger into his chest like she'd done with Lee. This time, she kept poking. "I want to know what's going on." *Poke.* "I don't care about waiting for a deal." *Poke.*

Strum took a step backward, trying to get away from her finger.

She followed and poked on. "You better tell me right now that you're not involved with Veritus." *Poke.* "Is that why Mom went crazy? Because she knows you're a murderer?" *Poke. Poke. Poke.*

"Of course I'm not involved with Veritus!" Strum exploded, unable to hold back. "But they're the reason I'm out. And I'm not about to go back in!"

Mina gaped.

Lee gasped.

Norm grunted.

Now they were getting somewhere.

Chapter 10

"WHERE'S THE DEAL, Lee?" Mina asked for the third time. Maybe the tenth? She'd lost count.

She'd managed to calm everybody down. After Strum's initial explosion, he'd gone stony again. He absolutely refused to say one more thing until he was guaranteed immunity. It was turning into a cluster, and time was streaking away like a meteor across the sky.

"McAllister hasn't responded," Lee replied from the table. "I'll let you know the moment it comes through."

Mina turned back to Strum and tried to reason with him some more. "If you aren't involved with Veritus directly, we have nothing to pin on you."

No tells. He wouldn't even look at her.

Harmony tried. "If the colonel-in-arms of the French Protectorate gets hurt, and we could've stopped it and didn't, I'm going to be upset. That's not exactly a great start to working your way back into your daughter's heart.

Like Agent Kane said, you could say some things that won't get you into trouble."

Mina appreciated Harmony's determination, even if it wasn't getting them anywhere.

Norm sat on a stool across from Strum. "It must've been terrible in there," he commiserated. "Day after day with nothing to do, no one to talk to, nothing to look at. Sensory deprivation is no joke. I don't blame you for not wanting to go back."

Strum uttered a few choice words under his breath.

"It's here!" Lee said. "It just came through."

Mina rushed over to the tech table, followed by Harmony and a reluctant Strum. Mina read it out loud. "The US government hereby grants immunity to one Strum Littlefield in regard to the whereabouts of Vincent Kramer, his involvement with Felix Bouchard, and the possible involvement of Veritus. Nothing he says in the course of this investigation will be held against him. We will support his freedom, no matter what is uncovered or the reasons why." It was signed by her director and the head of the entire federal agency, Cal Montreux. McAllister had gone all the way to the top of the chain of command.

"There you have it," Mina said. "A solid guarantee in writing. Right from the top. Now start talking." She glanced at her bare wrist. The habit was hard to quit. It'd taken more than an hour for this to come through. She was restless. "You said Veritus is responsible for your release. Please explain why, and do it quickly."

Strum paced back to the lounger. He sat, dipping his

head in his hands. He was weary. Mina couldn't imagine living the life he had for thirteen years.

"Over my many years in a box," he started, "I was visited by one man from time to time. He told me his name was Renaldo Patton, but I doubt that was his real name. He assured me that nothing he told me was being recorded and that nobody would believe me if I told them he'd been there. He was slick. He obviously held a position of power within the government, or he wouldn't have been able to access my box. Each time he came, he tried to convince me to use my hacking skills to help him. The more I said no, the more pissed he became. Over time, he admitted to being part of Veritus. He claimed he had the power to get me released if I agreed to help them, that the currency pull would be massive. I'd be set for life. A guy like me, he said, was just the right person for the job. After all, I'd already proven I would break the law." Strum shook his head. "All I had to do was secure digital documents and infiltrate companies Veritus was targeting. A master hacker in their ranks had recently disappeared. I told him to laser off. Every time. I thought he couldn't make my life any worse than it already was inside that shithole." He rubbed his face. "But that didn't end up being entirely true. A hearing release came up at the ten-year mark of my sentence. I was instantly denied. I didn't even get a chance to speak or plead my case. Renaldo showed up the next day and claimed he was the reason why the hearing hadn't taken place, and if I reconsidered, I could be out that same day." Strum glanced up, meeting his daughter's emotional gaze head on.

"I can't say I wasn't tempted. I was. After ten long years sitting with my own thoughts, I felt like I was at the end of what I could handle. But then your face came to me in a vision." He flashed a reedy smile. "I thought about the last time I was able to talk to you, hug you, hold you. Your face, your sensitivity, your innocence. You were so young when I left. I imagined the kind of woman I hoped you were growing into, and how could I be a good father and be involved with something like Veritus? So I told him to get out again. I didn't hear from him after that until about ten days ago. This time, he had something else in mind. He told me the government had impounded some ships in Greece and were investigating an illegal batch of chemis, enough to make hive bombs. Veritus feared it would be traced back to them shortly because the old guy in charge, the head of the whole thing, was getting lax. Renaldo was frantic. I told him I wouldn't help, and it was time he found someone else to hassle."

Strum went quiet.

"But you got out," Harmony said, frowning. "You said it was because of Veritus. They were responsible. So you agreed to help them after all, or you wouldn't be here." Her brain was obviously ticking through the reasons why her father would finally acquiesce.

Strum shook his head slowly. "In the end, I had no choice. I only did it for two reasons."

Mina already knew what those reasons were. She waited for Harmony to deduce them on her own. She wasn't disappointed.

Harmony gasped. "They found me! They found Mom!

They threatened to harm us."

"They did," Strum agreed.

"But they're just going to kill more people. You didn't want them to hurt me or Mom, and I can understand that, but they're going to kill more people."

"Not if I can help it."

"Once you got out, you contacted Vincent Kramer," Mina supplied, filling in some blanks. "You had no trust in the US government after your time spent in a box. You wouldn't even consider us as an option. Not to mention this Renaldo guy clearly came from the inside. You knew Vince from before. You sought his help in protecting your family, and in exchange, you'd give him information about Veritus and their plans."

Veritus was the reason Vincent Kramer had gone rogue.

Most likely, if Vince had gone to his superior, Ambrose Bernard, and explained everything he'd learned from Strum, Ambrose would've ordered him to stand down. US issues were not French issues. So, it seemed, Vince had decided to seek justice on his own, but was worried that if Veritus captured him—or, worse, killed him—no one would ever know.

To avoid bad press and political repercussions, Ambrose would've covered up his disappearance.

Vince had a backup plan. He'd hoped Mina would hack the Bow and find out about Veritus. He'd led Mina to Harmony, and therefore Strum, so she could help.

"Yeah, I contacted him to protect my family," Strum said. "Honestly, I felt I had no other choice. You're damn right I wasn't going to trust the US government. I didn't deserve ten to twenty in a box in the first place. They used my case as a deterrent for future hackers. I didn't kill anybody. My time should've been minimal. I was planning on it being one to three. I felt like that risk was worth freeing all those people of their unfair borrows."

"How are you acquainted with Vincent Kramer?" Mina asked.

"I was friends with Vince's dad, William. I only learned about his untimely death once I was out. He was a great man. A great mentor. It's a shame he's gone. I watched Vince grow up. I wasn't sure he would take a call from me, but he did." Strum shrugged. "He remembered me. I told him I could only talk to him in person. Coincidentally, he had been in town for another reason. We met up. He took what I said seriously. He believed me. He vowed to help. But he never said he was going to involve Harmony." Anger creased his face. "He promised to keep watch over her and my wife. He said he would make sure they were okay. I never gave him permission to involve you," he told his daughter. "I'm sorry he did."

Mina moved forward, but before she could speak, Lee said, "Vincent Kramer might not have had another choice. Maybe he learned something was imminent and had to take action." He glanced at Mina, then back at Strum.

"You know about their next plan of attack," Mina addressed Strum.

"I do." He ran his hands over his face and blew out a long breath.

This was what they'd been waiting for.

"What is it? What are they planning?"

"They're hell-bent on revenge," Strum cautioned. "When those agents took out their leader, Franco Tedesco the Third, they decided to do something big." He shook his head. "But I don't think you can stop it. It's too late." He gave his daughter a sad look. "I'm so sorry. I had to protect you. I had to pretend like I was helping them. In doing so, I set some things in motion that I don't think I can undo. I've been trying, but so far no luck."

"What did you do?" Harmony's voice rose toward shrill. "What did you *do*?"

His voice was sad. "They had me do some programming. They rushed me, told me lies about how they were doing standard demo on an old ship. Said I was going to program a small air-hydro. I didn't realize what I'd done until it was over. I've been out of the hacking game for too long. I didn't check and recheck the threads. It all happened so fast." He rubbed his eyes. "I've made a lot of mistakes in my life. I squandered my talent. I sacrificed my family for currency gain. But this might be the worst offense yet. I'm sorry. I don't want anyone to die."

"What did you program?" Mina's voice was cold.

Strum looked up. "A hypersonic missile. According to the instructions I saw flash briefly on screen before everything went blank, it's filled with poisonous gas. I wasn't supposed to see those notes. When I realized what I'd done, I tried to backtrack, but they'd already cut off my access. My tech went cold. I've been trying to get back in ever since. I meant what I said. I don't want anyone to die. I'm so sorry."

Lee surprised everyone by lunging toward Strum and grabbing him by the shirt, yanking him up off the lounger. "Where is this missile headed?" When Strum just stared at him in shock, Lee snarled, "My father was killed by Veritus, and I'm not about to let anyone else die the way he did."

Mina stepped between the two men, calmly placing her hand on Lee's forearm, giving Harmony a warning look to stay back. "Lee, release Mr. Littlefield." She stared right into Strum's eyes so he could feel her burn. "*After* he gives us the coordinates."

"I don't know. I swear!" Strum answered. "My task was to program the launch. To make sure what I thought was an air-hydro was powered on and ready to fly. If I can find a way back inside, I'm pretty sure I can find the coordinates. But I can't get back in. They locked me out."

"I can get us in," Harmony said confidently. "I'm excellent when it comes to gaining access where I'm not supposed to. We can find the coordinates, then we can program the missile to fly somewhere safe, like into the ocean, in case they have a way to launch it manually."

Strum smiled. He looked like he had hope for the very first time. "That's an excellent idea."

"You've been out of the hack game a long time," she said. "A lot has changed. Computers are more powerful, and hacking has gotten fundamentally more sneaky. If you have the original codes, the ones they gave you to access the portal where the programming took place, I can open up the trail on my Flow. The Flow was courtesy of your friend Vincent Kramer, by the way. I think he realized we were going to need it." She snapped her fingers twice when no one began to move. "Hurry up! We've got work to do."

Strum Littlefield couldn't look any more in awe of his daughter than he did right now. "I have the codes, of course. I can also bring my tech up here. It's not as... complete as your Flow, but we can connect them."

"What do you mean?" Harmony's face flashed confusion.

"I'm set up in the basement of this building. I wanted to be near you."

Harmony was incredulous. "You've been here all along? Right under my nose? And you didn't say anything?"

Ah, Mina thought, that would be why the team outside hadn't seen Strum enter the building.

Harmony slapped her wrist against his chest. She was a slapper *and* a snapper. "I'm not sure how I feel about that."

"I'm sorry. I told you before, I couldn't bear seeing you again if I had to go back in. It would've crushed you, and me, and I wouldn't have been able to cope. I was trying to protect us both. But I'm glad I changed my mind."

"Go get your stuff," Harmony ordered. "We have an agenda. We can fix this."

She was all business, and it was glorious to witness.

Before Strum could go retrieve his tech, Mina said, "You told all this to Kramer, didn't you?"

"Yes. But we're no longer in contact. He thought that would be safer for us both. I haven't talked to him in a few days."

"Where is Veritus working from?"

"I don't know."

"You had to have given Vince something." Mina had no doubt that the colonel-in-arms had gone underground to try to take out Veritus, to try to save lives where he could.

Strum shook his head. "Nothing solid. I told him I thought it was possible they were working from the ship that they told me was scheduled to be demo'd. That's it. That's all I had."

"Why did you think that?" Mina questioned. There had to be a good reason.

Strum scratched his head. "It seemed odd that they were going to blow up a ship in the first place. It would garner a lot of attention, especially since they told me they were going to do it right out in the harbor. Once the instructions popped up, and I saw it was a missile, not an air-hydro, I figured the missile was likely *on* the ship. In order for the programming to be as accurate as possible, they had to give me coordinates that were close to or similar enough to what they needed. They lied about the bomb, not the ship."

That made sense. "Franco Tedesco the Third owns a huge shipping company," Mina said. "Veritus would have access to his fleet. You're probably right. They plan to launch the missile from the ship. That would give them space and the ability to flee during the confusion."

McAllister had told them that Veritus was going to be acting within twenty-four hours. There was absolutely zero time to waste. Mina wasn't allowing anyone to die if she could help it. Her gaze met Lee's. Lee nodded once.

Mina was already taking a canal phone out of her pocket. She handed it to her partner.

At the same time, she asked, "Did you get all that?"

"Every word." McAllister's voice came from Lee's cuff. "Get to the harbor, Agent Kane. I want you in close contact. Agent Adams, get on those ship locations. I want to know how many ships of Tedesco's are in the harbor right now, how many are at sea within a ten-kilometer range. We will start there. Harmony Biggins?"

"Yes?" Harmony replied tentatively, placing a hand over her chest.

"If you can redirect the missile, a job in my department is yours, effective immediately."

"Yes, sir." She slid her fingers up to her forehead in a mock salute before realizing he couldn't see her. "I promise I'll do my best. And my best, you know, is pretty stellar."

Chapter 19

Mina exited the residence with Strum's black hood covering her face. Even though Veritus believed Strum was working for them, they could still have eyes on this building. She'd ditched her hat with hair extensions, so this was necessary until she was well out of the area.

She ducked down a side passageway meant for government utility drones, head down, finger-tapping Harmony's old cuff, trying to get it to work properly so she could communicate with the team. Mina wasn't too far from the harbor, so she was choosing to walk, blending in with the pedestrians going about their daily business.

This way, she could ascertain if anyone was following her.

It wasn't even noon yet.

"Work, damn you. If you don't, I'm screwed," Mina muttered to herself as she kept jabbing at the cuff. It was at least ten years old and sized for a child's wrist.

"Need a little help with that?" a familiar voice chimed next to her, causing her to startle, then grin. "Here, take this," Kaylee said, holding out a new cuff. "I have a feeling it'll work better. It's a gift from the US government to one of their top, incredibly gifted agents. Just make sure your wrist doesn't get blown off by a missile while you're at it."

Mina swiped the cuff out of Kaylee's hand. "What are you doing here?" She kept her voice low, glancing around to make sure they weren't attracting any attention. "And how did you get my cuff?"

"Oh, you know, I'm here doing the usual. Trying to save your ass. McAllister put out a summons for a team to protect you while you were inside that hovel, so I volunteered." She fell into step next to Mina as they began to walk. She wore a stretchy two-piece suit in dark navy and had a Kevlar fiber duffel slung over one shoulder, sunshades on, and dark red lipstick. She exuded a *don't mess with me* vibe. So very Kaylee. "He put me in charge. As for the cuff, I picked it up in tech while I was packing my duffel full of bad-guy-defeating goodies. They said you were without. I told them I'd remedy that situation."

"Does McAllister know you're with me?"

"Nah. But we'll tell him soon enough. As soon as we got word about the missile, I figured you'd slip out. Two more teams are already headed to the harbor, but this is your op. You aren't one to let everyone else have all the fun. So here I am. I like to run with the spec kids, but since they aren't around, I'll settle for you."

Mina snorted. "Hilarious. Just so you know, I'm the spec-*est*." She tossed Harmony's old cuff into a nearby grinder and donned her new one. Harmony would be getting an upgrade with her new job soon enough, and that one didn't work for shit. "Jeez. This is slick. I've never seen one on the civilian market with copper buttons." Mina tested some of the features. Everything was synced from her old cuff, so it was a seamless transition, like she'd never lost her other one. Not really *lost*, more like *was lasered away*. "Everything's so new and shiny, and it's extremely fast. Way faster than my other one. It's almost like it's anticipating what I want before I want it."

"That's because it's not civilian, you lucky b-train. It was custom-designed for you. Your DNA, your prints, your voice sig, everything. At least that's what the cute techie in R&D told me. I'm pretty sure it has some sneaky features you'll figure out later. It would cost a fricking fortune on the open market."

They crossed a busy intersection, moving fast. "How much do you know about what's going on with this op?" Mina held up her finger. "Sorry. Hold on. Let me let Lee know I have a new cuff." She pressed a button and brought her wrist up to her lips. "Establish contact to Agent Lee Adams."

A second later, Lee's voice issued out of her shiny new cuff. "You're not on the same tech you left with," Lee accused. "This is coming up as a ZenithGPX-C in your name. Holy shit. Did you get a new cuff already? A Zenith? And C means it's custom. Do you know who designed it? Zachary Zenith. He's one of the hottest tech—"

"Lee, I'm going to have to stop you right there. We can go into the awesome attributes of Zachary Zenith's design prowess another time. Though, I must say, you're coming in loud and clear. This is the best audio I've heard from a cuff." Mina held her wrist up to her mouth out of habit. "I met up with Kaylee, and she delivered it. Get your head back into our atmosphere. I need a status update."

While Harmony and Strum were working on missile coding, Lee was doing a search of Tedesco's entire shipping fleet.

"I just started the search. You left, like, three minutes ago. According to the updated harbormaster records, Tedesco has three ships active in the vicinity. Two are docked, and one appears to be anchored farther out, which matches with what Strum told us. According to the city, permission was granted to anchor *La Fortuna* in the harbor and perform maintenance of some kind yesterday evening. The type of maintenance is not specified." Lee paused as he typed. "*La Fortuna* is locked up tight. I'm not getting anything to break, and I don't want to alert them I'm trying. Shifting to the other ships now. Once I get more harbormaster information, I should be able to infiltrate their databases—that is, if they're not locked up as tight as *La Fortuna*."

"Keep on it. Get me intel on the docked ships as soon as possible. Voice comm is fine for now. I also need status updates on Harmony and Strum. This all has to work in tandem."

"Got it."

"Harmony and Strum?" Kaylee asked. "It seems McAllister left out a few details."

They were one block from the harbor. This area was a major thoroughfare for public transpo. They were forced to wait before they could continue because too many jetties and airchairs were hovering close to the ground.

"Does the name Strum Littlefield mean anything to you?"

"The famous hacker dude who blew up all those bank borrows? That was a long time ago. I was little and so, so adorable. What he accomplished was all anybody could talk about for ages. It's still designated as one of the greatest hack jobs of all time. That's the Strum you're talking about?"

"One and the same. He named his daughter Harmony, which kind of fits if you think about it. Veritus sprang him to do their dirty work little more than a week ago. He contacted Vincent Kramer and told him what was going on. Felt he had to tell someone and didn't trust the US government, especially since Veritus has people on the inside. Strum's been hiding out in the basement of Harmony's building, which is why you didn't see him entering."

"Tricky all around. McAllister told us Bernard reported through internal channels that Kramer is missing." She paused, processing. "Wait. So you're telling me the colonel-of-sweetness is trying to bring down Veritus?"

"Seems likely, but can't be confirmed until, well, he confirms, or we get physical proof." Mina looked warily at her pal. "If you connect this to Love Town one more time, you're off of the op. I mean it. Love Town stays a desolate, lonely place. Vince sent that Bow because he thought I could help, and it's a good thing I can." A traffic bot waved them across.

As they crossed to the other side, the piers, including landing pads for aircraft and dock channels for ships, came into view as far as the eye could see in both directions. The harbor had become very industrialized over the years. It was the true transpo hub of the city.

"Love Town is a classic. But I get it. This is Serious Town." Kaylee angled them to the side, stalling their forward motion. She peered around. "As far as I can tell, we're alone. No tail."

Mina scanned the horizon. "I didn't see one either." She glanced out into the harbor. "If Veritus is headquartered on the floating ship, it's going to be tricky to get to them unseen. We need to be out there, but if they spot us, they could launch that missile early, and that's a risk we can't take."

Kaylee nodded. "They definitely have a tactical advantage if they're floating. They'll have radar, NeuDAR, lidar, all the dars running, no doubt. They'd detect a drone or anything else that comes into their space. We can't take a boat either. Then, what, just draw up alongside of them like a couple of toddlers trying to crawl up a giant's tuck pant leg? Tedesco's ships are enormous. That won't work."

"You draw the most colorful comparisons. Why would a giant wear tuck pants? So impractical. Okay, so we don't take a boat. We take a ship." Mina clapped Kaylee on the shoulder. "You're a super-spec genius." She tapped her cuff as she hurried along. "Lee, I need those docked-ship locations. I want to know how many bodies are on board, what cargo they've got, if any, and when they're scheduled to leave."

Lee answered, "Working on it. This site is dense. I'm having to filter through all the other boats and ships." The quality of the cuff was so good Mina could hear the taps on his end. Usually, cuffs filtered out anything but voice to avoid feedback and interference. But this was so clear, there was no need to filter.

"We can't just hijack a giant ship, can we?" Kaylee bit her lip. "Or maybe we can."

"Hi, Kaylee," Lee called.

"Hi, The Wrong Turned Right Lee," Kaylee replied. "Looks like the gang's back together again."

"I'm pretty sure ships pilot themselves, like drones." Mina scanned the docks closest to where they stood. None of the boats looked big enough to be one of Tedesco's. "It would work best if one is leaving or on the way out, then we could hitch a ride."

"Ships that big have to cost a vomit-inducing amount of currency. Tedesco's crew will have tons of security in place. We might have a hard time boarding without being seen."

"Agreed. We won't know for sure until Lee gives us that info. Lee, where's the info?"

"You're a kilometer south of the first docked ship," Lee announced. "It's called *Dead Man's Game*. Kind of a bummer name for a ship. It's scheduled to head out to Europe tomorrow evening. Cargo looks to be super-computers, tech equipment, and, oddly, a few horses. Apparently, horseracing is still done in some places in the world. The next ship is a little farther up, maybe a kilometer and a half. I found it already. It's called *The Crafty Planet.* Better name. And we're in luck. It's scheduled to leave shortly, and it says something here about a scheduled rendezvous." Lee's voice echoed his confusion. "But...I'm not exactly sure."

"What?" Mina asked. "What aren't you sure about?"

"New orders just came in. They were approved less than five minutes ago by the harbormaster, but the orders aren't initiated the same way as the others. Kind of looks like they might've been entered manually by an air breather, which is weird because I know all this stuff is run by bots. I mean, computers don't usually make typos, and there are a few. Regardless, *The Crafty Planet* has requested, and been approved for, a rendezvous with *La Fortuna* by one Lloyd Barriweather. Running his name now."

"What are the chances?" Mina asked. "We need to get on that ship."

CHAPTER 20

"THAT SUCKER IS *huuuge*." Kaylee whistled. "I don't see a gangway or gangplank or whatever it's called. How in the hell are we supposed to board that mammoth thing?"

Kaylee was correct. It was the biggest ship Mina had ever seen up close. A great deal of it appeared to be submerged. She could see the reflection under the water. The top deck looked like it had a retractable cover that could make it watertight so that the entire thing could sink under the surface like a ghost. But Mina wasn't boaty, so she wasn't sure.

The entire outside was glossy white with chrome accents. Blue plexan windows were covered with a coating that mirrored the clouds floating above, meaning there was no way to sneak a peek inside.

"We can't stand here staring at it," Mina muttered. "Let's get into a position that gives us some cover."

Lee's voice came out of her cuff. "Lloyd Barriweather is a communication technician with Yardale, which specializes in personal security installation in high-rises. He sets up appointments and monitors things once they're installed. Nothing of note about him in his file. Single. Forty-four. Originally from Florida."

"There has to be something more about him somewhere, or he wouldn't be on Tedesco's ship about to head out to rendezvous with a ship full of Veritus members," Mina murmured. "Keep digging. We're also going to need to board that ship, Lee. Find us a way on. Where's Harmony at?" Time was ticking. Mina knew it in her bones.

"Making progress," the superhacker said from her position next to Lee back at her residence. Harmony's voice was crystal on the new cuff. So nice. "I'm inside their comp and almost through their security. It's blocked with the equivalent of fiber scraps and skin cement. Weaklings. I'm making extra sure they don't detect me, so I'm going slower than my normal hydro-hammer pace. But I'm confident that once I'm in, I'll be able to access the missile and the coordinates. There's no indication they're suspecting a breach. Confident asses. Once I'm done, you can go round up those ratty bastard killer asshelmets."

Mina was working on it. She eyeballed the ship docked in front of her. Who in the hell was Lloyd Barriweather?

"My daughter is a techno whiz," Strum interjected, his voice strumming with pride. "I've never seen anybody work so fast. I was a good hacker in my time, I admit it, but my pace was somewhere near extinct land tortoise and earthworm."

"It's good she's fast," Mina commented. "Lee, we need to get onto that ship."

"I just breached *The Crafty Planet*'s database. It's not secured like *La Fortuna*. It only shows a skeleton crew on board. Only three listed, not including Barriweather. Seems kind of slim. I can lower the stairway," Lee told them. "I can do it so it doesn't show up on their control panel, but it's an unknown how much noise it will make."

"Any more on Lloyd? Does it show any captaining experience?" Mina asked as Kaylee dug through her duffel and handed Mina a laser gun. Not as big as Mina's Gem, which was tucked away at her residence, but a huge improvement over the egg. A laser was Mina's weapon of choice.

"Nothing on captaining," Lee said. "But I think it's the right thing to do to board her." Why were ships and drones deemed female from the start? "You won't get closer to *La Fortuna* any other way."

Mina agreed. "Check in with McAllister, fill him in on everything you've told me. Tell him I'm awaiting instructions."

Kaylee gestured at Mina, who was still holding the laser. "Hide it so none of the civilians milling around here see it. Here's an ear node." She waved it over Mina's cuff. The cuff beeped once. "Cool. It synced up with no issues. Your cuff is now your mic, like spooky magic. Since I don't have an extra-special cuff designed just for me by some superstar named Zenith, I'm going to mic up the regular way."

Mina switched her laser setting to the lowest it could

go and lifted the hem of her shirt a couple centimeters to tuck the laser into her waistband. Then she placed the ear node in her ear so she could hear Kaylee. "I'm boarding first. I want you to stay dockside and keep watch. I can handle what's inside. Three, plus Lloyd Barriweather, who's a communication tech. I'll figure out who he is and make sure the ship doesn't leave. You coordinate with the teams once they arrive. Then everyone boards."

"You get all the fun jobs."

"The only thing I care about is that no one dies on our watch."

"Yes, I want that, too. But that doesn't change the fact you get the fun jobs."

"My op, remember?" Mina grinned.

"Report, Agent Kane," her director said from her wrist. "I have eight agents spread around your location, two teams of four. Just received intel from Agent Adams. I agree that this is the best option we have to get your teams close. I'm in the process of coordinating a larger effort involving the Navy and some commercial float craft. It's essential that once the missile is disarmed or redirected, or both, those on board *La Fortuna* are not able to flee. We have no knowledge how many personal craft they may have on board. The more agents in the area, the better. I'll be coming in on drone once the apprehension is in progress. Agent Adams says the ship has a skeleton crew. What are your plans to take control of the vessel without allowing them to alert their sister ship?"

There was that female thing again. As far as Mina knew, it'd been that way for hundreds of years.

"A laser set on sear," Mina replied. Kaylee handed her a stunner. "And a maxistunner. That should do the job. I'm choosing to board alone to keep as stealthy as we can. Agent Poston is going to secure the dock. I'll alert her when it's clear, and the team can board."

McAllister said, "Affirmative. I'll have satellite eyes on you for the duration. Keep your communication open. My goal is no lives lost. Not even a single soul."

"Good plan, sir," Mina agreed. "That's my goal as well."

"Good luck, Agents Kane and Poston."

"Where are you, Lee?" Mina asked.

"I'm here," Lee answered. "Should I lower the stairway now? The official term is gangplank. That's a pretty fun word, actually."

"Yes, go ahead," Mina said as she walked. Kaylee followed. "If I run into problems, I'm mic'd to Kaylee. She can board quickly. You'll be in charge of directing McAllister and the other agents if I get into trouble. Are we clear?"

"Crystalline."

Kaylee nodded with satisfaction. "Okay, the kid's catching on."

"Thank you," Lee responded.

"He's adequate." Mina smiled as Lee sputtered. She rounded the corner of the slip. She spotted where the stairway thing would open up. It was a long way up. It wasn't moving yet. "Okay, I'm here. Let's do this."

"I've got your back. I'll mic on as soon as I get a few

paces away," Kaylee whispered, breaking off to monitor the main walkway where pedestrians rode walkways or flew on personal jetties. "Don't get into any trouble. That cuff is too valuable to lose."

"Trouble's not my goal." In front of her, a staircase broke away from the side of the ship and began to float downward. It was almost soundless from where she stood. "No movement so far," she murmured for the benefit of those aiding and abetting her.

Once it was fully landed, Mina approached the railing, grabbing hold, trying to act like a tourist who was interested in seeing the nice, pretty ship up close. She peered into the interior at the top. It was too dark to make out anything inside. She took a few more steps, listening for movement or any talking.

"It's clear," she whispered. "I'm going in." She rushed the rest of the way up the stairs.

As soon as Mina stepped inside, she pulled out the laser and stunner. She had a pocket full of e-restraints as well. All she had to do was get anyone on board secured, then she was good to go. Then Kaylee and the other agents could board, and Lee could get them where they were going. Sounded easy enough.

Mina took a few steps down a long passageway. She knew she had to get to the top deck to get to the control room.

A tremor started under her feet.

"What the hell's going on?" Kaylee asked in her ear. "Why is the engine starting? You can't already be at the controls."

Mina couldn't risk speaking yet. Not spotting any movement, she took her chances and continued down the passageway, pausing in front of each open door with her weapons out.

"Why aren't you answering me?" Kaylee asked. "Holy shit! The footbridge thingy is going up, and the ship is moving. Mina! I need you to confirm you're okay, or I'm calling the military to stop this damn thing from sailing away."

Ships didn't sail, but that was a small point in the entire scheme.

Mina ducked into a tiny galley that held a couple of serviceable printers and not much else. She pulled the pocket door shut behind her. "I'm okay," she whispered into her cuff. "I haven't seen anyone yet. I felt the engines start, but I didn't know we were moving. Lee, what's happening?"

"I don't know." He sounded mildly panicked. "Nothing's showing up. It shouldn't be moving at all."

"Can you stop it?" Mina asked.

"I'm trying," Lee said. "But I just got locked out. Give me a minute."

"Until then, we proceed as planned," Mina said. "Lee, after that, I need directions on how to get to the control room. I'm assuming it's in the middle near the front. Keep me posted."

"Be careful," cautioned Kaylee. "You might want to turn that stunner up a few notches. As of right now, you're on your own."

Mina didn't answer. She eased the door back open, sticking her head out, glancing in both directions. She could feel the ship moving now. There was barely any motion, but it was there. Mina entered the passageway and could see through the plexan that the ship had just passed the end of the pier.

At the end of the hallway, she slid open a door. It was a big room. No one was inside. Loungers and seats were arranged in a conversational way. There was a bar in one corner. Maybe the crew quarters?

Across the room was a stairway.

She maneuvered quietly and began to scale the treads. At the top was a short landing and a single door. The door had a window. She peered through. No one was inside. It was another room, but more upscale. Likely for the passengers, not crew.

Instead of a stairway inside, there was a tube.

"Lee," she whispered. "I'm in a nice room that looks like it's for passengers. There's a tube on the other side. I need to know if that will take me up to the control room."

"I believe there's only one tube," Lee confirmed. "It does go to the control room. I'm still locked out of the controls, but I can get back in. I just need a little more time. The block is strange—it has some foreign words in it—but I'm figuring it out." Mina had faith in her partner hacker.

"You're getting super far away," Kaylee said. "I'm in touch with McAllister. He's concerned, but holding. He doesn't want to intervene if you can ultimately gain control of the ship. If you run into trouble, he'll send in drones. They're already in the sky, awaiting orders. So there's that."

"Got it," Mina said. "I'm on high alert. I have no idea if the tube will work without validated DNA. Lee, find out if there's another way to get up to the control room that's less conspicuous than a tube." She eased open the door and slipped inside the room. It was dark. This was clearly intended for passengers of the ship. Very upscale. Screens on the walls, greenery dotted here and there, gel-cush everything.

The tube was a single ride, no bigger than two- or three-person capacity. Oddly, the palm plate had been pulled out of the wall. "Okay," she whispered. "I'm in front of the tube, but the palm plate is dangling by a few wires. Some have been cut. Two are fastened back together."

"Are they black and yellow?" Lee asked.

"Yes," she confirmed.

"Somebody ripped it out and set it up manually," Lee said. "There are two other ways to access the control room. One is from the top deck stairway, but it will take you directly in front of the windscreen. The other involves a ladder. It's a maintenance shaft, basically. A small, cylindrical space that runs parallel to the tube you're standing in front of. That's your best bet. Look for an inset door to the left of the tube."

"I see it." Mina walked over to it.

"You should be able to open it. All the security protocols on the ship have been deactivated. Not by me, however."

"It's pretty obvious this Lloyd guy didn't have prior authorization from Tedesco to power this thing up," Mina whispered as she pulled open the service door. It was a small space. A shiny, white ladder was embedded into the far wall. "The ladder is here. I'm heading up." The element of surprise would be helpful right about now, though she wouldn't be kicking any doors in this time. She grabbed the first rung. "Voice off for now, Lee."

Mina moved up the ladder quickly. It was at least three stories. She didn't look down. Not hard when she was focused on getting control of this ship and trying to stop a missile from killing innocent people.

At the top there was a small trapdoor. Thankfully, it swung upward with little sound. She didn't dare alert her team. They would hear if she was in distress.

She eased out of the opening. The room was tiny, but well lit. Lots of odds and ends needed to run a ship were piled in here, along with some cleaning supplies. Mina placed her ear against the door.

No movement she could detect. No voices. No sounds.

Mina placed her hand on the lever and very quietly eased the door open.

She'd like to think she didn't gape, but she totally gaped.

She lowered her weapons. "What in the hell are you doing here?"

Vince Kramer sat at the controls, grinning. "I figured you'd show up sooner or later."

CHAPTER 21

"LLOYD BARRIWEATHER IS Vincent *comet-streaking* Kramer?" Kaylee yelled in her ear, hearing Vince's voice clearly through Mina's mic'd cuff. "Don't you dare take me out of your canal either. Don't do it!"

Mina yanked out the ear node. She couldn't do this in a three-way. She needed to think. Lee and Kaylee would still be able to hear her and Vince, Mina just wouldn't be able to hear Kaylee.

She stepped out of the storage closet. "Are you alone?" Mina glanced around the otherwise empty control room.

"Yes. The crew is secured downstairs." Vince was hunched over the control panel, engrossed in his work. His compucase was out, and super-thin optic cables were threaded between it and the circuit board, which had been pried up. Seemed Vince had some tech abilities Mina hadn't known about.

"You know, there are easier ways to communicate than leading me on a wild-galaxy chase around the city."

She moved toward him, stashing her weapons.

"I didn't feel like I could take the risk," he replied, glancing up, giving her another smile. "Every step of the way, I've been monitored by the French Protectorate, with just a few moments here and there to complete a couple of vid chats. Until about twelve hours ago, when I finally lost my security detail for good. Based on your talent for following clues, I hoped you'd figure it out. If not, I would've managed."

Mina glanced out the plexan windshield in front of them. The ship was cruising at a steady speed. "We need to turn this thing around. I have a team waiting."

"We can't." A hank of hair fell in his eyes. She'd never seen him without it slicked back or fingers running through it. "I've already initiated contact. As you know, I'm posing as Lloyd Barriweather, a member of Veritus. They're expecting him. If we abort, they'll get suspicious."

That wasn't ideal. "At the very least, we need to slow down. We can't arrive before Harmony disarms the missile."

His face went slack. "What missile?"

She stared at him incredulously. "The missile loaded with noxious gas that Veritus is planning on launching into the city? We can't arrive until it's disarmed. If they feel like this is a setup, they could fire it before we're ready."

Vince ran a hand through his hair to get it off his face. Mina closed her eyes. She had work to do. "Strum said they had him programming an air-hydro. He didn't say anything about a missile."

Strum had told Mina he'd been out of contact with Vince for a day or two. "Well, they lied, and you ended communications with Strum. It is really a missile, and it's filled with Tedesco's favorite killing substance. It's not surprising they would lie." She gestured to the controls. "And I'm not kidding. Slow it down. Or I can have my partner do it. You shut him out. Give him access so he can pilot this thing again. Or captain it. Whatever you do with ships."

Lee's voice came out of her cuff. "Actually, I'm back in. That was a good patch of code, sir, but the French words gave it away. I'm rusty in *code Français*, but I got there. I'm slowing the ship down now." Their forward momentum eased considerably. "*La Fortuna* is within your sights. You're about nineteen minutes to rendezvous at this speed. I'd advise not to abort. Vincent's right that they could get suspicious. On our end, Harmony is almost finished."

"I am!" Harmony agreed, her voice upbeat. "Just a few more millisecs. I'm inside their system now, and I'm redirecting like a snake about to pounce. Do snakes even pounce? Whatever. I'm redirecting like a girl about to save some lives. Not only can I redirect, I'm pretty sure I can make it like an ice cube. Freeze it so it won't work at all. Looks like someone was smart enough to add in a kaput protocol. Maybe one of those killers has a conscience after all." Wouldn't that be nice? "I'll keep you posted."

Before Vince could respond, Mina held up a finger as she put her ear node back in. She had to keep this moving. "You're back, Agent Poston. Tell me what's happening on your end. I need the full picture before we make any decisions."

"McAllister commandeered a boat for us," Kaylee responded immediately. "We'll catch up to you shortly. It's disguised as one of those drunken-tourist-floater things. The ones that look like giant marshmallows. I'm ready to put on a show for those missile-launching lunatics. We're backup now, not front line. The Navy is taking front with you two. Can't win them all. Ask Agent Cupid how he's going to pass for this Lloyd guy. The minute he steps out on that deck, any one of those Veritus guys with half a brain cell pinging around will know it's him. He pretty much sparkles."

It was true that he was recognizable, but he definitely didn't sparkle.

"McAllister is waiting to hear from you, and not so patiently, I might add."

"Got it." Mina turned to Vince and asked, "What's your plan, Kramer? Run it down for me before I report to my director." McAllister wasn't on constantly with Mina, because he was busy organizing the entire operation, from Navy to air reinforcements.

Vince reached into the duffel settled at his feet and pulled out a flexible face mask made of a strikingly realistic poly-compound skin cement, complete with long blond hair and a full beard. "Meet Lloyd Barriweather. He joined the Veritus organization seventeen years ago. He's a loyal member, but is currently e-restrained unhappily back at his residence. He's in charge of Veritus' tactical communications. When he says there's a problem, they listen. I managed to speak with those on board the ship last night through Lloyd's comm, with Lloyd doing the speaking." He shrugged. "People tend to follow the rules when they have a laser at their temple."

Mina had no doubt Vincent Kramer, colonel-in-arms of the French Protectorate, could be persuasive when he wanted to be.

"There are twenty-three members aboard," Vince went on. "A few more were scheduled to drone in later that evening, including Lloyd. But Lloyd managed to convince them that they needed some specialized cloaking tech, which only he could deliver. He told them it would keep them unseen if they decided to launch the air-hydro from the ship. It's fictious cloaking tech, but they bought it. Mostly, I think, because of fear. There was little cohesion, at least from what I heard. They are clearly without a leader."

"Air-hydro is a cover for a missile. Lloyd left that helpful tidbit out."

"He did. Not very friendly of him." Vince ran a hand over his face. He looked tired. He'd been at this for days. "An air-hydro would do damage, of course, but not missile-type damage. I guess I should've assumed there would be gas involved. That was shortsighted of me. Once Lloyd did the convincing, whoever is in charge on *La Fortuna* contacted the harbormaster and requested for this ship to rendezvous with theirs, and here I am. My plan upon hookup wasn't very in-depth. I was going to board as Lloyd and take down people as I went. I have two Trois Flux Stunners, French for 'three stream.' They take down three to four people at a time." Impressive. "The stun time is temporary, about thirty to forty seconds. But I'm a fast worker."

"How did you get intel on Lloyd Barriweather?" If the US government had Lloyd's residential address, he would've already been in custody.

"I have my ways," he answered. "It helps that I'm a colonel."

"Like Strum Littlefield?"

"Exactly. Except he contacted me, not the other way around. If he hadn't, I'd be back in France right now and not in danger of being fired or incarcerated for insubordination for my role in trying to bring down a threat to humanity."

They'd get to that in a minute.

Mina glanced out the windshield. They were getting closer to *La Fortuna*. "I hope you were planning on calling in the US government if I hadn't shown up."

"Of course." He stiffened. "I had a plan."

He was holding something back.

Instead of questioning him, because the colonel-in-arms was an agent of France with his own secrets, she knew it was time to get down to business. "Your Lloyd face may come in handy after all. I need to report to my director now. And, just so you know, drones are in the air, and the Navy is awaiting our signal. Once Harmony has redirected or nulled the missile, we will proceed with your plan to pull up alongside of *La Fortuna*. Normally, I would make this call privately, but you're in it now, just like the other civilians." Norm, Strum, Harmony. So many civilians. "We can discuss parameters for confidentiality after this operation is complete." Mina would leave it up to McAllister to decide. Sometimes the government had civilians sign an NDA. But Vince didn't really qualify as a civilian, so it would be up to him to honor whatever decree McAllister came up with. "Lee," she said. "Where we at?"

"You're fourteen minutes out."

Mina ordered her cuff, "Call Director McAllister. Mark as urgent." McAllister would get an amber star.

"Report, Agent Kane."

"I'm here with the colonel. Agent Adams and Agent Poston are remote. There are approximately twenty-three to twenty-seven Veritus members on board *La Fortuna*." Mina was guessing based on the intel Vince had given her. "The colonel had no prior information that there's a missile. He was going on Strum's earlier accounting of an air-hydro." Which could do an eighth of the damage of a missile, and that was if it didn't blow up on its way in, which they were known to do. "Lloyd Barriweather is Veritus' tactical communications guy. He's currently awaiting government pickup at his residence. The colonel's plan was to use a lifelike mask of Mr. Barriweather's face to gain access to the ship and detain members as he went. If I hadn't arrived, he confirmed he would've called in for backup." Mina studied Vince's face. His eyes flittered away. "Harmony's job is almost complete. Agent Adams has slowed the ship down. We are about thirteen minutes until rendezvous."

"Thirteen minutes should be enough time. The Navy is prepped and ready. They're in civilian boats. Fishing boats, tourist cruise ships, and ferries. None of which should be a red flag for Veritus. They're armed and have jetties. They can board *La Fortuna* within two minutes of tactical call. That ship won't be leaving the harbor."

"What are your orders for us?" Mina asked, inclining her head in Vince's direction. He nodded once, indicating he would follow their lead. "The mask is a convincing likeness of Barriweather." Which was unfortunate for Lloyd. Mina had no idea how Vince had had it made so quickly. Secrets were secret for a reason. "If the colonel boards the ship as Barriweather, it could be used to our advantage. Distract them while the Navy descends."

"Standby with that," McAllister said. "It's not out of the realm of possibilities. We've located Renaldo Patton, real name Martin Van Beal, the man who dealt with Strum. He's a superior warden in charge of well-known criminals. We're bringing him in now. I've just issued manual orders to pick up Barriweather. I want more information about who's on board this ship and what weapons are available to them. Report back when you're within five minutes of rendezvous or have significant information to share." Then he was gone.

"Where did you stash the crew?" she asked Vince.

"They're restrained downstairs in a storage room," he replied. "They're all safe, no injuries. I don't think any of them are connected to Veritus. They appear to be hired hands. Unfortunately, they might've recognized me, so some debriefing will have to happen before they're released.

We can deal with that later." Vince bobbed his head toward her, indicating her cuff and, Mina guessed, her total package. "This suits you. I have to admit I was disappointed to learn that you'd given up on your dream. It's nice to see you haven't."

Mina peered at him curiously. He really was an enigma. So different from the boy she remembered so long ago. And yet the same. He exuded confidence, was charming and smart. He believed wholeheartedly that he could get the job done and save lives in the process. That was likely why he'd risen so quickly through the ranks of the Protectorate. "Was your security detail the reason you had a black eye when you contacted me the other night?"

It might have seemed like a strange question, but to Mina, it was important.

"They were indeed the reason," Vince confirmed. "You'd think the colonel-in-arms of the French Protectorate would be given some leeway, but you'd be wrong. Bernard is precise about his control and the power he wields. Everything I do must be approved by the Protectorate from the top down. If I'd requested to act on Strum's intelligence, I would've been denied. A killing ring, even though international in scope, operating on another nation's soil is not a concern of ours. We protect French providences and French people, that's our line. The Protectorate doesn't operate like agencies in your government. We're military to the core. The French do have secret internal agencies like yours, but we deal with them rarely. Only if they need force, like you utilizing your Navy. My core guard didn't see my reasoning for coming to the aid of Americans. At the end, they were actively trying to stop me."

Before Mina could question this line further and get to what exactly Vince was holding back, the control panel began to blink.

Then a few static bursts erupted out of the speaker next to them, followed by a male voice.

Chapter 22

THE VOICE CALLED, "Lloyd, what the hell is taking so long?"

Vince shot Mina a concerned look, and they both moved toward the panel.

"We have this thing timed to go off soon," the man continued. "Then we need to get out of the frickin' city. Monique won't let it fly, though, until you deliver the tech we need. Half of us are going to board your ship once it arrives. That way, we can split off and avoid the feds."

There would be no avoiding happening.

Mina gestured to the unit, encouraging Vince to respond.

He shook his head, not toggling on the lever to respond to the man yet. "I can't. They'll know I'm not Lloyd. I don't sound anything like him. I wasn't planning on speaking above a whisper once I arrived."

Mina knew if whoever was speaking didn't get confirmation soon, things could escalate fast, especially if the missile was ready to be *let go.*

"Is there a female crewmember downstairs?" she asked Vince.

"Yes. One."

"Did she have a name etched on her uniform anywhere?"

"Not that I saw."

"How old?"

"Early twenties."

"Lloyd?" the man asked. "Where are you? We can see the ship moving. Stuart is paranoid that the feds are involved, so if we don't hear from you—"

"This is Leta," Mina intoned, notching up the pitch of her voice a few octaves to sound younger. "Lloyd is on the leeward deck." Mina had no idea what or where a leeward deck was, but it sounded right. She was counting on the fact that the other Veritus members didn't frequent ships either. If they did, it might be an issue. "We should be rendezvousing with you momentarily."

"Um, okay." The guy was thrown off. An image entered her brain of a bunch of Veritus members not normally part of in-person kill sessions wandering around, trying to figure out how to make this work.

This likely wasn't a well-oiled operation, which would work to their benefit.

Mina said, "If more of the members want to board *The Crafty Planet* once we arrive, they are welcome to do so. Lloyd has entered a destination for the Colonies of the Bahamas with the harbormaster, which was just accepted. We will be heading there immediately."

"Yeah, okay. I'll run it by Monique and Stuart. Who is this again?"

In a more precise tone, Mina answered, "My name is Leta McElroy. I'm the second mate and a valued employee of Mr. Tedesco's." Name-dropping the boss couldn't hurt. "I'll be there to greet you when you arrive."

"What do you look like?" the man asked.

Mina shot a glance at Vince, who mouthed the word *blonde* and set his hand in the air at shoulder level.

"I'm blonde, hundred and fifty-four centimeters. I'll be the one waving. See you soon!" Mina clicked off the comm. Then she was on the move. Before Vince could say anything, Mina ordered, "I need to see the crewmembers. Is the tube safe to use?"

"Safe enough."

Mina pressed the button, and the door slicked open immediately. "Let's go. We have less than ten minutes to get a plan primed."

He followed her on, selecting the lowest floor. "How did you get the name Leta? They're probably checking it right now."

"I hope they are. I saw her name on a plaque in the crew quarters on my way in. Looks like something they change depending on who's on board. Next to it read 'second mate.' That doesn't mean that's her downstairs, but the name should check."

"Impressive. You really don't miss a thing, do you?" Vincent Kramer nodded in seeming wonderment. "What next?"

"If we can confirm the crew below deck is not with Veritus and are indeed hired hands, I'm going to encourage them to work with us. If that doesn't take, I'm going to threaten them with obstruction of a federal investigation. If that doesn't work, I'm going to gather information and swipe a uni. It'll be Lloyd and Leta greeting that ship, no matter what. There's no way I'm going to allow them to launch that missile on my watch. I'll do whatever it takes."

Including pulling in more civilians, apparently. It couldn't be helped.

In Mina's ear, Kaylee hissed quietly, "*Yes*. Tell him who's boss, girly. Getting on the marshmallow now."

The tube opened, and Vince rushed them down an interior hallway. "I know I don't have to tell you this, but it's risky to involve the crew. How will you know for sure they aren't with Veritus?" He stopped at a door.

Mina shouldered past him, opening it. "I'll know." The room was dark. "Ultras on." Lights blinked on a moment later to reveal three worried-looking crewmembers in e-restraints. Two males, one female. All fairly young. Mina had already engaged her badge. The crystal-clear holo floated right above her wrist.

This cuff was *awesome*.

"My name is Agent Kane. I work for the federal government. We're sorry we had to detain you like this, but it was necessary. I have a few questions, and if you answer them quickly and honestly, I'll let you go immediately. How long have you worked on this ship and for Mr. Tedesco?" Her gaze landed on the first guy. His hair was dark, and he had a short, medium build. He looked the most fearful. Why not start there?

"Um, we don't work for Tedesco," he squeaked. It

wasn't every day you were tossed into a dark room by a stranger. It was scary. "We work for a temp agency. We were hired to make sure no one boards and everything stays clean and ready to launch."

"How long?" Mina asked.

"We've been here for eight days, ma'am," the other guy answered. He was blond, skinny, bearded, and slightly less scared. He'd actually pass for Lloyd at a distance. "It's been pretty quiet. We were joking that this job had been a way to earn sweet, easy borrows. Then that guy came on board, and everything turned to a plate of printed shit." He'd angled his head toward the doorway, where Vince stood.

Maybe they hadn't recognized him as the international heartthrob after all. That would be a solid bonus credit.

Mina realized it was *not* going to be a bonus at all when she turned her attention to the girl, who was staring up at Vincent Kramer with her mouth dangling open, mumbling, "You...you...you..."

"What's your name?" Mina squatted in front of the girl. The blonde reluctantly ripped her eyes away from Vince and forced herself to look at Mina.

"Mabel," she answered.

Damn. Not Leta.

"Have any other crewmembers been on the ship since you arrived?" Mina asked the group.

"A couple of guys here and there, but they never stayed long," the first guy replied.

"What's your name?"

"Sam."

"And you?" She peered at the blond guy.

"Wesley."

"Mabel, Sam, and Wesley." Mina stood as she addressed the group. "Have you been following recent news events? Do you have screen access here?" They seemed confused, so she added, hoping to hurry them up, "Tedesco owns this ship, and he also happened to be the head of Veritus. Have you been following the newscasts?"

Mabel gurgled, "Holy super carbon balls! You're the girl! You're the *girl*. Vincent Kramer. He...he...was out with a girl." Her head pinged between Vince and Mina. "You're her." She looked pleased with herself.

Clearly, Mabel wasn't following along *at all*.

Mina got in her face. Lives were on the line. "Damn right I was out with him. On a secret government mission. Have you heard any of the words I just uttered? Tedesco and Veritus. Killing ring. I'm a government agent."

The girl slinked back. "I...I...I..."

Sam said quietly, "My uncle was killed by Veritus about fifteen years ago. I'd do anything to rid the world of those bastards."

"Good." Mina stood. "That's exactly what I want to hear. What about you?"

"Of course," Wesley answered. "Who doesn't want to rid the universe of coldhearted killers? I'm thinking that having fewer of those in the world is a sweet idea."

Mina's gaze landed on Mabel. "This is a top-secret intergovernmental operation. I'm working in tandem with the colonel-in-arms of the French Protectorate to bring down a Planet's Most Wanted killing ring for good. I'm the one who took down Franco Tedesco the Third last night."

Vince made a sound from his spot by the door. She'd left that tidbit out of their interaction upstairs. Her association with the case would never be splashed around the media, because it was a secret. But these civilians would be offered a nice deal to sign, along with an NDA, and she needed their loyalty. Right now.

"The government requires your help," she went on. "Very shortly, we'll be pulling up alongside another Tedesco ship, *La Fortuna*, that has Veritus members on board. They have a missile full of their signature gas ready to launch at the city." She needed to be honest. No holding back. These civilians had the right to say no. There wasn't a zero percent chance of danger. "If you help us now, I will ensure that the government repays you. It will make the easy borrows you were earning here look like a tot with a printed treat. Along with that, you'll be required to sign a document limiting what you can say about your involvement. I need verbal agreements from all three of you. Your word will be a binding contract. Violating it will earn you time in a box." She gestured down at her cuff. "Everything I'm saying now is being recorded."

Sam nodded readily. "I'm in. Whatever you need."

"Me, too," Wesley said, struggling up onto his knees.

Mabel remained dazed. She kept blinking like she couldn't comprehend what was happening.

Mina knew this was a lot. Once again, she crouched in front of her. "Mabel, I'm really sorry this is happening to you. But I really need your help. If you agree, I'll personally guarantee that Vincent Kramer gives you a digigraph along with personalized media of you posing together. You'll be able to show all of your friends. You just won't be able to tell them the reason you met him. But we can come up with a better story later."

Mabel's eyes sparked wide with incredulousness as they darted between Mina and Vince.

"In order to get that," Mina said, "you must do exactly what I say. Do you think you can manage?"

"I...think I can. I really want to. I'm just...pretty scared."

"That's totally understandable." Mina took a step back while Vince moved in to unhook their e-restraints.

"Hello, Mabel," Vince said in a placating tone. "I'm very sorry I put you in this position in the first place. There was no way for me to know if you were Veritus members or not. I apologize, but I promise to make it up to you. All you need to do is follow the directions Agent Kane gives you so we can put the bad guys away for a very long time." He guided her into a standing position, then went to free the others. "How does that sound?"

"Really good." She nodded vigorously. "I want to help. I do. I promise."

"Follow me," Mina directed as she left the room. "Does anybody here know how to captain this ship? Hooking up with another huge boat might take more finesse than operating it like a holo game."

"I'm doing a decent job," Lee said from her cuff. "It's way easier than a holo game."

"You are doing a decent job," Mina agreed. "We're still afloat. But two ships banging together with a loaded missile full of killer gas on board one of them doesn't sound like what we want to have happening."

"You're right," Lee said. "It might be nice to have a little backup. In case, you know, things get tight."

"Lee, can you link directly into the comm up in the control room so you can all work together?"

"Yes."

"How much time left?"

"Seven minutes."

"Um, I kind of know how to captain," Sam answered. They were all following Mina down the hallway. "I've spent a lot of time in the control room since I've been on board. I've read some of the manuals. I'm really interested in captaining, even though I haven't had any formal training."

"Perfect. Thank you," Mina said. "You can head up to the control room with Colonel Kramer. Wesley and Mabel, come with me." Mina didn't wait to see if Vince would follow her order or not. She had too much to do. Seven minutes would barely be enough time. "I need access to the large deck situated on the bow. The deck where visitors from another ship can board. Can one of you please show me how to get there?"

Wesley took the lead. "There's only one place that can take on passengers like that." They meandered through a few rooms and down a few more hallways until they hit a door.

Just before Wesley opened it, Mina stayed his arm.

"I'm not exiting with you. The other ship has eyes on this one. You're both wearing unis that say you work here, which is exactly what we need. Once you're out there, act like you're getting ready to greet visitors. The other ship believes some of the members will disembark onto this one once we rendezvous. Roll up some rope, appear busy. I don't care what you do. Once we get close, Mabel"—the girl seemed more confident now—"I want you to wave a few times. Look eager. That's it. We just have to project the image that everything is fine. Do you both understand? No looking panicked or scared. Just pretend to be working. Doing an easy job, for easy borrows. Do you think you can handle that?" Mina peered into their faces. She had to be sure.

"We can." Wesley nodded. "Totally. I'll keep an eye on Mabel." He reached out and patted her upper arm. "Remember that game we played before? Where we counted all the rings on the railing because we were so bored? We called it counting for borrows? We can do something like that again." He glanced at Mina. "We'll be fine. If I feel like she's having a hard time, I'll bring her back inside. There's an intercom right inside the door that links to the control room. I'll be in touch."

"Thank you. I appreciate that. The government is grateful for your service. My plan is to come back down here very soon. If you don't see me, and the other ship is getting close, or you feel uncertain, or anything at all goes wrong—and I mean *anything*—get down to the storage room where you just were and lock the door. Do it as quickly as possible. Are we clear?"

Wesley nodded. "I understand. I get that it's dangerous. I'm still in."

"The water and air are crawling with Navy operatives and government agents. In a matter of moments, I can have you whisked away. I don't want you hurt. Please know that."

"I can do it," Mabel said. Her voice held a little quiver, but she was resolute. "Even if I wasn't getting Vincent Kramer's digigraph, I would want to do this. My father served in the military, and so did my grandfather. Even though Veritus hasn't hurt my family directly, they have hurt so many people. I won't mess it up."

"Perfect. Now get out there and look busy. I'll be in touch shortly." Mina turned and hurried toward the tube, confident in Wesley's ability to keep things controlled.

This was turning out to be one of the most serious ops Mina had ever been involved with, as well as the most civilians she'd ever personally recruited to work with her. It almost never happened like this.

As she moved, she said, "We rendezvous with that ship in less than five. Lee, I need a report. Please tell me Harmony has redirected that missile."

CHAPTER 22

"Almost...almost. There!" Harmony hooted on Mina's cuff as the tube door opened, and Mina stepped into the control room. Vince and Sam had their heads together.

Mina immediately walked to the windshield. The ship was about half a kilometer away, and they were closing in fast.

"I did it!" Harmony continued. "It's done. It's null. It's void. It's not going anywhere. Also, just in case there's a physical override switch, and those bastards do launch it, it will fly five hundred nautical miles straight over the ocean. My father checked satellite feed, and there are no ships anywhere near. I'm pretty sure the gas won't harm those poor fishes, but it's the best we can do."

"Superb work, Agent Biggins," Mina said with feeling.

"Oh! Yes! Oh, shit. It's really going to happen," she squealed. "Agent Biggins. Whoa. That's intense."

Mina spotted some other ships in the vicinity and felt

sure they had enough backup. "Now it's time to round up those rat bastard killer asshelmets."

Lee's voice came over both the comm panel on the ship and Mina's cuff. The echo was strange. "Once we get within twenty meters, I'm going to need you to—"

A siren roared above them. The shrill was incredible.

"What the hell is that?" Mina shouted over the din.

But she had a sinking feeling she knew exactly what it was. They all moved to the windows, straining to see. A huge, armored drone was positioned above them, hovering, siren still blaring.

Kaylee yelled in her ear at the same time McAllister's voice erupted from her cuff. She could barely hear either of them.

"That's not one of ours!" her director shouted.

"What in the torpedo hell is that?" Kaylee yelled.

Mina pulled out her ear node.

She knew exactly who it was, even though she didn't see any insignia. She didn't need to see a marker to know that the French Protectorate had arrived to rescue one of their own.

This was Vince's backup. His plan all along.

Mina sprinted toward the tube, and Vince followed. "Stay up here, Sam," she shouted. "Stay in contact with Agent Adams. He'll make sure we don't crash into the other ship and that you and your friends get out safely." Mina knew Lee had heard the order.

In the tube, the sound from above was a little more muted, so she had enough clearance to yell, "What the *hell*, Kramer? You put every one of us at risk! We're *incredibly* lucky Harmony succeeded not more than thirty seconds ago. How could you not tell me this was your plan?"

Luckily, the tube door slicked open, and she didn't have to hear his pitiful excuse. Hiding intel like that was dangerous. A guy like Kramer knew it.

Boy, did he know it.

Mina ran full speed toward the deck and Wesley and Mabel.

Vince was on her heels. "I had no idea *when* they would show up! I wasn't even completely sure they would."

She hit the end door, punching it open at a run. Vince, close on her heels, pulled a piece of tech out of his pocket. Mina veered one way, Vince went the other. Wesley and Mabel were nowhere to be found. Relief flooded through Mina as she pulled up. She was pretty sure they'd gone to the storage room like she'd instructed them. This development definitely qualified as out of the ordinary.

From her wrist, her director commanded, "I need a report, Agent Kane. What is happening?" He sounded as furious as Mina felt.

"It's the Protectorate," she told him, the cuff mere centimeters from her lips so he could hear. The siren was still going, but the decibels seemed a tiny bit lower. "Apparently, this was his plan in case I didn't show. I'm not exactly certain. But I *am* sure that Colonel Kramer knew this was a possibility and kept that to himself. As far as I know, he's in conversation with them now."

Blessedly, the siren stopped.

"Drones and Navy are closing in now," McAllister said.

Mina could hear myriad props coming from all directions.

"Prepare to board the ship," he went on. "Agent Adams is guiding you in. This was not the plan, but it's what we have. Let's take them down, Agent Kane."

This was about to get much bloodier than it ever had to be.

"I'm ready—"

An explosion ripped through the deck. Mina was thrown against the wall of the ship. She scrambled up, thankful the impact hadn't been more forceful. She had no idea where it had come from until she heard a shout.

La Fortuna floated less than ten meters away. A lone man stood on the bridge with a hydro-launcher perched on his shoulder.

As he met her gaze, he fired again.

She began to run right as Vince barreled around the corner. He grabbed on to her hand and pulled them both up and over the railing.

It felt like they fell forever.

Mina remembered her training, pointing her feet and trying to keep her body loose.

They hit the water hard.

She plunged deeply, kicking toward the surface as soon as was humanly possible, gasping for air as her head emerged. Vince popped up a second later.

There were at least thirty drones in the air overhead, several of them issuing orders through enhanced speakers. The ship they'd just leaped from had stopped.

As far as Mina could tell, the hydro-launching man had been subdued. No more bombs were exploding. That was a relief.

Treading water, Mina pushed her hair out of her eyes.

Vince swam up to her. "I'm sorry," he said on a long breath. "I'm so sorry. This was a miscalculation on my part. I didn't know for sure you'd show up. I had no way to alert the Protectorate I was okay. I tried through the comm unit while you were down below, but they weren't in range yet."

So the tech thing she had seen in his hand had been a range-finder communication.

Mina just shook her head. She had nothing to say. Vince Kramer, her childhood friend, hadn't trusted her with Protectorate intel, even though she'd let him—openly and willingly—into her world, even after he had led her on a long, complicated hunt.

She was saved from further conversation as a white, springy-looking boat puttered up alongside them. The flat deck had loopy railings and a plexan-enclosed box with one person, probably the captain, sitting in the center.

"Hey, looks like you two could use a lift," Kaylee called, leaning over the railing. "Quick," she called over her shoulder, "they need to get out of that damn water. It's a chemical slop. Hurry up! Toss them something."

Someone Mina couldn't see tossed two inflatables over the side. She grabbed one. Vince did the same.

As she treaded water, she watched as military agents swarmed *La Fortuna*. Not very fortunate any longer.

She should've been among them. Mina couldn't get a good look at the people on deck from her angle in the water, but the Veritus members didn't seem to be resisting. That was good. No bloodshed was optimal.

Her cuff was ruined. The impact had killed it. The circuitry inside was fragile, with so many intricately working parts. She wasn't about to get any updates until she got settled with Kaylee.

Mina coughed, spitting out seawater as she maneuvered to the side of the boat. If you could call it a *boat*. It really was a floating marshmallow. Agents grabbed hold of her arms and hauled her up.

Kaylee knelt next to her, covering her with a long cloth. "Step back, everybody," she ordered the other agents. Mina didn't recognize most of them. "Thank goodness you're safe. I saw that asshole hydro-launcher take aim. Then all of a sudden you and Vince were flying over the railing like two superheroes in some snazzy holo vid."

"Hardly. I need to contact McAllister. My new cuff is ruined." She lifted her wrist to show the new Zenith copper creation was cracked on top and dripping liquid.

"Well, isn't that just a sad crime?" Kaylee sat back on her haunches. "Not only did we *not* get in on any of the action to bring those bastards to justice, but your super-shiny new toy is grinder fodder."

They didn't have to wait long. McAllister's voice erupted through Kaylee's cuff. "Report, Agent Poston. I have eyes on your boat. I see you have Agent Kane and Colonel Kramer with you. Do you need a medi-team?"

"No, sir," Mina answered. "But if it hasn't happened already, three civilians on board *The Crafty Planet* need to be escorted to safety."

"Already accomplished. Agent Adams ordered it done. They're safe and in holding. The Veritus members were so distracted by the Protectorate's armored craft that our agents and military were able to board without them noticing. They were surrounded, and they surrendered without a fight. No lives were lost. We have two tech teams swarming the boat now. The missile is being carefully loaded into a vacuum-sealed chamber. It was a win." He was leaving out that it could've been a huge loss. But Mina would take the win. "You're to report to the Medi Center once you're off that boat, Agent Kane."

Mina began to complain. "I'm fine. I don't need—"

"That's an order. The amount of chemis and toxins in the water means you need a full purge in a medi-pod."

Ew. "Okay." Mina felt weary to the bone. She shivered. Then she coughed. Maybe a spin in a medi-pod wasn't such a bad idea after all.

"Ambrose Bernard has signaled a meet," McAllister said tersely, conveying just how he felt about the situation. His feelings were shared. "I will debrief you once I'm finished. That's it for now. Good work, Agents Kane and Poston."

"How do we get off this damn boat?" Kaylee yelled to someone behind her. "Can you please captain this floating eyesore back to the pier, please? This agent needs medical attention."

Mina refrained from commenting on Kaylee's natural mothering abilities.

Instead, she made the mistake of catching Vince's eye. She looked away. She wasn't ready. Then she looked back because he was moving toward her, a cloth wrapped around his waist, his hair slicked back.

Agents around them parted, giving him a wide berth, several of them wearing awestruck expressions. They were just lowly government agents compared to someone in his position of power—or that was likely their reasoning.

"Mina, we need to talk."

She stood, pulling the cloth tighter. "The op was a success. No lives were lost. We're all safe. You can go back to France knowing you did an amazing thing. I'm sure your followers will be thrilled."

He bowed his head, frowning. "I need to apologize. I didn't tell you it was a possibility the Protectorate would find me. I had no choice. I left them a few—"

No way was Mina doing this with an audience.

And it appeared Colonel Kramer was going to keep talking whether she wanted him to or not. Mina grabbed his elbow and propelled him to the other side of the marshmallow.

Harmony and her rapid finger-poking flashed into Mina's brain, but she chose to act like the adult she was. For now.

"You don't need to explain anything to me," she whispered, leaning in. "You already told me you do things differently in France. After what happened here today,

I got it loud and clear. The Protectorate does what it wants, when it wants. It's honestly not surprising. Lots of foreign governments operate the same way. No need to apologize." Mina understood that not everyone followed the same code of honor. "As far as I'm concerned, this op is over. The bad guys are caught, the good guys are safe. It was a success, and now we can go back to our regular lives."

"We just... Mina, please." His voice carried a fair amount of pleading. "The story doesn't have to end here. We were just getting reacquainted."

"I've enjoyed reconnecting with you." Mina had to actively try to unclench her beginning-to-clench jaw. She didn't want to do this now. Or maybe ever. "It's been fun to reminisce. Dinner was great. But I think it's best if we go our separate ways from here." She didn't think she'd ever *really* be able to trust him again. He had to know that. It was his choice, and he'd chosen to play a different game. "Don't forget, this story has a happy ending. Two children grew into adults, and both became successful in jobs they love." She wanted to make sure this sank into his head, which looked great with all the slicked hair, which wasn't fair because Mina knew she looked like a dripping-wet alpaca. "We're not the same people we were when we were children. We've grown in different directions." Much to her relief, they were pulling up to the pier. "I wish you well in all your future endeavors. I have no doubt you'll work your way up to head of the Protectorate one day." She awkwardly patted him on the shoulder as she turned and walked away.

"Mina," Vince called. "Please. There's more to the story. Let me at least try to explain."

She politely replied with a short wave. Mina was finished talking for now and certainly wasn't going to keep it up in front of a team of agents.

Kaylee met her at what seemed to be the only way off this boat, but unlike the big ship's sturdy stairway, this exit was a little more unusual.

"They can't be serious," Kaylee complained. "I'm not swinging off this thing by a damn tag line."

"I'm sorry, ma'am," the young agent next to them said. "We left the pier so quickly, the boarding plank snapped off. This is all we have. Apparently, the drunk tourists like to pretend they're pirates or something. I don't really get it. But it works. Either that, or you can wait for a drone. But you'll have to get a secure line up for that, too, since there's nowhere for one to land on this..." He glanced warily around them. "Floating cube."

"It's fine." Mina took hold of the line. "It's like a meter-and-a-half jump." She dumped the cloth from around her shoulders and leaped, swinging her legs and arching her back, letting go as the pier passed under her.

She landed easily, swinging the cable back to Kaylee, who snatched it out of the air with a perturbed look on her face. She landed next to Mina three seconds later.

Kaylee grabbed her hand, tugging Mina down the pier at a quick pace. "Don't look back. The wet, soggy puppy you left standing back there is too sad for words. His face is all scrunched up, and he looks like he's about to cry. Mother mercy on Mercury, it should be a crime to look that good after emerging from a chemi-soaked swim."

Mina started a rebuttal, but Kaylee deftly continued, "I'm not saying leaving him in his overflowing euroboots is wrong, mind you. That hunky mink rat deserves it. He compromised the op. His failure to disclose information could've gotten people killed. He deserves it. But—and this is just an itsy-bitsy but—he might have a point. I mean, there could be more to the story."

"I'm too tired to hear any more story," Mina said. "Honestly, it could be an entire novel, and I don't want to hear it. It's over. Any trust we'd built is gone for me. You said it, he comprised the op to a degree that people could've died. He lied by omission. Instead of reaching out for help once he got his intel from Strum, thinking I might be an agent, he led us on a chase. That's just not my kind of people."

"What if...and this is just a wild possibility, because he has no freedom inside the Protectorate, but what if he had to be super sneaky? I mean, it rings."

"He had time after he got away from his guards to contact me. Or Strum. Or Harmony. Or call the freaking PPF. Anything to keep the Protectorate from dropping out of the sky unannounced."

"What if, and here's another thought, he had no possible way of communicating? Because they can trace him through every single piece of tech he owns."

Mina shook her head. "If you keep bringing up Vincent Kramer, I'm calling Preston Jazz Hands on you."

Kaylee grimaced. "Oh, that's low. It's core-level underground."

"I'll go lower if I have to. I seem to remember someone by the name of Porcupine Jones."

A small shriek sounded, followed by rampant giggles, as Kaylee tugged Mina's arm. "You wouldn't dare bring up Porcupine Jones!"

"I so would."

"No, you're way too nice. And he was just way too crazy. How was I supposed to know Preston—of the animated jazz hands—was an embezzler? He was so cute and sincere. He was always complimenting my hairstyles." Kaylee let go of Mina's arm and did some jazz-hand moves. "Then he'd always break into an old-timey show tune. He loved his show tunes. He was probably watching old vids while he was trying to steal my data."

Mina stopped, pulling them both up. "You're *literally* a federal agent. Knowing he was trying to embezzle from you should've been a gimme."

"Okay. *Okay.* You win." She lifted her hands in surrender. Then they flicked back and forth. She was still jazzing. Mina tried not to laugh. She knew Kaylee was trying to make this all better. "I won't bring up Kramer... That is, until *after* you're out of the medi-pod. I'm sure then your head will be nice and clear, and you'll be more apt to listen to reason."

"If you do, I'll—"

"I jest! We are officially Kramer-free."

Mina headed toward the government medi-drone that had touched down to pick them up.

"Until tomorrow, that is," Kaylee snickered.

"I'm officially instating a cone of silence," Mina told her friend as she boarded the drone, nodding to the medi-workers. "Anyone who breaks it has to pay me *actual* currency."

"Baby, I can afford it." Kaylee smirked as she scooted Mina over and took the seat next to her.

Chapter 24

"EGGIE, MAKE ME a ham and cheese omelet. No, scratch that. Make me an ice cream sundae with extra hot fudge." Screw real food, Mina deserved a treat. More than weary, she was exhausted to the core. The Medi Center had insisted she stay several hours after detox fluid treatment so they could monitor her.

Apparently, the water in the harbor was a couple levels past disgusting, edging into frightening. But she'd checked out with no toxicity in her bloodstream, so they finally let her go. The twenty-second century had a lot going for it, but with the amount of traffic in the harbor, literally tens of thousands of crafts entering and exiting daily, on water and in the air, individuals ignoring safe protocols for dumping, and new chemi compounds developed to make the world even more efficient, they were losing the clean-water battle. It was disheartening.

"Would you like sprinkles and a cherry on top?" Eggie inquired.

Mina chuckled. "Yes, I would. The more sprinkles, the better."

"Printing ice cream sundae, extra fudge, lots of sprinkles, and a cherry on top. Printer must achieve zero degrees Celsius for this order. May take longer than anticipated. Please wait."

Mina took a seat on one of her gel-cush stools, settling her head in her hands. She was freshly showered, in her comfort clothing, and after she finished spooning in the delicious sweetness, she was going straight to bed. She didn't care in the least that it was only seven thirty p.m.

She'd received a debriefing from McAllister at the Medi Center.

His meeting with Ambrose Bernard had gone reasonably well. They'd been joined by the colonel-in-arms after he'd received some medical attention. Vince had admitted he'd gone against French protocol by coming to the US to take down Veritus. Ambrose had forgiven Vince's indiscretions on the spot, then backtracked and tried to claim that he'd known what Vince was up to, had secretly approved it, and had been in on the mission. He'd explained that the drone's entrance into US airspace had been planned down to the minute to ensure the op was a success.

Vince had been forced to go along with all of it. Ambrose, in order to keep France from looking like one of their own had gone rogue, needed a workable story to give to the media, who had swooped in like buzzards on a hot carcass.

Not only had they covered the story, they had gobbled

it up like someone with a maple-treat addiction.

According to Melissa Socorro, Vincent Kramer, international heartthrob and savior of the American people, had brought down Veritus single-handedly and had saved the city. She had been enraptured, stopping just short of describing Vince physically gripping his manly hands around a missile full of poisonous gas and manually stopping the thing from detonating with brute strength and the sheer force of his will.

The amount of gushing had been close to intolerable.

The op and everything about it had been so over-blown and embellished that Kaylee—Mina's super-mild-mannered best pal—got up and punched the screen in Mina's medi-room, earning her a swift rebuke from the staff. Kaylee had refused to apologize, telling them she would give them a currency draft to cover the damage and, much to Mina's relief, had finally dropped bringing up the colonel-in-arms.

Mina doubted any of this story had been cleared by Vince himself. She actually felt sorry for him. It would make his everyday life even harder. Mina had never in her life ever received public credit or accolades for completing an op, nor did she want to. Something like that would ruin any future undercover ops and was completely unnecessary. Lives saved was always enough.

"Your order is ready," Eggie intoned. "Hope you enjoy your sprinkles."

At least her meal printer was good company. Mina padded over to get her food, delighted to see an extra-long sundae spoon sitting by the dish.

She'd taken one dreamy bite when Veronica announced, "Incoming vid request from Lee Adams. Do you wish to accept?"

Lee had tried to contact her earlier, but she'd missed him while she'd been talking to the medi-team.

"Yes. Screen at forty." Mina cradled the sundae dish in one hand as she turned to face the wall, taking another bite. She tried not to smack too much, but it was super yummy.

"Oh, hi," he said. "I didn't mean to interrupt your meal."

Mina waved the spoon in the air. "You're not interrupting. I'm just having a quick bite before I hit the platform. I've been waiting to hear from you. First, how's Harmony?"

"She's fine." He shrugged. "I left pretty quickly after the mission was completed. McAllister complimented her and told her he would schedule a time to talk to her in the next day or two. She's excited to become an agent. I think she'll be good at it."

"I do, too. That was some pretty excellent hacking."

"It really was. Watching her work was amazing."

Mina didn't hear even a speck of jealousy. *Go, Lee.* "What about Norm? Since my cuff was damaged, I haven't been able to get a hold of him."

"He mentioned, rather cryptically, that he was going to visit a *dome center* to ask some questions, then meet up with *that kid* and keep an eye on him."

"Perfect. He's focused on Harri again, where he should be, and putting feelers out about others who may have exhibited the same reaction to Plush as Daphne." No news was good news on that end. She'd let Norm handle it for now.

As usual, Lee's cams were focused only on his face. Mina watched him move around. He finally began, "So, about Vincent Kramer—"

"Nope. Not talking about Kramer." She took a big scoop of ice cream into her mouth to prove her point.

"But he's taking all the credit—"

"We're not in it for the credit. And there's no way he wanted to be associated with that crazy, gushing narrative. He lied to us, omitted key details, but he's not a showman. That was all Ambrose." She chomped on some sprinkles. They were tasty. Texture was spot-on. "Honestly, I think it's a good thing. Vince in the spotlight removes our department altogether. Socorro and company are not even *trying* to dig for more details. They believe they have the whole story. It works for us."

"Yeah, maybe." Lee didn't pretend to be convinced.

"There was zero bloodshed," she pointed out, taking another creamy bite. "After Tedesco made it murdery and horrible, that was a cosmic blessing. To my knowledge, all the members of Veritus have been rounded up."

"I believe they have been, too."

"When they pulled in Martin Van Beal, aka Renaldo Patton, who tried to convince Strum to work for them all those years, he sang like a choral member in the Planetary Symphony. They rounded up five others in short sequence, each of them ratting out the others as fast as they could. The problem with incorporating greedy, narcissistic, parasitic individuals into your killing organization is they are only ever in it for themselves."

"You're right." Lee sighed.

Veronica intoned, "Delivery request, level twenty hub. Level two authorizations required. Government bot. Single package. Marked urgent."

Lee said, "Oh, that's from me. Well, from the government, but I had them send it over."

Mina's eyebrows rose. She reluctantly set down her now-melty, but still-delicious sundae. "Delivery approved. Have them send it up." To Lee, she said, "What is it?" She went over to the sink to wash her sticky fingers.

"Something you need." He shrugged. "It's no big deal. I just hurried up the process."

Lee remained evasive as Mina dried her hands. Then Veronica announced, "Bot delivery in thirty seconds."

Mina walked over to her door and performed all the necessary security measures to open it. A LiveBot, who looked exactly like a young twentysomething delivery boy with shaggy brown hair and a hat, stopped in front of her, producing a small package in his hands. It was black and not unlike the Midas box that Vince had delivered a few days prior.

She gave a DNA sample and a retinal scan, and the bot went on his way.

Mina shut the door and opened the lid as she walked back into her living area. Inside was a shiny new cuff with even more copper than the last. Not only were the buttons copper, but so was the edging on the entire band. It was beautiful. She carefully took it out of the gel-foam. "Wow. It's amazing." She moved it under the ultras and it sparkled.

Lee looked wildly uncomfortable, shifting more in his seat. "I didn't actually buy you this or anything. I just contacted Zachary Zenith and explained what happened. Since he works for the government, I kind of hinted that you were the one who took down Veritus." Mina raised her eyebrows. He shook his head. "Not outright or anything. Just that you were part of the larger group. He told me that he'd been working on this super-new, cool prototype. He had to get permission to get it coded to you, but apparently McAllister agreed pretty quickly."

Mina didn't want to think about the currency this had cost her department.

"I wanted you to get it tonight," Lee said. "I think he just finished it, like, ten minutes ago. I thought it would take a little more time to arrive. But I'm glad you like it. Zenith is a genius."

Mina had already secured the cuff around her wrist. It was lightweight, yet sturdy. Well, as sturdy as one of these could be with all the microscopic moving parts inside. Holo was a complicated three-point system, not to mention everything else. "I can't wait to try all the features. Thank you so much for doing this, Lee." She was genuinely thankful. It was a very nice gesture. "I appreciate it. I was sad to lose the other one so quickly."

"Yeah, that sucked."

Lee wasn't the only one who had intervened with the government on their partner's behalf.

"Have you received your new housing resident approval yet?"

He shook his head, trying not to show his disappointment. "No."

"Are you sure? Have you checked your internal messages?"

"My internal messages? You mean, like, my residence? I don't use a sim like you do. I keep it on standby. My place is not big enough, and my everyday household stuff isn't connected to it. I do things manually."

Not for long.

Mina sat back down and picked up her bowl. Melty was just fine with her. "Check it anyway." She took a bite.

Mina had directed the housing department to send the information via Lee's residence so it wouldn't interfere with the op. Lee was supposed to have gotten the message when he arrived home. She hadn't thought Lee wouldn't check his residence. Even if your home wasn't run by a sim, your address had the capacity to take messages. Everyone's did.

"Um. Okay." Lee addressed his residence, "Penny, have any messages come through for me?"

Penny. That was so cute.

A young female sim that sounded no older than ten answered, "Yes, Lee. Would you like to hear it?"

Lee blushed. "I programmed Penny after my little cousin, Jenny. She moved away when I was seven. It's her actual voice sig."

"No need to explain, Lee. I think it's adorable." Sims were very personal. Some people grew very attached.

"Playback, Penny," Lee instructed.

Mina listened as a male sim recited, "This message is from the Government Housing Department." The audio shifted to a message from a female clerk. "Agent Lee Adams, this is Muriel Greenway with the GHD. You've been approved for Level III housing in a high-rise of your choice within city limits. Please get back to me for details and virtual viewings. Once you make your decision, the government will procure the residence, install necessary security, and have the unit ready for you within three business days. Please reply at your earliest convenience. Thank you."

Shock flooded Lee. His face was an open data receptor. "Level III? A high-rise? No way. I can't believe it."

"Believe it. You've earned this. When we're talking about who *actually* took Veritus out at its very root, it was you. Without your quick thinking, your pixel mirroring capabilities, and everything else, you and I wouldn't be sitting here having this conversation. Congratulations. Have fun with the virtual viewings. Can't wait to see what you decide on."

"Thank you. I know you had something to do with this, and I appreciate it. My life has changed so much in the last year and a half. I'm really grateful."

"You're in a good position to help Harmony with her transition." Mina stood, bringing her mostly empty bowl to the grinder. The sundae had hit the spot. She was feeling much better. "She's going to need some guidance.

If I have any say, I want Kaylee to be her mentor. I'm going to have to convince McAllister and Agent Poston that it's a good idea to pair them together." Mina was already considering how to do it. Kaylee had sworn off mentoring a long time ago.

"Pairing her with Kaylee is a great idea. They're kind of the same."

They really were.

That could either be wonderful or disastrous. Mina was betting on wonderful.

Mina yawned. "I'll check in with you in the morning. I have no idea what McAllister has in store for us, but I'm hoping we get to continue the Plush case that's not a case. I promised Harri I would make this right, and I will do my best to fulfill that promise. At least I can go to bed knowing he's safe. Bliss Corp is like a bunch of hyenas picking off easy prey."

"It is. Sleep well. And thanks again." As Lee popped off her screen, he was looking eager to start viewing new residences.

Mina ground up her dish and walked to her sleep room.

Once inside, Veronica intoned, "You have five messages from Vincent Kramer. Do you wish to hear them?"

"No." Unlike Lee, Mina was choosing *not* to listen to her residence messages on purpose. "Engage sleep shades, enact Level V security, no interruptions by anyone other than Director McAllister or my family." Her bedroom shades began to lower. "And no delivery approval for anything from Vincent Kramer. Refusal without contacting me. Do not patch through any messages either unless I ask."

"Will do." Veronica stayed silent for a few moments. Then she said, "Are we adding Vincent Kramer to your excrement list?"

Mina laughed out loud as she crawled into her platform. She'd had no idea she had a shit list. "Please do." Thinking of her software system coming up with a shit list made her feel elated. Wait until she told Kaylee.

She snuggled into her silky sheets. "Wake up at eight a.m."

"Noted. Sleep well, Agent Kane."

"I plan to." She wasn't going to allow any dreaming.

Fat chance that she'd be successful, but she was going to give it her very best try.

VID STAR

A MINA KANE NOVEL: BOOK FOUR

AMANDA CARLSON

Chapter 1

"IT'S BUGGING ME that I have zero recall on this. I watched *A Crafty Planet* like two weeks ago. It vidstarred that one guy." Kaylee snapped her fingers. They looked enormous on Mina's sleep room wall screen. In her half-awake state, Mina had accidently ordered Veronica, her home sim, to place Kaylee at one hundred percent. "Paul—no, too normal. Pica? Prancer? *Crap*, his name has completely escaped me." She shook her head, her straight black hair skimming the tops of her shoulders. It was seven thirty a.m., and Kaylee was already dressed and ready to go. Mina snuggled farther under her silky, soft sheets. She wasn't ready to start her day just yet. "It was something weird and vidstarry."

Mina giggled as she tracked Kaylee's hands, which her pal and fellow CIU agent, kept moving animatedly, in between snapping.

"What?" Kaylee frowned, leaning forward. "So I don't know vidstars? You try to name one. Honestly, if there's not a dolphin frolicking or a marmot hunting for a nut, you rarely pay attention." Mina chortled. Marmots didn't eat nuts. But maybe? See, she didn't know everything about every animal. Kaylee was right, she did have terrible attention span when it came to watching people vids. Naturecasts were her favorite. "I mean, his name could've been Pez or Posty. But, come to think about it, maybe it was Petra. Yes—it *was* a girl. Petra Pebbles! That's it. What a ridiculous name. Vidstars take the printed frosting when it comes to identity-chipping themselves after dumb things like rocks or fingers."

Mina snorted. "Fingers? Come on. You're taking it too far."

"Cuticle Cantrell. Knuckle Knot. Or maybe it's Cuticle Knot and Knuckle Cantrell?" Kaylee swished her hand, then pointed, shaking her finger. It was the size of a small child on Mina's huge screen. "And if you don't stop that annoying hyena cackle, I'm going to drone over to your super sweet lux suite in the sky and give you a five-fingered knuckle sandwich. Honestly, it's the only time we should ever say the word *knuckle* in a sentence." She balled her fist and fake-punched the air. Dag, her dog, jumped up barking, thinking Kaylee was going to throw a ball, which was his fav.

Mina had to wait a few seconds to catch her breath.

She hadn't laughed this hard, this early in the morning, since she was in elementary programming and woke up from a girls' sleep party. "I'm not laughing because you don't know vidstars. I promise. I'm laughing because I found you the perfect partner. One you can mentor and hone to a fine, sharp tip. You'll enjoy it."

"No, I won't. I don't mentor."

"She's a snapper and a hand-waver. Honestly, she's a hydro-cracker and you're going to love her. There's no one else she should be paired with in the entire agency."

"Our department hires new recruits like every six years or so," Kaylee chuffed. "Maybe in six years I'll be ready to handle a baby."

"McAllister offered her a job."

Kaylee sat back in her chair. "Offered *who* a job?"

"Harmony Biggins. Strum Littlefield's daughter. I forgot to tell you. With all the jumping off the ship stuff, and getting detoxed from a chemi swim stuff, and all the...other stuff, it slipped my mind." *Other stuff* was Vincent Kramer. Mina wanted to enjoy her peaceful morning and doing so meant not mentioning colonel-in-arms of the French Protectorate. "McAllister told her she had a job with the department if she could disarm the missile, which she did." If she hadn't, the serial killing group Veritus could've launched it into the city, killing thousands. Harmony deserved compensation, and she'd chosen to take it in the form of a job with the CIU. "And because he's hiring her without any training, she's going to need a *really* good mentor. So naturally, that's you."

"Flattery will get you very, very far. Yeah, she made it all happen and saved a lot of lives," Kaylee said pensively. "How old is she? I never saw her, only heard her through your cuff."

"Almost twenty-two," Mina answered. It was a teensy

stretch. Harmony had told them she was twenty-one and a half. Close enough. "She's a Level XIV hacker."

"Level XIV? I thought they just went by *super* after XIII? So you're telling me, my baby agent hacker is better than your baby agent hacker?"

"Way to spin it." Mina chortled. "I don't pretend to understand their ranking systems. But yes, that means she is technically at a greater number." Hackers determined their own inner workings, it remained a mystery to everyone else. "Lee's right there, though. He let Harmony and her father do all the disarming, even though I'm certain he could've figured it out. The kid's brilliant at code. He just is."

"Is that pride I hear leaking out of your cackle?"

"It might be." Mina scratched her head and debated tossing off her covers. "Just between us, I'm not sure how I completed some of my other cases without him. He saved my backside on the Tedesco op. I wouldn't have been able to breach the penthouse at all. He figured out the military security cam switcheroo in like thirty seconds. If that hadn't happened, I shudder to think of where we would be right now. Tedesco would've gotten away with all of it and Veritus would still be operational."

"Yeah, don't let your brain go there." Kaylee scratched Dag behind the ears as the lovable dog draped himself across her knees. "So, in effect, you're saying that having a baby hacker partner makes you a better agent."

Mina chuckled. "I guess I might be saying that. Seriously, you're going to love her. You're almost the same person."

"It'll be up to McAllister." Kaylee shrugged. "We'll see what he does."

"I'm going to tell him I think you'd be the perfect mentor. She needs someone strong and levelheaded," Mina said. "Harmony likes doing things her way." That was something of an understatement. Mina chuckled thinking about the two of them together. Harmony was going to meet her twin gravitational force in Kaylee. "She's supremely confident, which is an incredible asset, as well as a hindrance when she's coming in so green. She'll respond well to your style, and therefore err less than she would with someone else."

"Levelheaded is quite the compliment coming from you. I like to think my lid stays in nice equilibrium at times of crisis," Kaylee chuckled. "But the erring part is what gets me. That's the reason I don't mentor. Taking care of babies is not my thing. They make kilotons of mistakes, which in our business can get you killed, and they tend to irritate me overmuch when they cry. And from what you're describing, there's a high likelihood I will make this girl cry. Not my thing. No enjoyment there."

"She doesn't strike me as a crier," Mina said. "And don't forget, you're talking to someone who went in fighting like a marmot trying to hold on to its nut when she was forced to deal with a super rookie. I can tell you from the other side, it's not so bad. I really like Harmony. She's strong, intelligent, confident, and would benefit from someone who keeps her on task. You won't be sorry. She'll probably end up helping you much more than you thought."

"So essentiall-*eee* you're telling m-*ee* that Harmon-*eee* may b-*eee* a real-l*eee* good train-*eee*?"

"Sthap!" Mina chortled, finally throwing off her covers. She couldn't fight it any longer. It was time to get up. "All that's missing is some finger snapping."

"Happy to oblige." Kaylee started snapping to a quick beat. "Harmon-*eee* is my new ment-*eee*, but only if sh-*eee* can face scrutin-*eee*, not my fault if I make her w-*eee*p, it'll be up to her to k-*eee*p it together." Kaylee stood, shaking Dag off. "Okay, that last part needs work."

Mina rolled to the edge of her platform, chuckling as she hefted a leg over the padded edge. The cush was still too cushy. It was like being stuck in a lux cage.

It was Kaylee's turn to cackle. "Watching you get out of that thing is like watching a roly-poly from *Mar Bots* trying to wobble out of a shallow crater. Just fix it already."

Mina made it up and over. She was in her comfort clothing, because she'd been too tired to change before bed last night, so she was covered. "I sleep like a baby in that hole." She gestured to the interior of the platform that was now a rumple of silky goodness. "I don't want to mess it up, but trying to get myself out each morning is becoming an issue. I think it quietly swallows me during the night."

"Can't you just raise the interior? I'm pretty sure that platform is top-of-the-line. Everything on it is adjustable. Not just the cush."

Mina glanced quizzically at her bed. "Huh. I never thought of that. Veronica, raise platform base up eight centimeters." Veronica, Mina's home sim, was connected to all of the operational tech inside her residence. Most everybody's sim had similar compatibilities, if they chose to pair them. People had been living with this convenience for over fifty years. Hard to imagining life without it.

Almost immediately the interior of Mina's platform began to rise.

"See, I told you," Kaylee said. "What would you do without me?"

"Sleep later." Mina tested it by sitting on the edge and bouncing twice. "Hey, same cush, new height. And, look, I can slide right out." Mina scooted off. "You're a genius." Mina headed into her closet to figure out what to wear for the day. "Why did you call me so early anyway?" she called. "I never asked."

"*The Crafty Planet* popped into my head. Not Tedesco's huge-ass ship you jumped off of yesterday, but the actual vid it was named after. Then I decided to check on my bestie. You were on an emotional dronecoaster last night. First, you thought you were working on equal euroboot footing with your old childhood pal, then he pulls a double cross and almost screws up the entire op." By screwing up, Kaylee meant he could've gotten a lot of people killed. He'd held back necessary information from Mina that had compromised her op. "Plus, I was curious—okay, downright insanely curious—if the colonel-in-arms, after all this dronecoaster drama, had the guts to show up last night."

"Here?" Mina came out of her closet with a pair of

mustard-colored tuck pants and a black tunic over one arm. "He can't get up to this level without authorization. So I'm not sure if he had the guts. I've got his calls on mute. Deliveries shut down. Veronica even added him to what she called my 'excrement list' last night without even being asked. So, no he didn't show up." Mina probably wouldn't have let him in. The fact there was a probably attached bugged her.

Kaylee hooted, slapping a knee. "That's hilarious. Poor Kramer. Though, the man is basically royalty. He could get up there if he wanted to." She shook her head. "He really zapped himself into a black hole with his glaring omissions."

"Omissions is just a fancy word for lies. I've gone over it in my mind." Like, all night. He'd swirled around Mina's dreams like a much too good-looking specter. "He made a kiloton of bad choices. From how he contacted me, to involving Harmony, up until the end when he deliberately kept important details from me. There's just no way I can trust him again. He blew it."

"Agreed. He shanked it big-time. But hearing his reasonings for what he did isn't out of the realm of the cosmos. He could have some good explanations."

"Why are you so intent on pushing team Kramer?"

"Because he makes you happy. I saw it before you could tuck it away. I like you happy."

"I like me happy, too. So that means Kramer stays on the list."

Kaylee chuckled as she rubbed Dag's ears and he tried to lick her face. "We're going out soon, you big lug." To

Mina she said, "I'm going to have Kevin make a stinky list too. Preston Jazz Hands is definitely on it."

Preston was Kaylee's one-time short-lived boyfriend who tried to embezzle from her. "I can think of a few more who would be right there at the top."

Kaylee's finger came shooting out, waggling. "Do *not* say Porcupine Jones. Do not."

Mina mocked running a finger over her lips. "I'm sealed. I will not bring up the weirdest, horniest guy you've ever dated."

"I went on *one* date with him. There was no whisp of a relationship. He doesn't even qualify for the shit list. I hardly knew him. It didn't work out because he was just too...prick-*ly* for me." Kaylee laughed as Dag barked. Porcupine Jones, was of course, not his real name. After all, he wasn't a vid star. They'd deemed him so after he continue to bring up his favorite boy part. He had a fondness, bordering on obsession, with using a specific prickly term for it which—*solar flare here*—is a turnoff to just about every woman on the planet. "And we were never intimate. You better remember that. But boy did he try. It was like it was his mission to land that pokey spaceship."

"Yeah, he couldn't wait to get his quill dipped."

"*Ha.* I seem to remember something about your lips being sealed? We vowed a long time ago we wouldn't bring up that prickly bastard. Let's move on. What's your plan today?"

"Not sure," she said. "McAllister debriefed me about Veritus and his meeting with Ambrose Bernard and

Kramer last night, but he didn't give me any further instructions. I'm planning to follow up with Norm and Harri first thing. Harri got fired. He thinks Bliss Corp is spying on him, which is likely true. If they're experimenting with Plush on unwilling people, they will try and keep it secret at all cost." The implications of that were vast and scary. "Norm is keeping watch over him until I figure out the next move." Norman Webb was an ex-marshal who Mina trusted with her life. Harri had worked at a pleasure emporium until yesterday when Mina had gone to interview him. "But the Plush case won't become a full op for a while." Likely a long while, since big-money corporations had their elbows locked with the federal government. "I'm assuming I'll get a new op designation at some point today. Have you received yours?"

"Nope. Still waiting," Kaylee replied. "McAllister said he'd get a hold of me this morning."

Mina changed into her clothes behind her closet door, peeking her head out. "I'm kind of hoping for a case with a little less drama. Maybe a nice extortionist or a placid forger or even an elderly thief."

"Yes," Kaylee chuckled. "Running down an airchair is a lot easier than motoring after a gigantic ship full of serial killers. But don't count your moon rocks before they arrive. Speaking of which, I ordered mine over a week ago. Sputnik Deliveries has been slow lately. I've got a cousin who goes crazy for them. Her birth year celebration is coming up, and I happen to know a moon cultivator who owes me a favor."

"Of course you do."

Veronica, Mina's sim announced, "Vid chat request coming in from Norman Webb. Do you wish to accept?"

"Yes, hold for thirty seconds, living room wall, forty percent," Mina told Veronica. To Kaylee she said, "There's Norm now. I have to go."

"Gotcha. And, just in case Kramer tried to crawl back, don't be too hard on the guy. Deep down in his black heart he meant well." Kaylee threw Mina a three finger salute. "By-*eee*."

Mina snorted as her friend disappeared. *Meant well* and *did well* were two entirely different things.

Nothing is completed without a great team.

My many thanks to:

Awesome Cover design: Damonza
Digital and print formatting: Author E.M.S
Copyedits/proofs: Joyce Lamb
Final proof: Marlene Roberts

*Head to my website to sign-up for my Book Alert
newsletter to receive new release info in your inbox so
you don't miss a thing!*

About the Author

Amanda Carlson is a graduate of the University of Minnesota, with a BA in both Speech and Hearing Science & Child Development. She went on to get an A.A.S in Sign Language Interpreting and worked as an interpreter until her first child was born. She's the author of the high-octane **Jessica McClain** urban fantasy series published by Orbit, the **Sin City Collectors** PNR series, the contemporary fantasy **Phoebe Meadows** series, the dystopian **Holly Danger** series, and the futuristic thriller **Mina Kane** series. Look for these books in stores everywhere. She lives in Minneapolis.

FIND HER ALL OVER SOCIAL MEDIA

Patreon: Patreon.com/authoramandacarlson
(Get my books early & for less than retail)

Website: amandacarlson.com

Facebook: facebook.com/authoramandacarlson

Twitter: @amandaccarlson

Instagram: @author_amanda

www.ingramcontent.com/pod-product-compliance
Lightning Source LLC
Chambersburg PA
CBHW050807190726
48285CB00005B/1828